"Very interesting and well written."

William Edelen Syndicated Columnist, Author

"A wonderful story is woven around two distinct periods in history, the Baroque and the 20th Century. Joseph Mastroianni's love for music and especially the *Chaconne* of Johann S. Bach reveals the power of music in dealing with today's struggles and hardships. Tremendous insight and an enjoyable conception."

Ron Purcell D.M.A. Professor of Music,
California State University, Northridge, CA,
Specializing in Lute and Guitar

"A fascinating journey that reveals a life and a lesson."

Richard F.X. O'Connor Editor
Author, *How to Market You and Your Books*

"Joseph Mastroianni's *Chaconne* is an engrossing and exciting tale of guilt, atonement, and realization. Rich with life-changing events and memorable characters, it chronicles a young man's coming first against obstacles, and finally to awareness through life's lessons subtle and manifest, wonderful and terrible."

Karl Leopold Metzenberg Story Analyst,
Local 700 Los Angeles, CA (Ret.)

CHACONNE

Chaconne

Joseph C. Mastroianni

9/10/05

DamianPress

This is a work of fiction. Some historical figures are represented in the story, but their actions within the pages of this book are purely from the author's imagination.

ISBN 0-9770484-0-3

First Paperback Edition

Printed in the U.S.A.

10 9 8 7 6 5 4 3 2 1

Dedication

*This book is dedicated to
my mother, Madeline Mastroianni,
who supported and encouraged me, no matter
how far-fetched the endeavor. My grandfather, Tito
Tassi, whose lessons appeared to be lumps of coal, but
were diamonds of wisdom, and to my children;
David, Mark, Steven, Traci, Carmen Ann,
and Damian. They taught me how
love without condition feels
by their gift of it.*

Contents

Prelude

Chaconne is really two novels in one, a tale of two lives separated by centuries in time. It is a love story — Milo Damiani's love for life and the music of J. S. Bach. Milo's world swirls with the sights, sounds, and tantalizing aromas of the big city. From shoeshine boy in the Italian ghetto to chopper pilot in Vietnam, Damiani thrills to adventure — more importantly, wrestling with the burning questions of life: how did we get here, what went wrong, and how can it be fixed? Finding answers to these questions in music, Milo fixates on Bach's sublimely melancholic *Chaconne* for solo violin, a series of continuous variations his father had played since before he could remember.

Through the tapestry of Milo's fascinating life, the author threads the story of Johann Sebastian Bach, one of the world's best-loved composers. Bach's was a world where death touched everyone, and often. After the Thirty Years' War, a tumultuous period when the Holy Roman Empire declined from sixteen million souls to fewer than ten million, Bach's ancestors endured waves of plague. His parents died when he was ten; his first wife at thirty-five, only half of his twenty children survived to adulthood.

History implies that the Chaconne was Sebastian's private consolation, an antiphon to the death of his first wife, Maria Barbara. Bach's story is told with great tenderness, accuracy, and contemporary worth to the novel's protagonist. Students of Bach cannot help but admire the sensible dialogue that today could only be imagined.

Joseph Mastroianni's masterpiece rings true, like one who saw it happen. Milo's experience comes alive in the vibrant and earthy language of one who knows Damiani's world well. He portrays a flesh-and-blood Bach, refreshingly knocked from the quotidian academic pedestal. The counterpoint between Milo and Bach is vital, original, and satisfying. In the harmony of that counterpoint, Milo finds redemption and peace. Mastroianni has composed a beautiful and gripping novel — a spiritual work, to those who know how it should be read.

Tim Smith, D.M.A. Professor of Music Theory,
Northern Arizona University
Author, *The Canons and Fugues of J. S. Bach,*
The Fugues of the Well-Tempered Clavier

~ ~ ~

Acknowledgments

If someone had told me I would write a novel someday, I'd never have believed it. I probably wouldn't have accomplished it without the help and encouragement of my dear friends. Without their countless hours of advice, encouragement, and ideas, it would never have been a book at all.

Karl Metzenberg, a gifted story analyst, read five hundred pages of ranting and helped structure it into readable form.

John Dooley, who wrote a fascinating and powerful Vietnam tale. He helped me remember things about that war I'd long buried. His keen eye for trash turned me into a garbage man. Richard F.X. O'Connor, editor, author, helped me focus; find my voice, and the voice of Johann Sebastian Bach.

A special thank you to book designer Christine Nolt who understood the symbolism behind the image. Thank you my friends and nit-picking fellow authors of Writer's Way. You are my ghostwriters and a light in the dark.

There is hardly a way to thank Tim Smith, Professor of Music Theory, Northern University of Arizona. A fellow Bach lover, he encouraged me to venture beyond the known Bach literature to give Sebastian a first person voice, while holding fast to the historic facts. My hope is the work will meet the high expectation raised by the eloquent Prelude he wrote for this novel.

Finally, Jose Maria Gallardo del Rey, *the* guitarist of his generation and my brother. He taught me to understand the wonderful music of our favorite composer, Johann Sebastian Bach and gifted from his heart the secrets of the guitar.

Author's Note to the Reader

Chaconne: the Novel is a work of fiction, an adventure about two men; Milo Damiani, a helicopter pilot and John Sebastian Bach, the sixteenth-century Baroque composer.

As a small boy, Milo hears his father play Bach's *Chaconne* and intuits a resonant truth which guides his life thereafter.

The first chapter finds Milo on a dangerous rescue mission. The following are chapters revealing the life path that brings him to that point in time. An historically accurate but fictional account of Johann Sebastian Bach's life and how he came to write the music that so deeply inspired Milo is told alternating chapters in counterpoint to the contemporary narrative; two lives separated by centuries connected through Bach's timeless *Chaconne*.

CHAPTER ONE

The Mission

Helicopter rescue missions are never routine, especially at sea in volatile weather, but faith in the ability of Sandy Peters, his co-pilot, allowed Milo's thoughts to wander from the business at hand — a big mistake. Sandy seemed to have everything under control. A hiss in the earphones indicated he'd keyed the mike.

"Much smoother now. With luck, we'll be snoring in a couple hours. You know, when I checked in at Morgan City tonight, I heard that music you played on your guitar. Sounded cool. What was it?"

Milo rarely spoke about deeply personal stuff. But because he didn't expect to ever run into Sandy again after this shift, he opened up.

"It's called *Chaconne*. It's a great piece of music, very complicated, but when I heard my dad play it — my first memory actually — something stuck."

"Like, what?"

"I haven't really thought about it much. In a strange way, I heard in his music a kind of invisible thread between Sebastian's heart and my senses."

"I don't get it."

"To put a tag on it, I'd say a perception of truth, I suppose."

"Who's Sebastian?"

"*Chaconne's* composer, Johann Sebastian Bach."

"That's a wimp name if I ever heard one. What do you mean, by your senses?"

"You know, it sort of led me along, that feeling of truth. Whenever I sensed it, things, decisions, seemed to work out better. Believe me I've had some bad shit go down in my life. I mean, my dad split before I'd turned ten, left me in charge of my brothers and sister, and some other heavy crap."

"Yeah, that's tough. I wish my dad had taken a hike, the prick. Maybe all dads are love batons."

Milo laughed. "Mine was okay. My mom drove him off, I think. I prayed like hell he'd come back, but knew he wouldn't. Prayed about a lot of things, but the big G had his phone off the hook."

"C'mon man, you can't blame God for that shit."

"I don't; there's no one there to blame."

"That's cynical."

"Anyway, we went to live with my grandparents in Boston. That worked out. Talk about a prick! My bad ass, grandfather was first-class, but if he hadn't taken us in, we'd have starved to death — and he taught me a lot."

"Parents always seem to screw us all up."

"Nah, I figure it doesn't do any good to blame anyone. Sure, life has dumped on me, but when I look around, everyone's shoveling out from under."

"Don't you think your parents or anyone had anything to do with it? Do you think stuff just happens?"

"Maybe, but what's the sense in whining? It doesn't solve diddly."

Sandy had the controls when lightning struck. The cockpit exploded with a million lumens. All went black but for tiny points of light shimmering in Milo's retinas. The illusion was no substitute for the lost instruments in the violent storm above a raging sea.

Another flash lighted the cockpit. The helicopter lurched into a roll and then shuddered. No lights; no instruments; only blackness.

Panic filled Milo's headphones. "Take it! Take it!"

Milo sensed Sandy's terror. A chill overcame him from his toes up, as if sucked into a cold muck, but reflex overcame inertia. He seized the stick frozen in Sandy's grip and whacked him on the helmet with a clipboard.

"Goddamn it, Sandy! Get off the fucking controls! I've got it."

Unloading his thoughts on Sandy gave some kind of relief, like taking an Ex-Lax on the day after Thanksgiving, it contrasted with the S.O.S overloading his brain and the fear shredding his belly. No matter. Survival depended on defeating panic, and there were no fear pills in the first aid kit. He'd been on that train before, but not in a storm gone mad and a co-pilot gone south.

~ ~ ~

Bach had a lifetime to create an everlasting legacy — Milo, but seconds to figure out how *not* to be first at a crash scene.

~ ~ ~

CHAPTER TWO

Baptism

Spring poked and prodded its way through the snow-covered ground of pastoral Eisenach. In the still morning air, smoke curling from chimneys carried whiffs of bacon and freshly baked bread from breakfast fires. The promise of spring could be seen everywhere: in sprouting flower gardens, bud-tipped branches, and shedding live-stock. Cows ritually sauntered to their milking sheds, eager to empty a good night's work. Born in this idyllic setting on March 21, 1685, Johann Sebastian Bach would become one of the world's most important musicians.

Founded in 1150, Eisenach was located in the region of Thuringia, central Germany. The small town of about six thousand occupants, had a claim to fame. Martin Luther studied at Eisenach's Latin School and began his translation of the Greek New Testament into German over 180 years earlier. The Church of St. George stood proudly, one of Eisenach's most significant edifices. Built from slate-hued stone, harvested like potatoes from surrounding fields, the ancient place of worship became a center of activity with the ability to seat a third of the town's residents.

The Thirty Years' War had caused untold destruction in the gradually recovering area. The burden of reconstruction fell primarily on the workers who were taxed for money and labor.

Though conditions had improved, Johann Ambrosius Bach carried on as generations of his family had, following a tradition as a musician, something that shielded him from the many hardships of the time. He held the post of town piper of Eisenach.

A rotund man, Ambrosius had a round face with a natural flush to his cheeks deepened by the chilly morning. He was impeccably dressed, his stout calves bulging in the knee-high stockings. His body-build confirmed the fact he could walk for hours in all types of terrain without fatigue, and often did. A serious-minded man and a harsh taskmaster with students, Ambrosius tempered it with humor, always ready with a smile or hearty laugh.

Today, a month before Easter, Johann Sebastian Bach would be baptized in the Church of St. George's. Ambrosius proudly carried his son towards the place of worship. His wife, Maria Elizabeth, did not attend. In accordance with strict Hebrew custom embraced by the Lutherans, she was forbidden to enter a church until undergoing a rite of purification six weeks after the birthing. Ambrosius walked with his good friend, Sebastian Nagel, who held the same position as he in nearby Gotha.

Nagel ambled along on spindly legs. His hunched shoulders spoke of countless hours at the keyboard. His eyes shone through thick bushy brows with the love and devotion he held for music. He admired Ambrosius for his natural ability, in contrast to his own hard-won crafts-manship, but harbored not an inkling of envy.

Ambrosius dearly loved his friend, giving freely from his musical well of ancestral knowledge. He looked at Nagel. "It is fitting my son should carry your name, though my hope remains strong he will surpass your feeble talent."

"Your comment is like a fart in the middle of a beau-tiful melody."

Ambrosius guffawed and doubled over, his effort causing him to slip and almost drop the infant.

"Oh, that you were as good with music as you are with words, my friend, you might be rich."

Nagel countered, "As would you if the Duke had granted you permission to take the job in Erfurt. But alas, you did such a good job duping him of your greatness, he couldn't part with you."

The commotion startled the baby. He began to wail and his aunt hurried forward, worried for the child.

"Don't fret, Mary. He's singing."

"There you see, Nagel? He is already a candidate for the choir."

At the entrance they were met by the co-godfather, Johann Georg Koch, the Ducal Forester of Eisenach, and by Ambrosius' twin brother, Johann Christopher, who'd arrived a few minutes earlier from Arnstadt where he held the position of musician to the court. The brothers were so alike in appearance and manner that their wives couldn't tell them apart but for the different clothing they wore.

Koch, a deeply religious man and serious of nature, looked at Ambrosius and Nagel dourly as a stern teacher would unruly students. "Have you two no respect for this holiest of days in the child's new life, joking and carrying on so?"

Ambrosius flipped him a backhand gesture. "Give your face a break and smile for a change, Herr Koch." Then he embraced his twin. "Hello my brother, it is so good to see myself again!"

Koch managed a hint of a smile; the remainder of the group guffawed and gave him *der Rüffle*, the raspberry!

Unheated, the interior of St. George's would take all summer to become a cool sanctuary. But now, the breathing of the minister, Johann Christoph Zerbst, and that of the guests could be seen floating about in the chilled air.

Zerbst, whose white hair sprung from his head at ungodly angles, could put half the parishioners to sleep, the remainder to daydreaming about anything but the service. Since many men held the popular name of Johann, they were addressed by their middle or last names. But the minister's middle name was Christoph, also common, so he became known as Zerb. His dreary monotone especially assaulted the fine ear of Ambrosius. Having paid him a groshen, two pfennig for the baptismal and then to suffer his unrelenting drone added to the annoyance. He would have preferred being put to sleep with the equivalent in grog.

The frigid fingers of the organist played softly, if not precisely. The pipes discharged wisps that formed a pocket-sized cloud overhead. Zerb began the service with Nagel holding the infant over the baptismal font. The child and perhaps a guest or two slept peacefully through the tedious sermon. The others shivered in their seats, restless for it to end. Finally, Ambrosius whispered, "Get on with it, Zerb. We're freezing in our knickers, man."

Koch shot him a malevolent glance and shook his head in disgust. Zerb reluctantly ended the homily and brought the boring ceremony to a close. Johann Sebastian Bach, now irreversibly launched on the Lutheran path and bound in the family tradition of music, had only to fulfill his destiny. A contract with God was sealed, but not of his own hand or choice.

~ ~ ~

Similar to Sebastian's, the known history of Milo's family went back to the 1600s. But with documented migrations to Rio de Janeiro and the United States, the Damiani clan did not confine themselves to a small geographical area as did the Bach's.

~ ~ ~

CHAPTER THREE

The Barraca

Milo's great grandfather, Vincenzo Damiani, arrived in America from Calabria, Italy, in the early 1800s in search of work as a *scalpellino,* a stonecutter. Families were started, children born, traditions continued, a business created. Until then, the Damiani family had spanned three centuries, living and thriving on three continents.

Carlo, the youngest of three brothers and a sister, took his first breath in Brooklyn, New York. His father, Giuseppe, or "Joe," also a *scalpellino,* carried on the long tradition of sculpting, and wanted to pass it on to resistant sons. Joe's brother, Raffaele, made mandolins and guitars as a hobby. To nobody's surprise, Carlo showed a keen interest in music and art. He began taking violin lessons at ten and knew then his life would be music.

Carlo idolized the great Arturo Toscanini, conductor of the New York Philharmonic Orchestra. One day, Carlo should have been cleaning the *Barraca,* a drab, mustard-colored, clapboard building reminiscent of an Army barracks, where after tiresome eighteen-hour workdays the laborers often slept.

An opportunity to emulate his idol arose; he could not resist. A parade, organized by local Fascists was to take place. The director, taken ill, couldn't lead the band, and designated Carlo to replace him. The route would take them past Carlo's house. As they marched towards the neighborhood, many people lining the street, who were obviously, not sympathizers shook their fists and shouted obscenities. Oblivious to politics, Carlo conducted his heart out.

Beaming, he timed the parade to stop precisely in front of his doorstep. To Carlo's dismay, his father strode angrily out of the crowd, grabbed him by the ear, and marched him home. Joe spoke in sonorous, broken English. The words echoed in the chambers of his large nose. He shouted above the noise of the confused and leaderless band.

"Stupido, why in hell do you march with these pigs? Especially when you should be cleaning the *Barraca*. Imbecile!" Joe, a Communist, wasn't amused.

Carlo tried hard to conform to his father's wish that he learn the family business, but dreams of being a musician would not allow it. At every opportunity he played with friends or organized concerts. He knew the price would be his father's wrath.

Carlo failed to do his part to support the family, though he lived at home, and his father's anger and frustration increased. The tension and continuous arguments escalated.

Carlo had recently met Maria, Milo's mother-to-be, fell in love, and asked her for her hand. Neither family approved. They thought Carlo rash and irresponsible.

At a typical Sunday family gathering, Carlo decided to

inform his father of their plan to marry. A big man, his father, whose large nose somehow did not dominate his face, had shaggy white hair and huge hands with thick fingers. He talked loudly in a deep voice that commanded respect. Joe owned the Ridgewood Monument Works, the *Barraca*.

The family gathered for Sunday dinner. Joe played the mandolin, his brother, Raffaele, the guitar, and Carlo's brothers sang "Mama," a popular Italian folk song. Homemade wine made the rounds; the aroma of cooking floated to every corner of the house.

Carlo's mother, Luisa, stood at the stove. She smiled at the rendition, sung with enthusiasm and purposely out of tune. It always made her laugh. Strands of graying hair fell into her eyes as she stirred a large pot of tomato sauce. Meatballs, sausages, beef, and pork simmered in the thick savory mix. Carlo came up behind her. Feigning a hug, he filched a meatball. With a stern look, she slapped his hand, then grabbed the corner of her apron and wiped the sauce from her son's chin. She also spoke broken English, but in a high-pitched melodic tone and often implied a question at the end of a sentence though it may not have been one at all.

"Don't be such a pig, eh? Your hands are dirty. The pasta, she's finish. Go drain it to put on the platter."

"Meatballs are fantastic, Ma. You're the meatball queen. Nobody, but nobody makes meatballs like you, Ma."

"Shut your face. You can't have another. We're going to eat now."

"Come on, Ma, one more."

"No. Drain the pasta before it gets over-cooked."

He smiled, licked his fingers, and kissed her on top of the head.

"You're a hard case, Ma, but I love you anyway."

After dinner, the men sat around the table, busy at cards. Luisa brought espresso to the table and poured. Joe put a shot of anisette and a twist of lemon peel into the strong brew. He and Carlo went onto the balcony. They quietly smoked Chesterfields in the cool evening air. Carlo broke the silence.

"Pop, can we talk?"

"Talk, talk, all you do is talk."

"Pop, I need to borrow five hundred dollars."

"What! Five hundred dollars?" he bellowed. "What for? So you can blow it on your stupid idea to start an opera company? Goddamn, Carlo, what's the matter with you? Your brothers and me bust our balls ten hours a day to survive. We can't depend on you for shit." He got more agitated by the minute.

"But, Pop . . ."

"No! Don't 'but, Pop' with me. You live in my house, eat like a pig, have parties with your friends, and don't show up to work half the time."

"Pop . . ."

"There are four jobs waiting for you to do the art. We won't get a dime from the customer until drawings are done. When are you finishing, huh? Borrow five hundred dollar? You got big balls."

"Pop, listen to me . . ."

"No, you listen to me, Carlo. It can't go on anymore, understand? This shit has to stop now."

Carlo shouted, "Pop, for Christ's sake! I'm getting married."

His father threw his arms in the air in frustration with a look of disbelief, and then lowered his head, shaking it slowly from side to side.

"Married? You're getting married? What the hell is wrong with you? You don't have a pot to piss in and now you want to get married? Where are you going to live? How will you eat?"

Joe raised his head and held his son's gaze. In a softened tone he said, "Carlo, that woman, she's too old for you. You'll ruin your life if you marry her. You think you can support a family playing violin? Think, Carlo! Think what you're doing."

"I *have* thought about it, Pop. We found a little place on Melrose Street for sixty dollars a month. It's right close to the shop. With the five hundred, we can buy some used furniture. Maria has a job at the laundry. I promise to work every day and will do my music at night. Pop, we love each other."

"Carlo, Carlo. You live in a dream, but dreams won't put food on the table or pay your rent. I'll loan you five hundred, but the designs have to be finished by the end of the week. No more excuses. Twenty-five bucks a month comes out of your pay every month until finished. No more talk about it. Finito!"

"Twenty-five, Pop? That's . . ."

"That's how she goes. Twenty-five!"

"Fine, Pop . . . Thanks."

Though Maria wanted a church wedding, they married in a private ceremony three months later, but only after he promised the children would be baptized Catholic.

From Maria's savings they purchased furniture and set up housekeeping. With the borrowed five hundred, Carlo started an opera company. After staging two operas, it folded. Heartsick and discouraged, Carlo would one day try again.

Ten months later a newborn made their family a three-some. As the first grandchild, Milo became heir to the family business, if only in the vision of his grandfather.

Milo's diminutive, white-booted, pink legs kicked in spasms. They seemed to imitate those of a frog attempting to swim but going nowhere. The infant, swaddled in a white-lace dress, clenched and unclenched his miniature fingers. His eyes scrunched closed as he sucked air until his lungs filled near to bursting. Buried in his white bonnet, his face looked like a Chapeau de Napoleon rose on a satin pillow. The echo of a wail ricocheted between saint-frescoed walls in the sanctuary of St. Joseph's. The ornately vested priest made the sign of the cross over the baby. In a loud monotone he chanted.

"*Benedictat vos omnipotens. Deus Pater, et Filius, et Spritu Sanctus.*"

"*Amen.*"

"*Dominus vobiscum.*"

"Et cum spiritu tuo."

With that pronouncement, Milo became a child of God. From that moment on, he bore the yoke of faith and the mantle of tradition. The lines were drawn in Milo's battle for freedom from both.

With money sparse, the *Barraca* became the venue for a baptismal celebration. Only Milo's mother objected. She thought it morbid. Everyone else in the family felt perfectly comfortable.

Carlo and his brothers cleared a large area in the main building. They covered the clay floor, hardened by many years of use, with fresh sawdust for the dance area. In the yard, large tables fashioned with worn wooden planks supported by granite markers served their purpose well. They'd borrowed wooden folding chairs from St. Joseph's. Carlo's mother and aunts prepared a feast.

His uncles provided the music. Homemade burgundy and red zinfandel flowed freely. The sounds of guitar, mandolin, accordion, and the music of laughter soon filled the dusk. Neighbors from windows of surrounding tenements clapped and sang. Dancers made the sawdust fly to the rhythm of a tarantella.

Grandpa Joe, holding the sleeping Milo securely in one arm, swung him to and fro. In the clear sky, millions of stars seemed to foretell Joe's vision. He sipped from his glass, and then waved his arm in a gesture as if to encompass the entire *Barraca*. He spoke softly to his grandson.

"Bambino mio, look what your grandpa has done for you. Your father . . . your father, he dreams only about

music. Your uncles, the bums, they don't want this. They don't want to learn how to be *scalpellini*. So, it's up to you to make beautiful art from these stones. I will teach you."

He grasped the tiny fingers in his own, gently messaging them.

"Look at those *scalpellino* fingers. Some day they will make great work. Some day they will make me so proud." He bent his massive head and kissed the child, who never felt the tears. Three more children were born to Carlo and Maria in rapid succession. The second, a girl, arrived twelve months and twelve days after Milo's birth. As a child, she always thought Milo to be only twelve days older. It would become a joke between them. Two more sons were born within the next three years.

Carlo continued to work for his father. He hated it and took out his anger and frustration on Maria. Milo would listen in terror as his father and mother screamed at each other, the arguments often ending with a resounding slap and his mother's sobs. Then his father would play the *Chaconne*, a refrain that would echo throughout Milo's life, and the music would soothe him to sleep.

Because his father and mother both worked, Milo spent the better part of his earliest years with his father's parents. Carlo designed tombstones and mausoleums, and Grandpa Joe and Milo's uncles brought the designs out of great chunks of Vermont granite.

Some of the most memorable smells and sounds of Milo's early childhood were associated with the *Barraca*, especially the fresh-baked Italian bread and pastries from the bakery on the corner of Melrose Street. Behind the bakery stood a brewery, which filled the air with steam and whistles.

On the opposite corner was Ingoglia's Market where Milo picked up sandwiches for his grandfather and uncles. Old man Ingoglia would give him small pieces of Italian cheeses, prosciutto, and an occasional olive when he came to the store. Each day Milo looked forward to lunch: his favorite sandwich, ham and provolone with mustard on fresh Italian bread. He'd always remember the aroma of cheeses and prosciutto hanging from the ceiling and freshly scattered sawdust on the wooden floor.

Before the granite could be made into headstones, it needed to be cut into workable pieces with a large stone saw. A constant supply of running water kept the screaming, diamond-edged blade cool. As the water hit the spinning blade, it caused a mist. Mingled with the granite dust, it had a unique earthy odor and taste and felt like a fresh breeze in the hot afternoon sun. Once cut, the stone could be chiseled by hand or with air tools. Used for carving letters and designs, the chisels were driven by a large compressor. He loved the rhythmic ker-thumping as it filled the air tank, its hiss when shut down, and the delicate tremolo of air tools contrasted with the solid hammer against steel, steel against granite. Both were like music to Milo.

Sandblasting, another method, would also be used. Milo watched his grandfather stencil letters and art onto a sheet of rubber bonded to the stone. "Can I try, Grandpa?"

Joe wiped the moisture from his goggles and propped

them above his forehead. He never pushed his grandson, but patiently indulged him when presented the opportunity. "Take this and you rub on the paper."

Milo rolled the graphite over the stencil. As his grandfather lifted the template, Milo's eyes widened in wonder. He smiled and clapped his hands excitedly. Joe said, "Wait a minute, then I show you something else."

When the rest of the artwork appeared on the rubber, Joe lifted his grandson onto a bench so both were able to reach the surface of the stone. "This thing, she can cut off a finger if you don't take care. Never touch here."

He pointed to the gleaming triangular blade on the end of a pencil-like knife. "Now keep your hand loose and I show you. Hold it like you draw a picture."

When Milo had a grip on it, Joe guided his grandson's hand precisely along the stenciled letters. The first word finished, he said, "Now, you put the point of the knife under the corner here, like that. Good. Now you can pull out the rubber. See?"

Milo exposed the granite beneath the rubber, barely able to contain his delight. "Now, you see what happens? When we blast with sand or steel particles, the air pressure, she makes them cut the stone where the letters are, but the rubber, she protects the rest of the stone, you see?"

"Can we do some more, Grandpa?"

"After lunch. So go wash your hands."

Milo thought the smell of rubber combined with the cement used to bond it to the granite a most interesting odor. He also liked the smell of his sweaty dust-covered grandfather and uncles as they sat casually on tombstones, eating lunch, goggles perched upon their heads. His uncle Remo had the same unique body odor as his father. Not unpleasant and very masculine. Later, his uncle's scent reminded him of his father. It elicited a memory of being on his father's lap, head nestled in his shoulder.

Milo delighted in going to the *Barraca*. His chores included sweeping the sandblast room, watering, and going to Ingoglia's for lunches. He never considered it work and was paid with a sandwich and a cold Pepsi. It was enough.

He spent endless hours watching his father draw designs of flowers, crucifixes, angels, and other religious figures. It seemed like magic as they were transferred from paper to granite. He watched with awe as his grandfather carved the raw stone. Joe would first rough-out designs with hammer and chisel then refine them with air-driven tools. Sometimes he would create entire works by hand.

Carlo despised having to work at the *Barraca*. An accomplished violinist and a conductor, he'd studied hard to become a musician. The house seemed always full of music and musicians. They had a piano and Milo played it, but disliked lessons, preferring to push the pedals of his grandfather's old player piano. He'd spend hours pumping and listening. It exposed him to many fine operas and music, and some of the greatest composers — Vivaldi, Mozart, and Beethoven. Most of all Milo loved Bach.

~ ~ ~

CHAPTER FOUR

Shoeshine Box

Milo's years up to the present were relatively happy, but for the arguments between his parents. Constant bickering between them kept the boy on the edge of anxiety. Adored by his grandparents, with whom he spent a great deal of time, the eight-year-old felt secure and loved. As the oldest child, Maria relied on him to safeguard the others until she arrived from work. Resentful of the responsibility, he grew defiant.

Milo cherished his father, tried to please him, especially with piano studies. Though he loved music, he hated the confinement and discipline of scales and exercises. In a struggle for notice he often did forbidden things to get attention. On one such occasion came an angry shout, "Milo, come here. Now!"

Duly subdued, he watched the belt slip slowly from its loops. It hadn't taken a degree in forensics to find remnants of peanut butter and jellied fingerprints on the back arc of the Guarneri. "How many times have I told you not to touch my violin? Pull down your pants."

Milo found himself folded over his father's knee. On the first blow, his bottom twitched and legs flailed. The next closed his eyelids tight. With the third, came a firm resolve not to cry out. He bravely bore the pain and indignity. Never been punished unless deserving and never thought his father cruel. Maria, on the other hand, would often rebuke him for no apparent reason. It confused and angered him.

Adding to Milo's angst, an embarrassing condition caused his schoolwork to suffer. No matter how he tried, he couldn't control his bladder. Self-assurance sifted away like flour through a sieve, in an episode of shame he'd not forget.

One day Milo raised his hand and kept it in the air attempting to get Mrs. Rhodes' attention. With a look of exasperation that transposed to her tone she said, "What is it, Milo?"

"May I please go to the bathroom?"

"No, you may not. This is the third time today. You haven't finished your work. You can go at recess. Now don't ask again."

Milo squirmed in agony, crossed his legs and squeezed. Then he rapidly moved his knees together and apart, to no avail. Warm urine gushed down his leg, ending in a puddle under his seat. With relief came tears. What had happened could not be concealed. The girl sitting next to him laughed. With no place to hide, cruelty compounded humiliation. Milo sat mortified and soaked. His flagging confidence caused him to spend more time alone or with his best friend, Barnaby, who never made fun. They understood each other.

One day, playing stoopball by himself, Milo threw the pink Spaulding against the concrete steps of the building in which his family rented a flat. He caught it on the rebound, quickly fired it back and fielded it again. It could be quite a challenge, depending on where the ball struck. This time it hit the sharp edge of the brick step and bounced high over his head.

Milo chased it down the street. It came to rest near a cat sprawled on the pavement. The cat looked as if sun bathing. As he got closer he saw the blood oozing from its mouth. Warily, he poked a foot at it. Eyes open but oblivious, it didn't respond. Milo would remember its eyes, an unsettling first encounter with death.

A few days later at the pool hall on the corner of his street, Milo noticed the chipped, faded, lopsided tin sign that hung from the roof of the old brownstone building. A prominent eight ball sat dead center in a field of red. Under it, the word "Billiards" jumped out like the bull's-eye of a target. It swayed in the breeze, suspended above the dark glass storefront on the right side of the entrance. As he often did, Milo stood, hands cupped around his eyes, nose flattened against the glass. A silent movie unfolded.

The smoky room contained two billiard and three pool tables, all of them worn and tattered. On top of each massive leg, a carved lion's head stood guard. A large paw at the bottom rested on the bare wooden floor. Bronze spittoons that had long ago lost their shine to poor aim were strategically placed. An old black fan in the far corner of the room labored to cool the players but served only to churn the steamy haze from one place to another.

Milo peered through the dark glass into the billiard

parlor. Sweat-soaked players chalked their sticks. Some leaned, intently aiming to bury a colorful, numbered ball into a pocket.

The man closest to Milo stood near a billiard table. He leaned on the cue in one hand and held a beer in the other. Milo couldn't see his face, only the smoking cigar in his mouth. Another very fat man, whose pants could not contain a large stomach that overhung his belt, faced him. Rage-contorted features barely contained eyes that seemed to bulge from his head. Everything appeared in slow motion. He slowly raised his arm. There was a flash of light and a loud report. The cigar man toppled backwards. As he fell, the still-smoking Havana seemed to float towards the ground. Bits of brain spattered the glass in front of Milo's eyes. He jumped back terrified but couldn't resist another look. Once again he saw dead eyes.

The ultimate inevitability of death had not yet occurred to him, but its finality filled him with a fear more menacing than that of punishment for wrongdoing, even his fear of heights. A stalking, redolent fear, it would shadow him, foul his existence thereafter. Carlo had told him to stay away from the pool hall. Now Milo understood. He ran. Days later he confided only in Barnaby.

A few weeks later Milo wanted to go to the movies of an afternoon. He asked his father for twenty-five cents. He fidgeted waiting for the usual response, "No." Not this time. Without explanation, his father took him to the hardware store. Milo watched his father purchase a shoeshine box with a black, cast iron footrest.

"What's that for?"

"Wait till we get home."

Then Carlo bought two soft-bristled brushes, a dauber, two buffing cloths, and a bottle each of black and brown wash, polish, and sole dressing. No words passed. He still hadn't received a quarter or a "No."

"What's that stuff for, Dad?"

"I said you'd find out when we get home. Button up."

At least it wasn't no, thought Milo, but could barely contain his curiosity.

When they arrived home, Carlo tossed him a brush.

"Here we go. Kneel down in front of the box. Use it to get the dirt off my shoes."

Milo knelt and took the brush, a bit large for his hand, but he managed.

"How's that, Dad?"

"You have to get it all off. See how you missed the back?"

"Yeah, but it's too hard."

"Stop whining. When the dirt's all off, take this, put a bit of that stuff there on it and rub it into the shoe real good."

Carlo handed him the dauber. Milo sighed, resigned to see it through, but not happily. He applied the wash, a consistency of watery jelly. It had a unique, almost sweet odor. He touched a drop of it to his tongue. Grimacing, he wondered how something could smell so good and taste that fusty. He daubed it onto the leather. Milo looked up for more directions, but hoped to be done. His knees hurt.

"Okay, then. Now dry it off with the cloth."

Frustrated, Milo tried to no avail. The shoe remained damp. "It won't come dry."

"Well, don't use half the bottle next time. Keep going."

Milo learned quickly; the other shoe took a fourth of the time. He smiled at his father.

"Done," he exclaimed gleefully. "Can I go to the movies now?"

"Nope, you're just getting started."

Milo's shoulders sagged. "But this is too hard, and my knees hurt."

Carlo cuffed him lightly on the head. Milo's lower lip began to quiver. He swiped at his running nose, smearing black over his cheek. Carlo, hard-pressed to remain stern, stifled a laugh.

"Now, take the can of polish, put some on your finger tips and rub it in good."

"Am I almost done? I'm tired."

"Not yet. Stop whining. After the polish is on, use the clean brush."

Milo applied the polish with his fingertips, rubbing it thoroughly into the leather. His fingers were aching and blackened. He held up his hands, looked first at one then the other and began laughing. Mischievously, he wiped them on his father's shin. Carlo feigned a malevolent smile.

"That's it. I'm going to . . ."

Milo cringed and closed his eyes. "Are you gonna spank me?"

"No, I'm gonna choke you."

All seriousness gone, they burst into laughter. Feeling comfortable in his father's good mood, Milo jumped at the opportunity to ask a question he wouldn't have otherwise.

"Why do you and Mommy always fight?"

Carlo took a deep breath."

"Never mind, just pay attention to what you're doing."

The moment vanished. Milo brushed, and as if by magic, the shoe shone. After a second coat of polish, his father handed him the buffing cloth.

"Hold it in both hands and pull it across the shoe like this."

In a rapid, conveyor belt-like motion, Carlo ran the cloth over the toe of the shoe and buffed it to a high gloss. "You try." Milo caught on quickly. He clumsily did the other and smiled at the shiny shoe.

"Am I done now?"

"Almost. Now take that little bottle, unscrew the cap and pull out the little brush. Be careful and don't spill it. Brush it on the edges of the heel and sole."

Milo applied the finishing touch of dressing and sighed.

"Am I done yet?"

Carlo smiled and gave him a hug. "You're done."

Over the course of several days, Milo cleaned and polished all four pair of his father's shoes. Each night he'd polish the ones his father had worn that day. With practice, Milo was able to pop the buffing cloth like a cap pistol.

He took delight in making them gleam and especially loved making the rag snap.

Satisfied, Carlo sent him to a local Italian club where his father played cards with his cronies.

"Find the dirtiest pair of shoes and ask the man if you can shine them. Listen carefully. Say, 'If you don't like the shine, there's no charge, but if you do, pay me what you think is fair.'"

"I don't wanna. What if they don't like it?"

"Just do a good job, and they will."

Milo recited the line over and again until he had it down. Milo ran down the block shouting, almost singing at the top of his voice, "Baarn-a-bee-eeey, come out. Baarn-a-bee-eeey."

When he got to Barnaby's house, Mrs. O'Leary stood with hands placed on hips as if to admonish him.

"Now you hush, Milo. You'll be wakin' the dead, you will."

"Sorry, Mrs. O'Leary. Where's Barnaby?"

"I'm coming. Be right there, Milo."

"Barnaby!" Milo gushed out of breath, "My dad made me a shine box and I'm gonna go to my grandpa's club to shine shoes. Wanna come? Can he Mrs. O'Leary?"

"I suppose there's no harm in it. But you'd best be back 'fore supper now, or it'll be a warm bottom if you're not."

"I promise, Mrs. O'Leary. C'mon, Milo, let's go."

They walked four blocks to the club, talking excitedly. When they got there, Milo found his Grandpa Joe.

"Grandpa, your shoes are real dirty. If I shine them,

you don't have to even pay me. No, I mean . . . you can pay me if ya wanna."

His grandfather laughed. "You do a good job or I'm gonna break you face."

When Milo finished, he earned fifteen cents and his grandfather got him another customer. With tips, he earned a dollar and ten cents. He felt proud and happy. When Milo got home, Carlo took the money he'd earned. Stunned, through welling tears, he shouted defiantly, "That's my money. I made it by myself."

Carlo showed Milo a receipt for nine dollars and twenty cents and spoke gently,

"Milo, you're a young man now. Only babies cry, so stop. I paid for the shoe shine box and the supplies with money I earned. You have to pay me back the other eight dollars and ten cents."

"That could take forever."

"It depends on how hard you work. But afterwards you can keep everything you earn and won't ever have to ask me or anyone for money again. Don't go running off yet, there's one more thing. Wait here, I'll be right back."

Angry, Milo muttered, "It's not fair," but inwardly he knew different. It didn't make him feel any better. Carlo returned with a piggy bank.

"Make sure you save half of what you earn."

On a Saturday, weeks later, Milo paid the remainder due his dad. Puffed like a blowfish, he said to his sister and brothers, "C'mon, me and Barnaby are takin' you to the movies."

To their delight, Milo treated them to the movie and ice

cream cones as well. He couldn't have been prouder.

One morning soon afterwards, Milo's father called him to the couch. Nothing good ever happened when summoned to the couch. Milo braced for the worst, sensing something was about to change. Carlo minced no words.

"I'm going to California to start a new life for us. I'll get a job and a house for us to live in. Then I'll come back, and we'll all take the train to our new home. Now, you're the oldest and you have to be in charge while I'm gone. Take care of your mother and your brothers and sisters. Do you promise?"

Milo froze. He looked into his dad's eyes. He saw sorrow and pain — and something else. Milo could barely stop his tears. Nor could he quell the fear. He looked at his high-topped red sneakers "I promise."

As they watched the car disappear, Milo turned to his mother. "Ma, he won't be back."

Shocked, Maria stung him with slap. "Don't ever talk about your father like that again."

Milo stood quietly and hung his head. He didn't care what she said. He knew the truth. Refusing to cry, he stormed off. Milo went to the abandoned lot down the block where he and Barnaby had built a hut from cardboard and odd pieces of wood. He climbed the fence and went to the hut. There, alone in the dark, he allowed his tears to fall. He'd never hurt as much or felt so alone. He vowed he'd be strong and take care of his family as his father had asked. The burden weighed heavily — the price, his childhood. It was Barnaby who helped him fill the void.

~ ~ ~

CHAPTER FIVE

Barnaby

S adder than he'd ever been, Milo sat forlornly in his pew, staring at the small coffin holding the remains of his friend. Who would there be to tell his secrets to now, he thought. Barnaby never made fun when Milo imitated flying an airplane. He'd use an old leather, ear-flapped flight hat and a broomstick between his legs. He vowed he'd fly someday. Barnaby believed him.

Both orphans, Barnaby and Milo shared music, solitude and secrets. That Barnaby also had no father gave Milo some consolation. His own troubles seemed smaller, more bearable in comparison. Barnaby lived three houses down on Melrose Street. A loner, he never joined in play with other kids on the block. They wouldn't have become friends had it not been Barnaby's penchant to hide on the fringe.

Barnaby never knew his father, and his mother died before his fourth birthday. One night Carlo had taken Milo to an opera rehearsal in the hall of the church where he presently sat mourning. This day was filled with sadness — that earlier night with music. Milo discovered Barnaby half-hidden in the shadows, listening. "What's your name?"

Startled, the boy stammered, "Barnaby." He stood

awkwardly, still partially hidden with his head lowered. "That lady sings nice. It's Vivien Goulette. She's my favorite."

"Wanna come inside?"

"Okay. Are ya sure it'll be all right?"

"Sure. C'mon, my father's the conductor."

When they got inside, Barnaby burst into a smile and stood agog at what he saw. They sat quietly on the dusty wooden floor, watching and listening intently. They were fast friends from then on.

Barnaby couldn't play roughhouse games, such as ringo-livio, which required chasing, capturing, and putting other players in "jail," but he could shoot skullys, a game played in the middle of the street, as most games were. A large square, with a smaller one in each corner and another in the center, was drawn on the pavement with chalk. Bottle caps were weighted with orange or lemon peel. Players flicked their caps with the forefinger. The object was to get the cap into the corner squares first, then into the center. Knocking another player's cap away from its target took skill. The first player to reach the center won. Constant interruptions by cars and an occasional horse-drawn cart didn't lessen the game's popularity. Barnaby had become expert at skullys the only game he played. He beat Milo regularly. Milo thought they'd be friends forever.

~ ~ ~

A dwarf, Barnaby walked bowlegged to the wooden park bench, kicking up dust on purpose. Placing his palms on the plank seat, he clambered up, first one knee, then the other, and plunked down on his rump. He sat panting, hunched forward, staring at the ground, his legs dangling.

"Can't reach the cookie jar, can't look out the window, and can't even reach the ground with my feet on this freaking bench!" he mumbled. "And nobody my age should be getting bald." Barnaby slouched on the bench, resting, his shoulders bent with his burdens. Tears rolled down his cheeks and splattered the dust below. At last he took a deep breath, sighed, and said to himself, "Oh, well, better go meet Milo and get my pretzels 'fore there's none left."

He jumped down and kicked. Dust rose and hung in the air. Barnaby trudged away.

He walked the three blocks to Jefferson Street, humming an aria from *Madame Butterfly*, one of his favorites. He loved opera, and knew the most popular female leads by heart. He and Milo eagerly anticipated the rehearsals of the Queens Opera Company at the church hall.

Would she be practicing today? he wondered.

The aroma of fresh pretzels hung in the air like a delicious cloud. Holding a handrail, Barnaby took the steps two at a time, hopping down to the bakery. Max stood busily scrubbing the oil well of the deep fryer. Beads of sweat rolled off his shining head into the sparse white hair above his ears. Perched on the end of his ample nose teetered batter-speckled glasses.

Wiping his hands on his apron, he turned towards

Barnaby, smiling broadly. His tangled brows shot upwards.

"Barnaby, how's it going? You're late this morning. Milo's been here and gone."

"'Lo, Max. Yeah. Still got some pretzels?"

Max chuckled. "Only three dozen for you, kid."

"Thanks, Max."

Mrs. O'Leary, Barnaby's guardian, hadn't planned to be. A kindly neighbor, she'd watched after him while his mother worked. When his mother died, there was no one else. She kept him rather than see him placed in an orphanage.

When she first sent fourteen-year-old Barnaby to buy pretzels, Max had given him a dozen on account. Next day, having sold them, Barnaby paid Max in full. Since then, Barnaby's order had more than doubled in less than three months.

"How's old Mrs. O'Leary doing, Barnaby?"

"Cranky."

"That's just her way. She's entitled. She must be near ninety, I'd guess."

"Uh, do ya know the lady who sings opera, down at the end of the block?"

"Yeah, that's Vivian. Damned good, too. She comes in here all the time. Loves hot pretzels."

"She sang with the opera company my friend Milo's father used to conduct."

"Hmmm . . . wouldn't surprise me to see her at the Met someday. The neighbors bitch about her, but they got no class."

Barnaby doffed his Dodgers cap and slapped it against his thigh. He ran his stubby fingers through the frizz on his head. He'd become increasingly aware of the balding. It embarrassed him. He quickly put the cap back on.

"Gotta get goin' Max. See you tomorrow."

"Bye, Barnaby. Say hello to Mrs. O'Leary for me." Max too, noticed a lot of scalp showing through Barnaby's hair. He decided to ask Mrs. O'Leary about it when he talked to her again.

That evening, Barnaby went back to Jefferson Street and sat on the curb across the street from the brownstone where Vivian lived. It stood apart from the other houses, a dignified, if worn, remnant of the prosperity it once represented. But for the lights atop the ornate lampposts, the street was in darkness. In the dim light, the line of garbage cans looked like soldiers on guard. The steaming manhole in the middle of the street could have been a campfire.

He felt the cat before he saw it. Back arched, it rubbed its head against Barnaby's leg. Softly he said, "Hi, cat, got sump'n for you."

He reached into his pocket, and pulled out a brown paper bag that held a sardine he had filched from Mrs. O'Leary.

"Here you go, cat."

The cat took the fish, sniffed it, gave it a couple of gentle pokes, licked it and crouched in front of him to eat.

Hunched against the chill, Barnaby rubbed the cat's ears. Not wanting to be seen, Barnaby thought they were hidden in the shadows, but a streetlight cast their silhouettes on the wall behind them.

"Hear that singing, cat? My ma used to sing like that, even better. Oh, she was fine, she was. Used to sing to me all the time, she did. Sure miss my ma, cat. Don't know what happened. Started looking real tired and pale-like. One day she told me she was going away for a while. Left me with Mrs. O'Leary, she did, and never seen her again. Mrs. O'Leary told me she died, and I never knew my pa."

~ ~ ~

Vivian, sat down, closed her eyes and relaxed. The lighting made her cheekbones appear even higher. Moving her tongue to the corner of her mouth, she ran it slowly over her full lips, leaving them glistening. Her fingers interlocked, she pushed them forward in a stretch. Sucking air deeply into her lungs, she slowly exhaled through her nose.

She opened her eyes. Wrists high, she placed her fingertips on the keyboard. Her dark eyes flashed. In one elegant swoop, she flung the rippling black tresses from her face and began. Scintillating bubbles of sound floated out through the open window into the crisp air.

~ ~ ~

The night came alive with her voice. Eyes closed and arms moving as if conducting, Barnaby sat entranced, humming the harmony. When she finished, he thought about his mother, fighting to control his emotions. Picking up the cat, he held its face to his cheek.

"What'd you think of that? Huh, cat?"

The cat licked a tear from Barnaby's face.

"Gotta go now, cat. Mrs. O'Leary will be wondering where the heck I am. Night, cat."

Putting the cat down, he jammed his fists into his pockets, and in his peculiar gait, ambled home. He could almost hear Mrs. O'Reilly sitting at home, railing at him.

The back of her hands was mottled brown, the sinews and bluish veins clearly defined. Her white hair was wound tightly in a bun with a brown and yellow hairpin through it. Through gold-rimmed bifocals, her flint blue eyes held the look of Ireland. The absence of teeth was made obvious by the set of her jaw. In her lap lay an afghan. It covered her legs to where her rolled stockings ended. At her feet were two rolls of yarn, one blue and the other white.

She sat rocking and knitting, the creaking chair and clicking needles the only sounds save for her muttered fretting.

"The boy's after bein' the death of me, stayin' out till all hours. Suppose if it's the only thing to complain about, I shouldn't be. Poor lad's off his color, too. Not eating like a growing boy ought to, either."

The clumping in the stairwell caused her a sigh of relief, but as soon as he opened the door, Mrs. O'Leary scolded.

"Barnaby, do you know what time it is? You missed your supper again."

"Sorry Mrs. O'Leary."

"You'd best eat it right off, lad. 'Tis warm on the stove. Then, be off to bed with you. Need to be at the clinic at

7:00 on the morrow, you do."

"Not hungry, Mrs. O'Leary."

Barnaby removed his jacket and cap and hung them on the wooden hall tree. He wasn't looking forward to the clinic; he didn't feel half as bad before the treatments as he did afterwards. Fatigued, he collapsed on the sofa.

Mrs. O'Leary took off her glasses and rubbed her eyes.

"Well, at least be takin' a cup of tea, and there's fresh oatmeal cookies by the kettle."

"Thanks, Mrs. O'Leary."

~ ~ ~

Tonight, Vivian would work on *Carmen*. As she sang, she glanced out the window. Again the silhouettes were there. It had been a month since she first noticed. But for her cat, she would have felt threatened. Who is he, she wondered.

Barnaby sat in his usual place on the curb when the staccato beat of the opera signaled the beginning of the aria.

"Hello, cat. Listen. This is the best part."

Barnaby sang the words along with Vivian, keeping the tempo by moving the cat to and fro. When Vivian had finished, the purring cat was nestled in his lap.

"What's she going to sing next? Huh, cat?" He heard her door open. Abruptly, he put the cat down. "Uh-oh, cat. I gotta go."

"Hold it!" she shouted from the doorway of the old brownstone. "Hold it!"

Barnaby stopped in his tracks, and stood sheepishly,

trying to hide between his shoulders. She towered over him, feet apart, hands on hips, frosted breath rising around her face. Her intimidating posture belied her kindly tone.

"What's your name?"

"Barnaby, Miss Vivian."

Her eyes widened. "How do you know my name?"

"I heard you sing at Milo's father's rehearsal, and Max told me you lived here."

"Oh, Max! Such a nice man! I know some nice things about you too, Barnaby."

"Oh? How?"

"I know my cat."

She stooped, picked up the cat, and hugged it to her chest.

"So, what are you doing out here all the time?"

Barnaby shuffled, shifting his weight from one foot to the other. His hands dug deeper into his pockets.

"Ah . . . Well . . . I . . . I come to hear you sing, Miss Vivian."

"Oh. Do you like opera, Barnaby?"

"Uh huh; my ma used to sing to me all the time."

"My mother sang to me too! Listen, it's chilly out here. Why don't you come in for some hot cocoa and cookies?"

"Uh . . . better not, Miss Vivian. Mrs. O'Leary, she's the lady I stay with. Well . . . she'd be awful worried. I better get home now."

"How about another time then? Just ring the doorbell, okay?"

"Thanks Miss Vivian. Night."

"Good night, Barnaby. Do come by soon."

~ ~ ~

Mrs. O'Leary poured tea. There came a knock at the door.

"Why, hello, Max"

"Mornin', Mrs. O'Leary."

"How've you keepin' yourself, Max?"

"Good as can be expected at my age."

She chuckled. "Och, you're but a babe. Don't you be complainin'."

"I've been noticing that Barnaby's hair is thinning, and his face's got a kind of yellowish tinge."

"Faith, it's the experiment treatments they be givin' him at the clinic, Max."

"Oh? What's wrong with him?"

"Don't rightly know, Max. Somethin' to do with a condition the 'little people' sometimes get, poor lad. Not bad enough bein' one. He's had his share of burden, with no father and his mother gone, God rest her soul. Been told it's serious, I fear."

"God, that's terrible. Well, just wanted to check with you. Let's pray everything will turn out fine. Have a good day, Mrs. O'Leary."

"And you, Max. Thanks for stopping by."

~ ~ ~

A week passed and Barnaby hadn't been to visit, leaving Vivian wondering why. Deciding to ask Max, she walked the short distance to the bakery. Max beamed in delight when she entered the shop.

"Good afternoon, Vivian. Nice to see you."

"Hello, Max. How are you?"

"Well, I've my aches and pains, but that's another story. How's about yourself, Vivian?"

"Fine, Max, but I wanted to ask about Barnaby. I haven't seen him lately."

"Yeah, he's been sick and getting treatments at the clinic. Mrs. O'Leary tells me it's serious. Such a nice lad too. Sure loves your singing."

"Oh, geez. Thanks Max."

Another week passed. One evening, Vivian had just finished dinner and started washing dishes. The cat, napping on the sofa, suddenly sprang alert, staring intently at the door. The doorbell chimed. Vivian dried her hands and spoke into the intercom.

"Hello. Who's there?"

"It's Barnaby, Miss Vivian."

Barnaby walked up the stairs, heart pounding, wondering if he should have come. No getting out of it now, he thought. When he reached the top, he knocked timidly at the door.

"Come on in, Barnaby. My! What have we here?"

Barnaby handed her a brown paper bag containing two fresh pretzels, and a fistful of daisies filched from Mrs. O'Leary's window box.

"These are for you, Miss Vivian."

"How sweet, Barnaby. Thank you."

Barnaby's cheeks glowed pink.

"Have a seat while I make some hot chocolate."

"Thanks, Miss Vivian."

Barnaby hoisted himself on the sofa and looked up at the high, gold leaf-sculpted ceilings. It made him feel even smaller. He glanced around the room. Sheet music covered the living room table and the floor next to the overstuffed armchair. Behind the piano were four rows of shelves filled with records. A mahogany cabinet containing a phonograph and radio stood nearby. Glossy oak floors framed the Persian rug, candlelight softened the room, and Barnaby felt as if he were in a painting. The cat jumped into his lap and licked him. Its rough tongue tickled Barnaby's hand.

"Hey, cat. Stop that."

Barnaby clambered down and went over to the piano. On top, on doilies, were two vases filled with miniature pink roses. The keyboard barely reached the level of his chin. He ran his fingers over the smooth ebony finish.

Vivian returned. "Come sit on the sofa with me."

She brought cocoa and cookies and poured herself tea.

"Well, Barnaby, where have you been? I thought you'd changed your mind about visiting."

"Ah . . . Been sick, Miss Vivian."

"Oh? Tell me about it."

"Well, I was getting bad headaches so I went to the clinic. They gave me lots of tests. The doctor told me there was a tumor on my brain. Now they are giving me stuff to fix it."

"Are you feeling better?"

Barnaby looked at the floor. His lower lip began to quiver and his eyes filled. Vivian sat quietly waiting.

"No."

Vivian placed a hand on his shoulder. With the other she gently raised his chin with the crook of her finger. She looked directly into his eyes. He blinked.

"Tell me about it, Barnaby."

It feels awful, Miss Vivian. It feels so bad. Don't want to be living any more. But . . . I miss my ma, but I'm afraid to die."

Vivian drew him to her. Placing her cheek on top of his head, she enfolded him in her arms. He made no sound, but the wracking heaves and her dampened breast wrenched her soul. She held him, singing softly, until he became calm. Then she spoke in a gentle voice.

"My mother used to sing to me, too. She died when I was fourteen. My father always traveled, didn't see him much. When I did, he did awful things to me. I wanted to die, too. I was afraid, just like you are, and I thought about dying a lot. Then I started to realize that everyone would die eventually. Nothing can change that. The more I thought about it, the less fearful I became. My life has been happier since. We live until we die, Barnaby. We can live in fear, but that is only an existence. Or, we can overcome our fear. Each of us decides."

Barnaby felt warm and safe in Vivian's arms. She smells even better than my ma, he thought. Vivian got up, took Barnaby by the hand, and gently urged him to follow.

They remained in the darkness a long while. Later, in

a small voice filled with gratitude, he whispered, "Thank you, Miss Vivian."

In the weeks that followed, Barnaby spent many wonderful evenings with Vivian, but his condition grew worse. Most of his hair was gone. He became weaker and could barely walk. His visits were at first less frequent, then soon stopped.

Mrs. O'Leary sat rocking with her lap full of work, but her thoughts elsewhere. The phone rang.

"Hello?"

"Good morning, Mrs. O'Leary. This is Max."

"Oh, how are you, Max?"

"I was just calling after Barnaby. He didn't come for his pretzels today."

Mrs. O'Leary's voice lowered.

"Been meanin' to call you, Max. Barnaby . . . he passed on last night."

After a long silence, voice cracking, Max said, "How terrible. I'm so sad, Mrs. O'Leary."

"Don't you be grievin' now, Max. Barnaby died peaceful. He's safe in heaven, and when he went, 'twas with a smile."

~ ~ ~

Max called Vivian to tell her about Barnaby. Saddened by the news, she poured herself a cup of tea, and placing both hands around the cup, took comfort in its warmth. It had not occurred to her, when she saw Barnaby last night she might never see him again.

That night he'd sat on the sofa playing with the cat.

Vivian worked at the piano.

"Hey, cat! Cut that out. It hurts."

"Barnaby, stop playing with the cat for a minute. Tell me what you think of this." She began to sing the *Ave Maria*. The hair rose all over Barnaby's body. The crystal clarity of her voice thrilled him. When she finished, she turned to Barnaby, grinning.

"How's that, Barnaby?"

"Ah . . . well, if you could just hold on to that last note longer till it sort of goes away by itself?"

Vivian's eyes widened, the response not what she'd expected. She turned back to the piano. With a toss of her head, Vivian flipped her hair from her face, and sang it again. On reaching the last note, she held it, holding it delicately, until it faded seamlessly, from sound to silence. Astounded, she wondered why she hadn't known that. Vivian turned to Barnaby smiling. He cried, but his tears were those of joy.

"Like that, Miss Vivian. Just like that."

~ ~ ~

Milo looked about the church. Mrs. O'Leary sat by herself in the pew in front of him, to his right Max and Vivian. So few people for such a big church, he thought. A chill crept over him. He shuddered, the church as cold and empty as he felt inside. Milo wondered if he would always feel that way. He spoke to God. "Why did you let my father leave? Why did you let Barnaby die?"

Milo felt ready to cry, but his well of tears had been drained. His best friend gone, any trepidation about moving went with it. In a few days, they'd leave for Tybourne. He loved the little farm in the country. He thought it wouldn't be as sad there.

~ ~ ~

Although Milo couldn't have known, a kindred spirit who had lived many years before him, Johann Sebastian Bach was a man who had struggled with similar losses, frustrations and anxieties. They had influenced his life, as would those of Milo. What Bach learned through those traumas was manifested in his music, a lasting gift to the world and a refrain that would become a guiding force for Milo.

~ ~ ~

CHAPTER SIX

Angels of Death

A well-worn clavier burnished by years of use filled one corner, across the room a harpsichord. Several violins, a cello, viola and flute were casually scattered about as if to lounge while awaiting their turn. Music scores were strewn about on every flat surface in the room. Sebastian, preordained to continue the long musical heritage of his ancestors, fidgeted uncomfortably. His ears reddened at his father's chiding. "How can you expect to play anything if you won't do as you're told?"

The violin felt many times heavier than it actually weighed. Sebastian wanted to smash it to smithereens and toss the fragments into the fire. He stomped in frustration, causing a stocking to fall. He tried to pull it up and dropped the bow. "I don't care if I play anything — ever."

Ambrosius took a deep breath, trying to control his anger. He's only seven, he thought. "Be careful with your bow. Do you think pfennigs appear out of thin air?"

In the German language of that time the word "Bach" had become idiolect for musician. "You are a Bach. Music is sacred, Sebastian. It comes from God. You are blessed. God will punish you if you do not heed its call."

"This isn't music. I'm tired of playing these silly scales."

The opportunity presented itself. Ambrosius chal-

lenged his seven-year-old. "Well then, lad, let us hear
what you think music is. The boy looked at his father,
smiled, then began to play.

Dumbfounded, Ambrosius likened it to the voice of
angels. "You are truly inspired by God. Of that, there is no
doubt. Now then, play the D major scale ten times the way
you played that."

"Then can I play my own music?"

"Yes, then you can play whatever you wish."

The exuberant boy flung his arms around his father,
almost dropping the violin. "Thank you, father. I do want
to please you, and God."

"I cannot speak for God, but you have pleased me
immensely. Now the question is how many flats are there
in the key of B flat major?" The boy looked at him coyly.
"Not one more than is absolutely necessary."

They laughed.

Being born to a family of privilege could not shield
Sebastian from the earthly hell of death. It surrounded
him like a posse of black angels. His first encounter came
with the death of Cousin Jacob, an apprentice under his
father. Sebastian looked at him, sweat-soaked, moaning in
his bed. "What's wrong with him, Father?"

"It could be the plague; the doctors are uncertain."

Sebastian looked at his father with sadness. "Is he
going to die?"

Ambrosius wished he could have said differently. "I'm
afraid he will."

"Why must people die, Papa?"

"It is God's plan."

Sebastian thought it strange that God would have such plans. The thought reoccurred two years later when he looked mournfully at the lifeless face of his mother. "Is this God's plan too, Papa?"

Ambrosius, filled with grief and pain, especially for his son, gazed at the pallid face of his beloved wife. "I know it is difficult to understand the way of God. You must have faith. What he does is beyond understanding."

Sebastian clutched his father. Ambrosius felt his son's fear. "I hope he doesn't take you from me, Papa."

Thirteen months later, his father looked to be in slumber, but by then, Sebastian knew well the look of death. Death and fear, now irrevocably interlocked, would shadow his life, one to be unquestionably accepted — the other courageously overcome.

A seed had been planted in an inquisitive mind. A litany of unanswered and unanswerable questions began. For a musical intellect that never permitted such ambiguity in his compositions, it would become an intolerable and haunting impasse.

Years later, when faced with those same unanswered and unanswerable questions, Bach as a young man; was able to resolve both in his superlative composition, the *Chaconne.*

~ ~ ~

As with Sebastian, Milo learned early on about the finality of death and each would question his imposed faith, but not before a lot of life had been lived.

~ ~ ~

CHAPTER SEVEN

Tybourne

The minute Milo walked into the candy store, he forgot all about the Double Bubble gum that he'd gone there to purchase. The girl standing on tiptoes at the cash register counted her pennies while trying to hold on to her crutches. The thin shapeless legs below her pink shorts were encased in shiny, hinged braces, making them appear more fragile than they were. His heart felt funny and so did the hole in his pant leg where his knee poked through. He hoped she wouldn't notice. Mr. Nat (that's what they called the proprietor) smiled and raised his brows at the expression on Milo's face. It showed embarrassment, delight, and fear all at once.

Milo quickly turned for the door mumbling, "Be back later, Mr. Nat. Forgot my money."

"You can bring it later, Milo."

The girl looked at Milo and smiled shyly, but Milo didn't turn back. He hurried out and crossed the street. His heart seemed to be doing jumping jacks in his chest. He hid behind a parked car and watched as she struggled to manipulate her crutches while carrying the books held with a brown belt in one hand and the bag of candy she'd bought in the other.

The books swung like a pendulum, causing her to

stumble. The bag flew out of her hand, dumping the candy onto the sidewalk. Milo ran over and gathered the candy, put it into the bag, and handed it to her. Her eyeglasses were cockeyed, threatening to fall off. Through them her large green eyes filled with frustration, embarrassment, and tears. Milo handed her the bag. She straightened her glasses and tried to reach into the bag of candy with the hand holding the books. The sudden movement almost toppled her, but Milo stopped her from falling. She stood knock-kneed, crutches askew, and began to laugh and cry at the same time. Milo stood stricken by puppy love. Her vulnerability overcame his shyness.

"Have to go get my money. Want to come with me? I live right around the block."

"Okay."

She handed him a chunk of Bazooka. He popped it into his mouth and smiled. "Double Bubble. It's my favorite."

"Mine, too."

The hole in his pants now seemed unimportant. He took her books and they walked to his house.

"What's your name?"

In the middle of a bubble, she popped it. "Madeline Heinz. What's yours?"

"Milo Damiani. Where do you live?"

"On Knickabocker Avenue, the next block up from Mr. Nat's. We just moved here."

Milo got a pang. He realized that in two days, he'd be moving. He'd been happy about it until now. "We're moving to my grandfather's farm near Boston on Saturday."

"Oh."

They didn't speak the rest of the way, each engrossed in thought. Milo opened the door to the hallway leading to his mother's flat.

"This is nice. No stairs. We live on the second floor."

There were two entrances. Milo opened the door that led to the parlor, a fairly large room. Its most prominent feature was a scarred but functional piano on top of which stood a plaster bust of Mozart and a bronze one of Bach.

Worn, flower-patterned linoleum covered the floor. On it sat a ragged, padded-armed couch and matching chair, also flowered. Two large windows opened to the street, which was obscured by partially opened Venetian blinds. The flower-patterned drapes didn't match the floor, couch or chair. Milo loved flowers but not these patterns that looked like dead flowers; he didn't want to be reminded of dead anything. The fragrance of flowers and odor of death seemed incompatible to him. He hoped his new friend wouldn't be mindful of the décor.

Madeline leaned her crutches against the wall, held an arm of the couch, hobbled around it, and sat down.

"Want a drink of water, Madeline?"

"Yes, please."

Milo went to the kitchen and poured a glass. With his mother at work and his brothers and sister out at play, the house felt serene. He returned and gave Madeline the glass. She dropped it, and her lip began to tremble.

Don't worry. I do it all the time. Milo wiped up the water and got her another glass. Madeline drank half of it, sighed, and smiled.

"Thanks. Do you play the piano?"

"My dad was giving me lessons before he left, but I hated it. Wanna hear someth'n?"

"Uh huh."

Milo went to the piano and opened the sliding doors above the keyboard. He placed a roll on the spindle and began pumping the pedals. After a short delay, the roll started turning and the keys began to move as if played by a ghost. Milo had his hands in the air with his fingers moving as if striking the keys. He turned to Madeline; in an imitation of his father's admonishment he said, "You must keep your wrists high."

Milo thought Madeline's timid laughter sounded like a song, more musical than the piano spewed forth, more than any melody he'd ever heard. When the roll came to its end, he got up and bowed.

Madeline clapped her hands and bounced gleefully on the couch. Milo sat next to her and looked into her eyes. Her hands were folded in her lap. Wisps of fine blond hair fell over her glasses. Her smile melted him.

In a natural yet awkward way, they hesitantly leaned towards one another, their eyes wide. Hearts quickened, lips as magnets drew slowly close until they touched in a brief meeting, seemingly an eternity. An innocent kind of magic, a first kiss that would never happen again and Milo would always remember.

They would not see each other again. Two days later, his family moved to Tybourne to live with his grandparents, the Tessinos. The move seemed a blur to him, due to the bitter cold in the back seat of his grandfather Nonno's car and his thoughts of Madeline during the long drive.

A week later, Milo and his grandfather were in the wine cellar. The smell of fermenting wine permeated the musty air. Gnats buzzed in the dim cool. Milo's grandparents had just returned from Modacio's Funeral Home where they had received the body of their son, killed in the Normandy invasion. Milo had been named after this uncle. He heard the thump of his grandmother Nonna's footsteps descend the wooden stairs; then he could hear her cry.

In Italian she said, "Dear God, our Milo is gone forever."

Till then, Nonno had managed a stoic façade, but now he put his hands over his eyes and cried as well. In a culturally symbolic gesture, they pounded their foreheads against one of the thick wooden columns supporting the floor above. Young Milo understood the monumental sadness that permeated the cellar. He had never seen a man weep. Now he also wept, both for his grandparents and himself.

In the 1940s, Tybourne, a picturesque New England town had as its principle industries a tannery, processing cowhides into leather, and a shoe factory (a natural offshoot). There were small family farms growing corn, beans, squash, and carrots along with lettuce, tomatoes, cucumbers, and the like. Families grew and canned their homegrown products, many selling at the open markets in

Boston, twelve miles to the south.

Having visited his maternal grandparents on a summer vacation, Milo was enchanted, loved the farm and was happy to live there. He quickly learned that chickens, ducks, goats, and rabbits were not welcome in the large vegetable garden.

Painfully, Milo discovered Nonno's fruit orchard was sacred. Nonna's flowers, especially roses that blossomed ubiquitously, were her pride.

Milo enjoyed fresh fruit more than candy. After a hot summer's day, he'd pick a ripe tomato warm from the sun, sprinkle it with salt from the shaker in his pocket, and scarf it down. Nonna always knew by the stains and seeds on his shirt. She never seemed to mind.

The self-sustaining farm provided the family with vegetables and fruit to can for winter. An abundant supply of eggs, chicken, rabbit, and goat's milk provided some income.

The new way of life suited Milo perfectly, but for Nonno's notions of instructing him in life's lessons. They appeared as lumps of coal, but later became gems of wisdom. The fine line between cruelty and compassion became obscure in the process.

One winter night, Nonno arrived home with a newborn fuzzy lamb. Broadly grinning, he placed it in Milo's arms. The creature flailed its legs and probed for nourishment, all the while bleating pathetically enough to break a heart. Nonno handed Milo a bottle filled with honey-sweetened milk. "Feed it."

It took some contorted maneuverings to connect the darting pink mouth to the elusive nipple, but soon the lamb sucked blissfully until it slept, occasionally suckling on reflex.

Milo turned to his smiling grandfather. "Can I keep it, Nonno?"

"It will die if you don't give him milk when he wants it. Do you understand?"

Milo knew well about dead eyes. "I will."

Without another word, his grandfather left the lamb in Milo's care.

The lamb and Milo became inseparable. Milo could hardly bear to leave it between feedings. The creature followed him like a long-legged puppy, and soon learned the art of matching butts. By spring, the lamb had almost become a four-legged appendage.

On the Friday before Easter, Milo evaded terrified hens, which were trying to dodge the lamb's attempts to batter them to oblivion. Nonna called from the pantry window. "Nonno wants you to bring the lamb to the cellar. Right now."

"I'm coming," he shouted. Milo managed to grab a hind leg, heaved the protesting animal to a shoulder and trundled into the cool of the underground room.

Nonno chomped on his stogie as he tied on a leather apron. He took the lamb and with a swift blurred movement, struck it behind the head with his fist. It went limp. Milo's eyes showed white to twice their normal size. With a flick of a knife, the lamb's throat parted, spurting a stream of blood into the galvanized bucket on the floor.

All Milo could think to do was run until the sucking for air stopped him. He collapsed in a tearful heap at the edge of Flask Pond. When he'd cried himself dry, he went home, locked himself in his room, and cried himself to sleep.

On Easter Sunday, lasers of anger shot from Milo's to Nonno's eyes. "Why did you do that?"

Nonno placed a firm hand on Milo's shoulder. "Lambs are for food; dogs are pets."

Milo had not tasted the bitter taste of hatred before. He never ate lamb again, and would not forget its eyes.

~ ~ ~

A traffic roundabout, the Center, dominated Tybourne. Many New England towns had those remnants of seventeenth-century English influence. Though he didn't understand why, they seemed somehow familiar and a comfort to him.

The salient features of the Center were two old white Protestant churches facing each other on opposite sides of the roundabout. The Catholic church his family attended seemed more holy to Milo. When he asked why there were three different churches, but only one God, none of the answers made sense. Milo stopped asking.

One day while helping his grandfather pluck the feasting beetles in the garden, Nonno harped at him. "When I was twelve like you, I already had a job. You should find some work. Nonno can't afford to give you money for spending."

It made sense to Milo. His father taught him the value of earning and saving. He went to Moore & Parker's on the east side, a gathering place where the newsboys would pick up their papers, and a coffee or soda could be had at the fountain.

Milo sauntered into the distribution office, a shabby and sparsely furnished place occupied by Billy Parker. Tobacco juice from the plug in his cheek permanently stained a scruffy gray beard.

"What kin I do fer ya, boy?"

"Do you have any routes?"

"Where do ya live?"

"On 28 Campbell Street. I live with my grandparents."

Billy nodded toward the canvas bag on the floor.

"Yer kinda scrawny there, boy. Think ya kin carry that bag of papers?" Milo didn't hesitate.

"Yes sir. I'm stronger than I look."

"Well, I ain't got nuth'n fer ya now, but I'll keep ya in mind." Billy spat into the spittoon at his feet.

"Thanks, Mr. Parker. Should I come back tomorrow?"

"Come back every day if ya want, and you kin call me Billy." With a wink, and a backhanded wave, he shooed Milo out the door.

As an added motivation to get a job, Milo loved the fantasyland of movies and the thought of going to the old Strand Theater, at the north end of the common, whenever he wanted to. On the hottest summer day, the dark cool of the Strand was irresistible, offering a double feature, newsreel, and three cartoons, all for twenty-five cents.

Milo made a pest of himself until Billy gave him a route. The bag turned out heavier than he thought.

Just to the south of the Center, almost anything could be bought at J. J. Newberry's. Farther down the street stood Sears and Roebuck, where purchases could be made with time payments. Milo and many of Tybourne's young people got their first real jobs there.

West of town, Flask Pond shimmered in the morning sun. Milo had learned to skate on its icy surface. Almost every winter evening after supper, the shore screeched with the sounds of children skating, and families sipped apple cider in the warmth of fires spangling the beach. Misty breaths framed ruddy cheeks in the sparkling New England night. Ice fishermen chatted and smoked pipes as they tended their holes and watched the kids.

On this late spring day, Milo decided to explore with a four-mile stroll around the flask-shaped pond. Loneliness seemed lessened by the oak, pine, maple, willow, and birch trees around him. The woods were rife with blueberries, mulberries, and rhubarb. All found their way into many a pie.

Milo picked a basket of plump blueberries, already tasting the wedge from the pie Nonna would bake the next day. A red fox peeked at him from a thicket of birch at the pond's edge. *Wow, he thought. I've already seen a skunk, deer, possum and raccoon. Maybe I'll see a bobcat, too.*

Milo headed for a stream winding down to the pond. He cautiously approached a family of beaver busy at work. Fed by springs, the pond teemed with bass, trout, and endless kibbies that would bite at anything. Not particularly tasty, they guaranteed a catch at the end of the day.

Flask Pond served as the town's water supply. Milo knelt at the water's edge and cupped a handful of fresh sweetness, wondering how it could be so, with slimy fish darting about in it.

Ambling past the old icehouse, Milo marveled at the massive wooden timbers supporting the building. Sided with winter slush-hued clapboard, it spoke of stability and permanence. Milo poked his head inside. A cold blast from the stacked ice blocks slapped his cheek. Pigeons warmly cooing in the eves took a bite from the chill. Flask Pond, he decided, would be a refuge, a place where he'd never be lonely.

Hard play burned his muscles, brightened his eyes, and splashed a tired glow over Milo's face. His cousin, Bunny, four years older at sixteen, was visiting for a week. Milo sat next to her at the supper table. He'd once borrowed her bike without permission. She ratted on him, which cost him a red-welted bottom, compliments of Nonno.

Nonno got up and went to the pantry for wine. Talking at dinner could cost him a thrashing, he thought, as she whispered in his ear.

"I'm sorry about the bike; you should have asked." Milo flashed an angry glance and kept eating.

"I have something for you."

That sparked his interest. "What is it?"

"Shhhh, don't talk so loud; you'll get us killed. I can't tell you now because Nonno's coming. After supper, go to my room and wait. I gotta do dishes."

His grandfather seemed to have radar and eyed them. Milo waited until Nonno began eating, and then gave Bunny a nod. She inched closer touching his leg with a foot. She's the one who's going to get us killed, he thought, staring her down with a chunk of bread hanging from his mouth. Bunny giggled.

Nonno looked like a statue with a throbbing vein in its neck about to explode. Milo, head buried deep between his shoulders, dug into his food. He got a faint whiff of a strange odor seeming to come from her, not offensive, and in some way exciting.

After supper Milo went to her room. Sunset brought with it a cool breeze that filled the curtain. Chilled, he flopped on the bed, covered himself with an afghan and fell sound asleep.

Milo thought at first the sensation to be a dream. He smelled that peculiar scent again, and felt warm moisture between his legs. *Oh no, I wet the bed.* He reached down and touched something soft and kinky. It moved. He didn't. There were strange sensations in his groin.

"Shhhh, be quiet."

Milo froze. What's happening, he wondered. Clumsily, Bunny hurriedly removed his clothes. Now both were naked. Not moving, for fear she'd stop, not knowing precisely why, Milo had a sense of anticipation. The scent about her somehow excited him.

"Does it feel good?"

Milo swallowed hard and nodded. Bunny got guttural.

He winced at the garlic breath tagged to the vowels of her *ooohs and aahhs*. She lay on her back and wrestled him on top. His body grew rigid, causing Bunny difficulty keeping him aboard.

She groped with frantic fingers, not gently, for his penis. Milo's eyes showed mostly white. Not resisting, he didn't know how to assist. The odor got stronger and so did his heartbeat. It caused him to suck in air, very large gulps in short intervals.

Bunny began to make strange noises, all the while trying to plant his penis into the soft excited wet place between her legs. Milo would have been frightened, but it felt so good. She bucked and snorted. Milo grabbed hold so as not to fall off, and then the squeals and groans got louder.

Milo flung a panic-struck glance towards the door, expecting Nonno at any second.

"Cripes," he hissed. "You're going to get us killed."

Bunny gave a last thrust, as if to fling him towards the ceiling. Her body spasmed and then, she squeezed him tightly. Alarm turned to terror, as his breath squirted out like toothpaste. Struggling, Milo pulled at her arms, got loose and rolled off.

Bunny rose to an elbow. Squint-eyed, she wagged an admonishing finger. "If you tell anyone about this, you'll get us killed."

Milo wouldn't have known how to describe the experience.

The next morning he tiptoed around Nonno, expecting

the inevitable, which never came. Nonno spoke only of the load of chicken shit they were delivering to Mr. Santullo as they drove along Lowell Street.

A sure-fire, bumpy country road plunked between woods, Lowell Street ran north and south, connecting Main south to the Santullo farm and then rolled picturesquely into the town of Burnham. Even up to the late fifties, Tybourne remained farmland except for subdivided lots. The Santullos owned several, which they sold as needed for their children's college tuition. Milo knew he'd have to pay his own way.

In three years, Milo managed to save a few hundred dollars for tuition. That, the darkening fuzz on his jaw, and his football prowess, gave him confidence. At fifteen, he awkwardly straddled the line between boy and man, but got a chance to test himself. One of his friends, Kevin Dolman, lived on Lowell Street. Milo's cousin, Chris, dated Diane who lived a few lot-lengths away. She introduced Milo to her cousin, Denise Forbes, who also lived on Lowell Street. Milo's only girl battle took place on Lowell Street with Denise's ex-boyfriend, Frank, a town bully.

After his first date with Denise, Frank owl-eyed Milo's car pulling up. Frank let it be known there'd be no giving up his girl to some jock. A group of neighborhood kids gathered to watch the duel.

Milo got out of the car. Frank swaggered over with hands casually tucked in his pockets. Greasy hair plastered Elvis-style gleamed like armor. A pack of Luckys bulged between elbow and shoulder. Frank thrust his face inches from Milo's and spittle blustered, "If you don't want your ass kicked, stay away from my girl, asshole."

Milo gave him the glue-eye — his eyes never left the opponent's and didn't blink. Before the last word escaped the bully's snarl, Milo's knee and the guy's groin had a meeting. Milo then popped him flush on the nose drawing blood, which redesigned Frank's shirt. Bravado gone, he fell to the ground bawling.

"It worked," he gloated under his breath. "My dad was right." But as he glanced down, he saw not an adolescent, but a little boy. A flashback to Mrs. Rhodes' class and the piss puddle at his feet on that day left him feeling Frank's humiliation. He reached down and pulled him to his feet. "I'm sorry."

On many occasions, Milo walked the six miles from his house to Denise's. One frigid night while walking her home from a movie, Milo kissed her and felt her breast for the first time.

The day he got his first car, a maroon and white '41 Ford, he and Kevin raced on Lowell Street. Milo had driven its length countless times. Some of the happiest moments in his life happened on Lowell Street . . . and some of the worst.

~ ~ ~

CHAPTER EIGHT

Father Flynn

Excited about becoming an altar boy, Milo trained under Father Flynn. Tall and scrawny with closely cropped, curly red hair, thick horn-rimmed lenses made his eyes seem to bug out. The glasses slid down Flynn's nose, compelling habitual push-ups. Milo wondered why he never got them fixed. Father Flynn reminded him of Ebenezer Scrooge.

Behind a facade of tough talk hid a gentle man of God. The priest always sensed trouble. Milo liked that most about him.

Milo had gotten into difficulty with his grandfather about chores. Nonno demanded everyone share the seemingly endless garden tasks. No matter. Eager to please, Milo did them willingly and cheerfully, but alas, tried too hard and planned a surprise that backfired.

Nonno had been busy and neglectful of his own chores, the ones he wouldn't let anyone else do. Rank with overgrowth, Milo decided to weed. With scythe, rake, and peach basket, he sweated away the greater part of a hot afternoon cutting weeds, grass, and what he thought was brush. Proud of his work, Milo didn't anticipate Nonno's response.

While Milo drank lemonade in the kitchen, Nonno

stomped in ranting. The Italian accent had a growl to it. Carrying a thin whip-like branch, Nonno bellowed, "What the hell you did in garden?"

The neck veins swelled and Nonno's lips formed a tightrope. Milo stood stupefied and stuttered, "I cut the weeds and brush."

Nonno raised the branch and struck Milo's calves. Milo jumped back astonished. Pain and anger flared in his eyes. "What did I do?"

"This is not a weed. Is my rubber tree. You know how long it takes to grow a rubber tree? Why didn't you ask before you cut it, you stupido? Get the hell out before I break your neck."

Milo had brought down a prized tree and Nonno's wrath. Tears of anger and frustration streamed from his eyes. *Fuck, he thought, big deal. What about all the clean up?*

That evening at religion class, Flynn asked him to stay. With lowered head, Milo stood fidgeting. Furious with Nonno, he did feel bad about the tree.

"Milo, what's wrong?"

"Nothing."

"Don't hand me that malarkey. You're not your usual self. Something's up."

Blood climbed to Milo's ears like mercury in a thermometer. Lip quivering, he told the story.

"Your grandfather probably had a bad day. Adults make mistakes. They are not perfect. He'll be over it in time."

Milo blinked. "Yeah, but it won't bring the tree back."

Father Flynn looked at Milo, dumbfounded. An accident destroyed the tree, yet the boy felt responsible. "It's all right, Milo. God forgives you, and so will your grandfather. The tree is in God's care."

Milo saved money from his paper route to replace the tree. Father Flynn drove him to the nursery and offered to help plant the sapling. Milo wondered why he still felt badly.

"Father, I know about accidents, but the tree still died."

"It was an honest mistake. If you had destroyed the tree purposely, that would be different, right?"

"Yes."

"Well, you've replaced the tree, paid for your mistake. Your grandfather will be pleased."

Nonno examined the new tree with great pride in his grandson, wished he hadn't lost his temper, but didn't dwell on it. He ambled into the house and found Milo in the pantry. Milo stood with a broad smile, salting a fresh tomato. Nonno placed his hand on Milo's shoulder.

"You look happy. It's a nice tree. Not as good as other one, but she's okay."

Milo felt a sense of approval, but was not entirely satisfied. Early on, he'd stumbled onto a device. When he spoke to God, he never got answers, so he spoke to his inner voice instead.

"I paid for my mistake. Even Father Flynn said so, so why don't I feel better?"

"It's because you feel guilt."

"But I was guilty."

"No, you made a mistake. I guess you can keep feeling guilty, or you can forgive yourself. You get to decide."

"I suppose."

~ ~ ~

CHAPTER NINE

The Cat

Up at the crack of dawn, Milo decided to feed the chickens to surprise Nonna. Fury, the black lab, rose to a half-squat and shook off the night. "Hey boy, wanna come help? Come on, that's it, come on, Fury."

With his butt-end doing the rumba, the lab snuggled its snout under Milo's armpit, as if trying to flip a pancake. Milo grabbed him by the ears. "You're slobbering all over me! Let's go"

The dog bounded away. Milo followed, as Fury snuffled, nose to the ground, until he found the perfect shrub. He looked at Milo nonchalantly, lifted his leg and gave the bush a steaming shower. Milo laughed, wondering why a dog couldn't just piss any old place. The rooster woke the hens as Milo approached the coop.

The rusty door latch wouldn't release. "Sit, Fury. Atta boy. You're a good dog. Guess I should oil this thing, huh? You stay here. Good boy."

Fury sniffed for a spot and sat on it with his head cocked quizzically, while Milo went inside and closed the creaking door. He filled a galvanized two-gallon pail with corn and went out into the fence-enclosed yard. Fury, ears at attention, watched unblinking.

"Might as well oil the hinges, too. Right, dog?" Fury

brushed the ground with his tail. Milo took a handful of corn and scattered it. The hens strutted, clucked, and pecked about him. "Look at these guys, dog, they're starving."

Fury looked and brushed. Milo kept tossing corn. "Dio mio!" sounded a familiar voice nearby. There stood his grandmother, gray hair poking from the red bandanna covering her head, bony legs, stark white above black stockings rolled about her ankles.

Milo laughed at the sight of her. "Mornin', Nonna. I'm feeding the chickens."

She placed her hands together as if praying, and lifted them to her large nose. Dark eyes peered at him between white, bushy brows. "How much you gave to them already?"

"The poor things are hungry — this is the second bucket."

She leaned towards him, hands on hips. "Dio mio, they gonna be dead. Go bring the eggs to the house, and don't say anything to Nonno, or he gonna kill you."

The next morning, after Nonno went to work, Nonna called Milo to the cellar. Three hens hung by their feet, draining blood into a bucket. Between her knees was a big pot of steaming water. "Bring those hens," she commanded sternly. Milo gingerly unhooked and tossed them to her feet.

"Sit there." She pointed to the stool opposite. Nonna plunked the hens into the steaming water.

"Don't you notice chickens, what they do all day?" All

day they scratch and peck, scratch and peck. What you think they do?"

"Scratch and peck, Nonna. What?"

She laughed. "Dio mio, they scratch and peck and eat, yes, eat! That's right," she nodded. "They eat! So, you only have to give them a little bit corn, just to get them fatter. You see what happen now? These ones, they eat themselves to death. Now we gonna have chicken soup, roast chicken, chicken cacciattore, chicken everything! And your Nonno, he's gonna be suspicious."

"I'm sorry, Nonna."

"Dio mio, you're sorry. I know you're sorry. Now, help me pull out these feathers. I hope you learn a lesson, because if no, Nonno is gonna choke you."

"Thanks for not telling on me."

She reached over, pinched his cheek and gummed a smile.

"You talk better with your teeth in, Nonna."

"Shut up you face, or *I* gonna choke you."

~ ~ ~

Milo enjoyed pigeons. Watching them fly, he wished he could soar. He became interested, not because of their song, but for their attitude. They were survivors thriving in all climates, fearless in pursuit of food, and weren't apt to eat themselves to death like dumb cluckers, he thought.

Pigeons couldn't get into the chicken coop, but sometimes hung out waiting for stray morsels inadvertently tossed. Within seconds two might arrive. In under a minute, a small flock competed furiously for fare. It amused Milo that by some mysterious means they sent an invitation to breakfast, only to fight the guests for a share.

Milo took pleasure in observing, especially tumblers and rollers, breeds noted for their aerobatic ability. He decided it would be a fun project to raise them.

Milo's friend, Bobby Cagino, about the same age and also interested in pigeons, lived across the street. Milo hummed happily as he walked to Bobby's house. He'd spoken with Nonno, who said he and Bobby could convert the shed, now filled with trash, to a pigeon coop. All they had to do was help Nonno dump the junk.

"Hey, Bobby, my grandfather said we can use the shed. All we have to do is help him take the stuff inside to the dump. How about helping? Then, we can start a flock."

"Okay, when?"

"Saturday morning."

"I didn't think the old fart would let you use his shed."

"Neither did I, but he did. Not only that, but he said we could use chicken feed for our pigeons too. How's that for a break?"

"He must be setting a trap or sumpin'."

Milo didn't agree. "Naw, he thinks it'll keep us out of trouble."

They looked at each other and laughed. But later, Bobby's statement would prove prophetic.

Working after school, Bobby and Milo finished the coop in a week. Now all they needed were birds. They decided to make a foray to the coal yard — pigeon heaven. The birds could roost and nest in the rafters of the large bins, and an adjacent grain yard gave them an easy food supply.

In the dark of night the boys climbed steep coal piles that reached to the rafters. Milo whispered. "You aim the light into its eyes. It'll freeze. I'll grab it."

"All right, but keep the freaking noise down; you'll spook 'em."

"Shit! Don't worry. They ain't goin' to fly at night."

Bobby aimed the light. Sure enough the bird became immobilized. Milo easily captured it and then checked for eggs, but there were none. They caught three hens but had difficulty finding a male.

Bobby shined the light into another nest. Suddenly, the bird flushed and flew into Milo's face. Milo slipped in the loose coal, and then tumbled in an avalanche of blackness. Unscathed, but covered with coal dust, he spit and sputtered. Hooting gleefully, Bobby suddenly rode another slide to the bottom. Just as Milo struggled to his feet, Bobby crashed. They fell in a heap. It was Milo's turn to laugh. "That's what you get for laughing, asshole."

"My father's going to beat the shit out of me."

They finally caught two males and went home to face the consequences of a haul over the coals.

The next day, they rode their bikes seven miles downhill to the zoo. The bird keeper, a kind old man, enjoyed their frequent visits. He told them they could exchange common pigeons for surplus domestic breeds. In exchange for the ones caught at the coal yard, they got a pair each of homers, tumblers, and white kings. Struggling on the uphill ride home, they hardly noticed the terrain, chattering on about their flock and what fun was in store.

Each day they'd check the nests for eggs, hardly able to contain their excitement when the first ones dropped. It seemed forever until they finally hatched. The bird keeper told them, once nested, pigeons would always return, as would their offspring.

Within months their birds flew every late afternoon. The flock would circle high, returning to roost at dusk. Tumblers would climb until mere specks in the sky, then free-fall, head over heels, recovering about fifty feet above ground. One evening one failed to pull out. Milo and Bobby were horrified.

They lost pigeons in other ways. White kings, the largest, were the price paid for use of the shed. Without asking, Nonno took two plump hens and suffocated them by clamping their beaks between his thumb and forefinger. To Milo's revulsion, Nonno cooked them in spaghetti sauce. Milo refused to eat.

Bobby and Milo also lost birds mysteriously. It remained a mystery until after school one day, a black and white tomcat fled with a fresh kill. Bobby hated felines. It meant war. They tried to discover how the cat got into the coop to no avail and decided to trap it.

The cat somehow had cleverly managed to find a way into the enclosure, then accessed the coop through an entry to the nesting boxes located high above ground. Bobby rigged a hinged door, triggered to close by dislodging a lock pin tethered to a cord. Each night they waited. Bobby whispered. "Hey, Milo, we've been here for two hours."

"Yeah, I'm starving . . . wait a second."

Milo put a forefinger to his lip and pointed. The cat slunk, belly to the ground, its tail imitating a metronome. Incredibly, the tom squeezed, Houdini-like, through a hole in the wire fence much smaller than its body. Once inside, it eyed the hole above. A coordinated force of rippling muscle and sinew gathered, then flashed upward. Milo yelled, "Now!"

Bobby pulled and the door slammed. Bobby looked at Milo in disbelief. "We got him! Be careful, don't let it out."

"You go in first."

"What's the matter, afraid of a freak'n cat?"

Milo opened the door. Feathered chaos engulfed them. Pigeons flew into walls and each other. Shrieking, the desperate tom climbed the walls but found no escape. It dove into a nesting box.

Bobby poked a shovel handle at the cat making sounds like water on an oil fire. Milo stood paralyzed while Bobby tried to kill the thing with the blade end. It didn't seem right. Milo screamed, "Stop it!"

"What do you want me to do with the freak'n thing?"

"We can't just kill it. It's scared to death. Maybe he won't come back."

"Screw you! It'll just keep on killing our pigeons."

"I don't know. It doesn't seem right."

"C'mon, Milo, we have to."

Milo felt ill. After a pause, he reluctantly helped Bobby

keep the cat cornered. Bobby kept hitting until it went still, couldn't fight back, and wouldn't die. Finally, they dragged it outside. Enraged, Bobby kept hitting the bloodied, moaning animal.

"Stop it!"

Bobby leaned on the shovel and looked at Milo as if in a trance. Milo dug a hole, grabbed the tom by the tail and flung it in but couldn't bury it. Bobby covered the still breathing cat. He looked up in triumph.

"We got the son of a bitch. He won't be killing any more pigeons."

For Milo, there was no celebration. After Bobby left, he reopened the hole hoping to find the tom alive. Matted with fresh dirt and blood, its eyes told him otherwise. Milo gagged, and reburied it. He felt something very wrong with what they'd done. It wasn't just the killing.

He spoke to his inner voice.

"What is it? Killing the cat is wrong, but there's something else."

"You didn't want to kill it."

"No, but I helped."

"That's because you let Bobby talk you into it."

"But I didn't know what else to do."

"You do now."

Milo knew the truth. Never again would he be manipulated into something he thought wrong. He promised no one would take his power again. Defiance of authority, especially of the Church, would force Milo to rely on that power.

~ ~ ~

Bach also spurned the shackles of the Church, but in subtle and clever ways through his musical compositions. For without their sponsorship, his freedom to compose would have been severely curtailed, perhaps leaving his genius unfulfilled.

~ ~ ~

CHAPTER TEN

Walk to Lüneburg

Without an alternative, Sebastian and his younger brother, Jacob, were taken in by their elder brother, Johann Christoph, the organist at St. Michael's in Ohrdruf near Arnstadt. Here Sebastian began his fascination with the organ. The loss of both parents deeply affected him. He became sullen and withdrawn. His only joy seemed to be when he accompanied his brother to St. Michael's. There he would lose himself among the wood pipes, wind chests, and bellows of the organ, observing with fascination the mechanical workings that produced the music he so loved. Only the sound of the organ, especially when his beloved brother Christoph played, brought a glint of delight to his eyes.

One afternoon on a dreary sunless day, Sebastian sat on the floor staring blankly at the flickering embers smoldering in the fireplace. Christoph plopped down beside the forlorn boy.

"What are you thinking about, little brother?" Sebastian looked up. His eyes flashed pain and anger.

"What could God's plan be to take Mama and Papa from us?"

"It is not for us to know, Sebastian, only to accept."

"I try, but it hurts and it won't stop."

"You need something to take your mind away from it. Music can do that. You haven't touched your violin since you arrived. How would you like to learn to play the organ?

The nine-year-old boy's face shone with passion. "Yes, and I want to know what makes it work and why it sounds so wonderful."

Christoph beckoned the boy to stay put. He rose and walked over to the library and returned with a well-worn book. He handed it to Sebastian. "Tomorrow we will begin your lessons, but today I want you to begin reading. It's Werckmeister's *Erweiterte und verbesserte Orgelprobe*. It tells all about organs and contains wonderful illustrations."

Sebastian took the book and ran his fingers delicately over it as if trying to capture the context of the pages through them. He looked at his brother and smiled. "I'm going to learn everything in it."

"Fine, little brother, but not all in one night. It's a lot of information to take in. You have a lifetime ahead."

Sebastian hugged his brother. With eyes tightly clenched he silently prayed. "Dear God, please don't take Christoph from me."

Sebastian hungrily absorbed the book his brother had given him. It became more important than the Bible. He mentally devoured each word and every drawing, often by flickering candlelight late into the night. By day, he'd spend hours examining the innards of the organ and its mechanics. One day Christoph sat to play the organ at St.

Michael's. After the first chord, Sebastian crawled from inside the instrument's structure, coughing and wheezing. Smudges of grime smattered his face and soiled his clothes. Christoph roared with laughter. Sebastian wiped his eyes, blackening them into a raccoon-like mask.

"I know why the tone is fading on some notes. There's a small hole in one of the bellows. I almost had it patched," he sputtered.

"Good work, little brother, but the next time you decide to diddle around inside, you'd best let me know first. You look a frightful mess. Get yourself tidied up. We'll go home and get on with your lesson.

Early on, Sebastian exhibited fierce independence and a streak of stubbornness. He'd grown tall and determined he would one day surpass his father's height. He'd lost his plumpness, but had a large-boned look and sturdy calves, as had his father. He wore his light brown hair long, which served to take the roundness from his face. Nobody could forget his eyes. Everything to know about him could be seen there and they never flickered when he spoke. On gazing into them, one immediately intuited truth.

Sebastian learned to play the clavier and also became skilled on the organ, something that required both hands and feet. Everything his brother gave him he played to perfection. Christoph had studied with Johann Pachelbel, a composer and one of the finest organists of his time. He had a notebook containing clavier pieces of Pachelbel and other great masters. For some unknown reason, he refused to give Sebastian access to it. Sebastian knew its location behind a cabinet with a grilled door. His hands were small and enabled him to roll up the manuscript and poke it through. For many nights he copied the score by moonlight, intending to improve his technique with practice. Unfortunately, Christoph overheard him.

"Sebastian, how did you learn that music," he scolded. The boy handed him the score. "I took it from the cabinet and made this copy. I didn't think you'd mind."

Christoph grabbed it angrily. He glared at his younger brother. "If I had wanted you to have it, I would have given it." You will not ever touch any of my things without asking. Is that understood?" Wounded, Sebastian nodded, then ran to his room and wept.

He'd recently completed two years of study as a choral scholar at the distinguished Lyceumn Illustre Ohrdruf. He stood awkwardly at the desk of the cantor, Elias Herda, a young and kindly man, whose soft, soothing voice belied his stern demeanor.

"Sebastian, as you well know, a scholarship is unavailable for you to continue here and your brother cannot afford tuition fees. There is an opportunity at Michaelisschule in Lüneburg."

Sebastian looked at the cantor quizzically. "If Christoph cannot afford to pay my tuition here, how will I be able to attend Michaelisschule?"

"I've recommended you and your friend George Erdmann as choral scholars with a stipend. Frankly, I think it wise for you both to complete your education there. Speak to your brother about it. I've summoned George and will speak to him after we've finished here."

Sebastian's brows shot upward and the dimple in his cheek deepened as a smile spread across his face. "Thank you, Herr Cantor."

As George entered the cantor's office, he wondered why Sebastian smiled at him. Sebastian paced impatiently in the hallway. The two lived on the same street, three doors apart. George came out of the cantor's office with a frown. His shoulders slumped forward to make a scrawny frame appear more fragile. Anxiety filled his dark eyes.

"What's the matter, George?"

"I'm not sure about this, Sebastian. Lüneburg is so far away."

"So what? We'll be on our own. It will be great fun."

"But I'm not even sure I want to be a choral scholar."

"Oh come on, George. It's a lot better than fiddling for pfennigs here. Besides, it'll be an adventure, and there may be lots of pretty maidens to fiddle there!"

George turned crimson and stammered, "We're too young for that sort of stuff."

"We won't be for long once we get to Lüneburg!"

They walked with arms over each other's shoulder, talking excitedly about the prospects. By the time they arrived home, they'd decided.

Sebastian burst through the door shouting. "Christoph, I'm going to Michaelisschule in Lüneburg!

His brother looked up over his glasses and put down his book. "What's this rubbish?"

"It's not rubbish, Christoph. I have a recommendation

with stipend from Herda."

"Slow down, little brother."

Sebastian spoke with exuberance, "With due respect, I understand you can't afford my tuition at the Lyceum. Now I can finish my education at Michaelisschule."

"You've had enough education. You can find plenty of work here, and you're already a better musician than any of your peers and . . ."

Sebastian cut him off. "I'm going and that's final."

Christoph looked at the determination in his younger brother's eyes and nodded. "I suppose it is, Sebastian."

For the two teenagers, Lüneburg, located about two hundred miles north of Ohrdruf, couldn't have been more daunting. Sebastian would be the first in his lineage to break the bounds of the small area in which his family had lived for centuries. Unless they were fortunate enough to hitch a carriage here and there, the trip would be made mostly on foot while carrying their belongings. They asked Christoph for advice about the trip. He warned they'd have to do some detail planning and agreed to help.

"You're going to spend many a night sleeping on the cold hard ground, so you'd best be prepared." The boys looked at each other in shock. It hadn't occurred to them, one of many particulars they'd overlooked. A fourteen-year-old of the time had minimal, if any education at all. Many worked to help support their families. Sebastian and George were privileged. Though older, George lacked Sebastian's maturity, leaving Sebastian to assume the role of leader. A trip of the sort they were about to undertake would move them closer towards manhood by the time they reached Lüneburg.

Reality hit when the packing began. Christoph put his hand to his forehead and looked at the pile the boys had placed on the floor between them. "Well then, I see you must have somehow come into a rather tidy sum of coin."

"What," they exclaimed in unison, looking at each other puzzled.

"It appears you must be going to hire a couple of menservants to lug all of that."

The boys looked at each other sheepishly, then Sebastian blurted, "Oh . . . umm . . . we were just trying to decide what to leave behind."

"Ah ha . . . I see what you mean. It seems as though you've a lot to decide here, so I'd best leave you to it."

Two days after Sebastian's fifteenth birthday, the boys made ready to depart. Their over-stuffed duffels would get lighter as they got stronger, but for now felt like bags of lead. At the last moment, as Sebastian patted the book Christoph had given him tucked away in his shoulder bag, he decided to leave his violin. The organ had won him over. The families grouped around the boys and gave last-minute bits of advice and thankfully, small gifts. After tearful embrace George and Sebastian were ready. Sebastian squeezed his brother tightly. "Thank you, Christoph. I love you."

"I love you, too, little brother. Write often and take care."

They did have the good fortune of early, if muddy,

spring weather. Fragrant steam rose from the warmed
fertile fields and dissolved quickly in a clear morning
breeze as they headed north to Lüneburg. The early
heating sun had them sweating profusely within an hour
and the duffel straps cut relentlessly into their shoulders.
They stopped to rest. In the refuge of a giant pine on a soft
bed of needles, Sebastian lay with head propped on his
duffel.

Above him, two chaffinches preened. The male began
to trill a repeated melody. George walked towards the tree
and opened his mouth to speak. Sebastian signaled him to
stop and be silent, then rose slowly to a sitting position
and listened intently. His keen ear immediately deci-
phered the haunting melodious sequence. Over and over
he hummed to himself, then placed it in memory. There it
remained to later be reborn as the theme for the
Chaconne.

Three weeks after departing, their loads no longer
seemed so heavy. They hadn't quite made the halfway
point, but their daily progress would improve as they got
stronger. Both were transformed. The greatest physical
change had taken place in George. His frail look had vanished and he now walked with an air of confidence.
Sebastian began to emerge from his shell.

Today they had the good fortune of stumbling upon
the rural farm of a hospitable Lutheran family. The boys
splashed each other playfully as they bathed in the warm
pool of a spring-fed pond. They'd been invited to supper
and a bed of hay in the barn. The aroma of the pig roasting

in the hearth drifted down to them and their stomachs grumbled in anticipation. "My God, how can a pig smell so good? I despise pigs."

"George, when you haven't eaten a hot meal for as long as we, a roasted rat would smell divine."

"I hope it's a very big pig. Maybe they'll let us take some with us."

"Let's not be greedy. We can eat enough to last two days!"

The boys feasted hungrily, which pleased their hosts. They'd made their beds in the loft, giving them a clear view of the star-filled sky out of an open bay.

"Did you ever wonder how many stars there are?"

Sebastian burped loudly and sleepily replied, "Not one more than is absolutely necessary."

They soon realized they could earn room and board along the way by chopping wood or doing other necessary chores. And then one day, they happened upon an easier way to earn food and shelter. They were at the woodpile on a small farm, Sebastian chopping and George piling. Sebastian wiped the sweat from his forehead and sucked a burst blister in the crook of his thumb.

"It's your turn, George." Sebastian walked to the well. He scooped a ladle of cool water and sipped as Heinrich Weldig, the landowner, approached.

"Bach, did I understand you're heading north to Lüneburg?"

"Yes, Herr Weldig, we are."

"If you'd be so kind to deliver something to my

brother, Franz, I'm sure he'd provide a hot meal and a bed for you both. He lives in Nordhausen, about twenty-six kilometers north, on your way."

"We would be most pleased, Herr Weldig."

Sebastian returned to the woodpile. "Hey, George, we're assured of a meal and bed in Nordhausen."

"That's good news, but how?"

"All we need to do is deliver something to Herr Weldig's brother there."

The tinkle of a bell sounded. Sebastian turned to see Weldig stumbling down the path waving a rope his hand. He never saw the goat, but felt its horns squarely in the buttocks. He tried to escape, but the goat dogged him relentlessly. "George, don't just stand there, you idiot. Get this insane animal away from me."

George got his laughter under control and grabbed hold of its stubby tail with both hands. He stopped smiling as a hoof struck his groin. Upon the arrival of Weldig, they managed to get the rope back over its head.

Soon after they departed and were out of sight, the goat, now subdued under a load of duffels, plodded along quietly the rest of the way to Nordhausen. From then on, the boys would always ask to deliver mail and news to villages and towns along their route, swearing to not take anything they couldn't deliver by hand — or ride.

A few weeks later they arrived in Lüneburg, tanned, healthy and prideful of their accomplishment. They reported to the cantor.

"Your duties will be as follows. You shall sing in the

matins choir on Saturday vespers, Sunday main services, as well as weddings, funerals, and all festive occasions. You will be given room and board, and a small stipend of twelve groshen, which I advise you save. You are hired as sopranos. When your voices change, as they inevitably will, you will relinquish your position." He looked directly at Sebastian. "I'd advise you stay out of trouble. We have little tolerance for troublemakers."

Sebastian defiantly looked him in the eye. "What is your definition of trouble, Herr Cantor?"

"You will know it if the time comes."

Sebastian fell happily into his life in Lüneburg. Along with his official duties, he played violin in the orchestra and accompanied the choir on the harpsichord. On his own, he continued to learn everything possible about the organ. Then, it happened. George and Sebastian were practicing. Sebastian's voice cracked. George looked worried. Sebastian laughed.

"Did you expect I would sing like a girl forever?"

"I suppose not, but what will you do now?"

"There is no recourse, I'll fake it until I'm found out and worry about it later!"

"Good plan, but what then?"

"My cousin, Johann Ernst, lives in Hamburg. Another relative of ours, George Bohm, lives nearby. He is a great organist and perhaps Johann can arrange for me to study with him. I may even get the chance to study with old J.A."

"Who in hell is that?"

"Fool, only the finest organist in Germany, perhaps in

the world, Johann Adam Reincken."

"Ah . . . I've never heard of him."

"Of course you haven't, you uncultured twerp. Besides, exciting things are happening. There is a fine theatre, and it is rumored that Handel will soon be the new opera director."

"It all sounds very exotic. When my voice changes, perhaps there will be opportunities for me as well."

"I wouldn't count on it. I fear you're destined to sing like a girl forever. You'll graduate before then."

George grinned, "Most likely you are right."

"Hamburg has a most magnificent library, hundreds of manuscripts, a feast of Buxtehude, Shutze, even Carrissimi and Monteverdi."

"Who are they?"

Sebastian ignored him and went on animatedly. "The most exciting thing of all is the Ritteracadamie where I can listen and learn about French music."

"It sounds great for you, Bach, but I'll miss you."

"Don't sound so gloomy. We will always be friends, and Hamburg is only sixty kilometers away, a mere stroll for you now."

Sebastian mouthed the lyrics for several weeks, but he couldn't escape the future. It obliged his confession. The cantor allowed him to complete the required curriculum by performing other duties. He graduated Michaelisschule shortly hereafter.

~ ~ ~

CHAPTER ELEVEN

Adventure

Like Sebastian, Milo's adventure came about entirely of his own doing, in defiance of a surrogate father. Well past midnight, he'd just finished playing hockey with his friends. The rink rental rates were lower in the evenings after 10:00. By splitting the fee, they'd rented the ice for an hour and thirty minutes. He'd taken a puck in the shoulder and it was sore. An ice pack would fix it, he thought, and slipped upstairs to avoid his grandfather. On the way, he decided to raid the pantry. He cut a wedge of Romano cheese and some pepperoni, ripped a chunk of bread from the loaf his grandmother had baked that morning, poured a glass of homemade wine and took a gulp. The odors were reminiscent of the produce market in Boston where Nonno and he had shopped the Saturday before.

Relatives living near the market provided an opportunity to visit and share a meal. He always looked forward to going there. Vendors, predominantly Italian immigrants, sold a wide selection, ranging from fruits and vegetables to all types of fish, fowl, and meat. Exotic fare, such as beef, goat, and pig heads hung from hooks with tongues lolling, were bought for the brains and considered a delicacy. A variety of animal blood used for sausage was available as well. Every imaginable comestible, spice, and herb from the old country could be found.

Milo was mesmerized by this magical maelstrom of colors and aromas. In a myriad Italian dialects, shoppers bustled about, vociferously vying with each vendor — a true feast for the senses.

Besides the weekly shopping, Nonno was there for another reason. They'd finished the shopping much faster than usual. Nonno seemed uncommonly buoyant, but Milo paid it little mind, enjoying the scene, watching dark-eyed Italian beauties who never seemed to notice him. He and his grandfather arrived at Carmen Perrotti's booth. After the typical cordialities, Nonno and Perotti got into an animated discussion about the attributes of various grapes on display. Nonno finally settled on the zinfandels. A deal was struck, the grapes to be delivered on Monday. They went on to enjoy a midday meal with family.

The wooden crates sat in the driveway, streaked ruby by the bleeding grapes, and swarming with gnats. Milo helped his grandfather carry them to the basement. Before sunrise they uncrated the grapes, loaded them into a large press, and squeezed them. Nonno hummed around a short stogie clamped between his teeth. Milo, who rarely saw anything but a stern old man set in his ways, smiled.

"In the old days, we did this with our feet. Now with the machine, it's easier and more fast but not so much fun as then."

Milo frowned at the thought of drinking wine that had been stomped. They poured the fragrant elixir into two fifty-five gallon oak casks, seeds and all. He could only help after school, and it took most of the week to get the work done. They ended with a ritual burning of the crates. He remembered the satisfaction as they tossed them into the fire.

Milo rubbed his shoulder and knew an ugly color would be reflected in the mirror the next day. Purple, green, and yellow were not great skin colors, but they were a badge of honor for jocks. Milo took the last bite of his snack and turned, startled to see Nonno at the pantry door. His grandfather pointed to Milo's glass.

"It's good vino, no? But, Perotti, he tells me the new grape we buy last week will make the best wine ever, even better than that one."

Milo nodded, but sensed something more from his grandfather's tone, something unpleasant would be forthcoming. He braced for it. His grandfather poured a half glass, held it to the light, then took a sip.

"Milo, you a good boy, but, I tell you a thousand times, you gotta be home by 9:30 on school days. You know the time now? What's the matter? Why you don't listen?"

"Geez, Nonno, It's not like I'm getting in trouble. I was playing hockey. I'm not a little kid, for God's sake. Leave me be."

Calm up to then, his grandfather flared. He'd waited for just such a response to make a point. He put his glass down slowly and rose. He spoke softly, but the nuance could not be mistaken.

"You live my house. You do what I say. If not, find

another place to live."

With clenched fists and tight jaws, a young buck and an old stag faced off. Milo threw his hands in the air. "You want me to go? Okay, I'm gone. This is bullshit." He stalked off without any consideration of the consequences.

~ ~ ~

Milo read that the Great Northern, a lumber company located in Maine, needed summer help. With his duffel of clothes and two hundred dollars, he hitched a ride towards Caribou. Upon reaching New Hampshire, the state police picked him up.

"Where you heading, son?"

"I'm on my way to Maine."

"How old are you?"

"Fifteen."

"Do you have permission?"

Milo lied. "Yes."

"No big deal, but I'll have to verify that. Okay?"

"Sure."

"Let's drive to the barracks. It'll only take a few minutes."

Milo had never been inside a patrol car. He glanced about, disappointed. Oh well, this is as far as I go anyway, he thought, actually relieved.

The patrolman spoke with Nonno. "Well, son, that's that. You're all set. My patrol extends to the Maine border. It's about a forty-five-minute drive. Want to ride with me?"

Milo hid his disappointment, defiantly bound to his

decision. He exhaled a thank you, sir.

Midway to the state border, they stopped at a diner.

"What say we grab some grub, young man?"

"Thanks. I haven't eaten today." Treated to a hot turkey sandwich with fixings, then pie, Milo couldn't believe his good fortune.

Drowsy from the meal, he nodded off. A gentle shake woke him.

"Last stop, son."

"Thanks for the ride, sir."

"No problem. Listen, your best bet is to stay at the YMCA in Caribou. It's clean and cheap."

"I will. Thanks for dinner and the lift."

"Good luck." The trooper drove off with a wave.

Alone in the night on a ribbon of black tarmac, he watched the taillights fade to pinpoints of red, then disappear into the night. The lights of Caribou blinked in the distance, lifting his spirit. After a cold hour, he caught a ride and found the Y. Slipping between hard-won sheets of fresh linen, Milo drifted to sleep, fearful of the future, but savoring the delicious taste of freedom.

The next morning he found the office of the Great Northern. He was hired at $.70 an hour with room and board: $33.60 per week, no expenses, and nowhere to spend it. I can save it all, he thought.

The outdoors always suited him. He eagerly rose before dawn and followed his nose to the kitchen. Pappy, the bent, bowlegged, and red flannel-attired cook, cussed as he plucked broken eggshells from scrambled mix. Milo barely stifled a laugh. Sensing his presence, Pappy turned and shouted, "Well, don't jus' stand thar, boy. Git over an' start squash'n those oranges."

Milo went to the crate sitting near a large contraption capable of squeezing eight oranges at a time.

"Jus halve 'em, put 'em in the holes, pull the lever until the juice stops, trash the skins, and do it agin."

Milo squeezed the entire crate. Afterwards Pappy told him to get a coffee. From then on, he spent mornings in the kitchen. Camp atmosphere and easy work suited him fine. Best of all, he enjoyed helping the toast-edged grill jockey with breakfast.

Pappy taught him how to make strong coffee, several ways to prepare eggs, and how to properly cook bacon. At home, Nonno did most of the cooking. Now eager to learn, the skills Pappy taught would prove helpful later that summer.

Amidst the whining saws, roaring front-loaders and logging trucks, days were chaotic. Milo worked on a cruising crew scouring the woods in advance of the lumberjacks to measure and chalk trees large enough to harvest. The smell of pinesap in the air, falling trees snapping and cracking about, Milo found contentment in the work.

After a hearty supper, he'd usually enjoy a steaming hot chocolate. Awestruck at the starlit sky, he wondered why he couldn't always feel the way he did at that moment.

With the harvesting done, saying goodbye proved difficult. Milo didn't want it to end, but there it was... Pappy made an attempt at indifference, then gave Milo an awkward embrace.

"Take care of yer'self, kid."

"I'm gonna miss you, Pappy."

Less apprehensive now that he'd added to his money cache, Milo knew he had to work. He returned to the Y in Caribou and asked the desk clerk about job openings in the area. The attendant referred him to a cobbler a few blocks away.

The bell hanging above the shop entry jangled a greeting. The compatible smell of dirty socks and old leather, not at all unpleasant, met him at the door. Two ornate, high-backed wooden chairs sat atop an elevated platform with cast iron footrests — not much more than a fancy version of a shoeshine box. Beneath, on wooden shelves, were the familiar tools of the trade. Milo could almost hear the rhythmic snap of the polishing cloth.

The cobbler Alphonso Midonni was known as Phonsie. Hunched over a workbench, in a leather apron, dark with age and use, the old man tacked a heel onto a delicate woman's shoe. The hammer seemed far too large for the job. Grime of the trade filled the cracks and fissures of gnarled and knotted fingers.

His white ashen hair looked like a storm cloud and a color-matched mustache hovered over his mouth like an umbrella. With spectacles perched upon a large, but finely shaped nose, he reminded Milo of Nonno.

"Good morning, sir. My name is Milo Damiani. The

clerk at the Y told me you were looking for help."

Phonsie squinted over his pocked glasses through bushy brows. He was soft-spoken, but his body language exposed intensity. Familiar broken English immediately put Milo at ease.

"Phonsie here. How old you are?"

"I'm fifteen, but I have permission to work. I just finished a job with the Great Northern, but I've been shining shoes since I was nine."

Phonsie tossed him a pair.

"You shine 'em up."

When Milo finished, Phonsie seemed unimpressed.

"Not so bad, Mr. Damiani. Now, you see those shoes, eh? You take the pliers, and then pull off the heels. I show you now."

He ripped off the worn heel. "That's how she goes, eh?"

Milo nodded.

Pointing to a row of shoes awaiting repair, Phonsie said, "Finish those all up. Do good job, eh?"

By day's end, Milo had his second job.

"So, Mr. Milo, I hope you don't want to be a shoemaker for your living."

"No, I'm going to be a pilot."

"Now you talk smart. The shoes, now they make them so cheap nobody wants to fix. They just buy new ones. A pilot, he don't have to worry about cheap shoes, eh?"

"Yeah, but I have to finish high school and get two years of college. I have to save money."

"Good, do good work and the money, she will come."

Summer lay ahead and Milo wouldn't worry too much about it for the time being.

Two weeks later, Kevin Dolman wrote. Kevin's uncle owned the Driftwood Fish House at Hampton Beach, and needed a pot washer. Milo wanted to go. A job beach would be fantastic, but he felt badly about leaving Phonsie and had difficulty broaching the subject. Phonsie sensed his unease and mumbled through a tack-filled mouth.

"Mr. Damiani. Your mind . . . she's not on heels and soles this morning. Something is bothering you?"

Milo kept his eye on the work, but tried to gather his thoughts. Phonsie had been kind and encouraging. Milo felt disloyal.

"Out with it, Milo. What problem you have, eh?"

"See, Phonsie, I got this letter from my friend. His uncle owns a restaurant in New Hampshire."

"Nice. So?"

"Well, he said I could work there for the summer, and living on the beach would be fun."

Without missing a hammer beat, Phonsie spoke. "Mr. Damiani, you have only one chance to be young. You know, when I was your age I leave school for to help my family, eh? I was apprentice with a shoemake in Padua. A big prick . . . he was one, oh yes. Work me twelve hours a day for very little money, peanuts. No time for play, only work. Then, more work — day in, day out for six years. Then we move to America. Here was hard work too, but the money was more, eh? But, for me, no fun, eh? Better you should go Hampton Beach for summer, but promise you gonna finish school, and be piloto, yes?"

"What about you, Phonsie? I can't go until you find someone."

"It's very slow in summer. I can handle it. Don't worry about me. Go have some fun, eh?"

Milo grinned while exchanging a hug with the old man. Phonsie spit out the tacks and went to the register to count out Milo's earnings, then added another $25.00.

"You go Hampton Beach, Mr. Damiani, but keep your promise to be a flyer, eh? Stay in touch. No need for you to hang around here now. You have the whole day to get to the beach. Call by collect when you get there. Be careful, stay out of trouble, eh?"

"Thanks, Phonsie. I promise."

Milo couldn't wait to get on the road. He'd barely raised his thumb when the spotless green and white Pontiac, a proud chief crowning the hood, rolled to a stop. An elderly matron wore a straw hat that filled the space between her head and the car roof. She hunched forward, both hands on the wheel. Blue-tinted hair straggled from under the hat. A stark white one sprouted from a wart on her chin, which seemed an extension of her neck. Speaking flat Maine, false teeth clacked on every third word.

"Come on, honey. I haven't got all day. Where are you headed, young man?"

"I'm goin' to Hampton Beach, ma'am."

"My. We're both in luck. I'm going to Rye, just the very next town and not looking forward to driving alone.

Hop in, and be quick about it now. Haven't got all day to spend waiting on you."

"Yes, ma'am; thank you, ma'am."

"Now don't you be ma'am'n me all the way to kingdom come. The name is Cornelia, and don't you try short'n it up either."

She chuckled while he figured it out. When the woman spoke again, he found himself focused on her rattling teeth. He hoped she didn't want to chat. He wanted to think. It wasn't to be. She clacked all the way to Hampton.

Fortunate to find a room in an old Victorian, it stood on the beach about a mile from the Driftwood. The widowed owner had converted the area under the porch into a studio. Small but comfortable, it had a shower, tiny closet, twin bed, a dresser, and a desk with a chair. There was no fridge or stove, but a cooler and hot plate would do fine, he thought. The only window provided a view of the sea. He paid four weeks rent in advance and moved in.

As Milo unpacked, a movement outside the window caught his attention: three guys tossing a football. Milo went outside to watch and without warning, the guy with the ball fired a bullet. Milo caught the ball, but ended up on the ground, butt first. The guy who'd thrown the ball offered a hand. A flaming redhead, his face and torso were dotted with freckles. "I'm Frank Murphy. Everyone calls me Murph." He pulled Milo to his feet.

"I'm Milo. Great pass."

"Great catch."

"Are you working here for the summer?"

"Naw, we have a cottage about a half-mile down the beach. I got a football scholarship to Boston College, so I took the summer off. Figure the beach is the place to get my legs in shape for fall."

"I was thinking the same. Maybe you could give me some pointers."

"Sure, kid. We're out here every day."

Murph, a high school All-American halfback, played Milo's position. Bound to take a lot of ribbing from Murph and his bunch, he thought it a small price.

The next morning Milo interviewed with the chef and was hired on as a pot washer to start immediately. Pots, pans, and utensils, though clean, were dull. These are bullshit, he thought. In a short time, Milo made them gleam and did the same with the kitchen. He scrubbed and oiled the wooden prep benches and dug grime from every corner. The kitchen sparkled. The chef tried not to let on, but Milo knew he was pleased. Everything had fallen into place, almost too easily, he thought. Milo had a great place to live, a job that provided meals, and Murph.

Milo had good football savvy, but Murph taught him how to switch the ball smoothly from one arm to the other when changing direction and to protect the ball when tackled. He coached him to lower a shoulder into the tackler. Most importantly, he helped to cure Milo's propensity to fumble. The new skills were a bonus added to a great job at the beach.

A few days later, the chef's helper spilled boiling water

on himself and Milo was promoted. Time spent in Nonno's kitchen and with Pappy paid unexpected dividends.

Her name was Talli. She, too, had come to the beach for the summer. Three years older and four inches taller than Milo, Talli's hair, closer to white than blond, was of such fine texture that only a ponytail or braids kept it away from her face. She chose the ponytail and it reached almost to the top of her petite buttocks. Not quite grown into her long, shapely legs, the fullness of her breasts was also unfulfilled, but the promise obvious. A smile contrived to hide a slightly protruding eyetooth didn't, but the result created a charming dimple in her cheek. A husky, soft timbre to her voice was innocent rather than calculated.

Given the task of preparing mashed potatoes, Milo used Nonno's recipe of anchovy and garlic crushed to a paste, then blended with olive oil and wine. He whipped it into the potatoes with butter, milk, soured cream, salt and pepper. He tasted. Perfect, he thought.

Dinner had been underway for an hour. Talli burst through the door. With a full tray balanced in one hand, she ran into Milo and broken glass and food flew. Angered, Milo could see only a mess — until he saw Talli.

"No problem," he stammered.

"It was my fault. I wasn't watching."

She wiped food from her apron. He thought her the loveliest creature he'd ever seen. "Naw, I wasn't paying attention; it's all right."

They faced awkwardly until both blurted names at the

same time. They laughed and shook hands. All four of Milo's grandparents were Italian immigrants, but his eyes and sandy hair belied the fact. Milo appeared anything but Italian except for a Roman nose. She stared into his eyes. It made him uncomfortable.

"Are you the chef?"

Milo smiled. "I'm the chef's helper."

"Oh. Well, my customers have been telling me to give compliments to the chef about the mashed potatoes."

Milo beamed. "I made them."

"Wow, Milo! That's great!"

"Actually, it's my grandfather's recipe. I'd like to talk more, but orders are piling up."

"I know, and there's a long wait line too."

"Maybe we can go to the beach or something?"

"Okay. I'm off tomorrow."

"Sounds good, I don't work until 3:00. Do you want to meet on the beach across from the Pelican Grill tomorrow?"

"What time?"

"Ten?"

"See you at ten."

All the time they spoke, his heart grew with each beat.

They spent the morning on the sand. Though older, Talli didn't seem to know how to breach the awkward silence between them. Milo's feeble attempts didn't work either. Then there were the teasing jibes from Murph and his bunch to contend with. With chances ebbing away like the tide and time, he mustered some courage.

"Wanna come over to my room for supper? I was going to make pasta."

Talli smiled shyly. "Okay."

In the room but a few moments, they couldn't get their clothes off fast enough. Milo knew nothing of foreplay, and Talli thought what they were doing was it. Trapped in passion, from the frantic throes of lust arose the voice of reason, and it wasn't Milo's. If it hadn't been for Talli's willingness, the act might have been considered rape. She spoke breathlessly.

"Do you have any protection?"

"Shit," he exclaimed. "I can get some."

Milo threw on some clothes and sprinted the distance to Murph's cottage, arriving breathless. Composing himself with some deep breathing, he walked through the door. Murph and his bunch were playing poker.

"Hey, man, what happened to the fox?"

Milo blushed. "Hey, Murph, can I talk to you in private?"

"I'm play'n poker, man. Speak up."

Milo turned pepper red-faced, but desperately blurted out, "You got a rubber?"

Cards flew about the room along with the guffaws. Murph went deadpan, his eyes rolling in circles.

"Hey guys, the half-pint's gonna get some pussy." Murph went to the dresser, poked about, and then tossed Milo a condom.

Milo caught it and bolted, covering the distance back at full speed. Talli had the sheet pulled to her chin, as if she'd changed her mind. Then they tore Milo's clothes off. Having never used one, he fumbled with the condom and spent himself on her thigh trying to roll it on. When he finally got the condom fitted, it was over.

There's the rest of the summer I hope, he thought, trying to rationalize his embarrassed disappointment. Not at all discouraged, Talli seemed willing to go forward with the relationship, but it didn't work out. Unable to overcome the mortification of his perceived inadequacy, he couldn't continue. To his relief, she left for college. But for a brief interlude, the adventure had been a grand experience.

~ ~ ~

On the last Sunday of summer, Milo invited his family for brunch. Afterwards, they sat on the patio overlooking the ocean. Nonno pulled Milo aside. "Let's go walk."

A warm sea breeze carried the familiar and comforting aroma of Nonno's stogie across the secluded beach, as he and Milo strolled to the water's edge.

Lazy rollers splashed foamy jetsam onto the sand. A flock of clamorous gulls, looking like a carpet of calico, blared like a cacophonous orchestra tuning instruments. Busy-bodied sandpipers scurried among them, intently immersed in whatever it is they do. Two large pelicans, beaks resting like saxophones on their breasts, posed as ancient sages.

Annoyed gulls scampered aside for the presuming humans to pass. Milo looked at the lovely scene and reversed a familiar cliché — *What's right with this picture?* he asked himself, and then thought, *Everything.*

When the noise died down, Nonno spoke.

"Milo, you make Nonno proud. You got a job and a little place to live on your own. Now you need to think about the future. You need finish school. You should come home now. We won't have any more trouble. Now you are a man."

Milo thought, *Not quite yet.* "Thank you, Nonno."

~ ~ ~

Chapter Twelve

End of Innocence

The tension between Milo and his grandfather ended. They established a nascent friendship based on mutual respect, but anger still lingered due to the way Nonno dished out wisdom. Milo missed his father and resented Nonno's surrogacy.

The wound of his father's departure still festered and a raw, avenging vulture-like anger possessed him. Like an arthritic joint, it flared in the cold dampness of anxiety and fear. Prowling within Milo's subconscious were doubts about the promise he'd made to Carlo and resentment for the obligation. Like an invisible load, Milo felt, but couldn't see the weight. Since living with his grandparents, the burden had lessened some, but it still governed much of his life.

Milo returned to school with immediate dividends. Earning a varsity letter in football made him proud and shored up his self-confidence, but his less-than-adequate academic grades were humbling. Milo's application for military flight school was contingent on attending a prep school first. Upon completion of a two-year college requirement, he could then apply.

An impassioned desire to fly dominated his future plans and, for the first time, Milo believed it would happen. His experience in Maine with Phonsie now allowed him to work at a local cobbler shop, providing some semblance of independence. Even after his contribution to household expenses and savings for college, he had spending money. A jock with a car paid in full, a steady girlfriend, and the softened air of spring left Milo feeling confident about the future. In respite from an emotional thrill ride, only the rancor between Milo and his mother continued to be troublesome.

For years, Maria had believed her husband would return, but over time she realized Milo's prophecy to be accurate. Conflict between them smoldered, a peat fire ready to explode. One day, while Milo helped Nonna shuck corn, his mother and siblings were on the patio. Maria raised an anger-choked voice.

"Don't listen to Milo when it comes to your father; he doesn't understand. Your rotten father didn't care about us. You don't know how much I suffered working in that hot laundry twelve hours a day so you could eat. He left us to rot in the slums. Not once did he call or write, the son of a bitch. Do you think he loved you? He didn't give a shit about what happened to us. If it hadn't been for Nonno and Nonna, you'd have starved to death, because I couldn't take it any more. I would have been dead. All because of that bastard! He never loved you kids. You were like a chain around his neck."

Milo flung an ear of corn into the distance and stormed to the patio. "That's bullshit, Ma. Dad did love us. I know he did. I don't know why he left, but he didn't hate us. I'm freaking tired of you saying that."

"You're always sticking up for your father, Milo. Someday, you'll be sorry. God will punish you, you'll see."

Milo wanted to strike her, but instead used his tongue.

"It's your fault, Ma. You *made* him leave."

Mimicking chicks around a hen, the children flocked around their mother. His sister spoke. "That's wrong, Milo. Can't you see how much he made us suffer?"

"This is bullshit!" Milo walked away furious and alone in his conviction.

After this emotional outburst, Maria started to accept the strength of Milo's feelings. The acrimony dissolved as salt in water. She softened and eventually expressed admiration for her son's steadfastness and beliefs.

A true friendship began between them. A simple, uneducated woman, innocent and naïve, vulnerable to jokes and teasing, Maria laughed most when the joke was on her. Milo admired that. Problems with Nonno and Maria on the mend, the seventeen-year-old felt more and more self-assured.

Spring burst forth and put a reluctant winter to bed. Just past dawn, with the sun on the rise, Milo drove to work one morning, full of joy. Often one of few about, he owned the road and woods, even the eagerly anticipated coffee shop. The warming sun splashed snow-swathed fir trees in crimson, contrasting with the dismal slush-splashed roads.

The mire spattered the sides of Milo's 1951 Ford coupe, annoying, but not enough to mar the day. Green shoots poked through everywhere. Milo opened the window, gulping air as if to suck the morning deep within himself. He felt the bite of fresh-ground espresso on his tongue.

Across from the café, a creek passed under the road through a culvert beneath an old fieldstone bridge. Spring rains and melting snow had swollen the stream, especially where it narrowed. The racing current and rocky bottom smashed and heaped the water, forcing droplets to form a mist over the boiling froth.

Sure enough, there wasn't a car in the lot, only a set of footprints to the door — Sharon's. He'd get the first cup; she drank tea. Relishing the thought, Milo parked and whistled a cheerful tune. Flashing a white toothed smile, he flung the door open and greeted the waitress with white teeth and a sweeping bow.

"Good morning, Ms. The usual, please."

"Coming right up, Mr. Suave." Sharon smiled.

With a wink back, Milo sat to read the paper. "Spring arrives on tail of winter storm." The headlines punctured the silence between word and thought. *Right*, thought Milo, *not soon enough*. He turned to Sports. It spoke of spring practice and the prospects for the new team. He felt nostalgic reading it, missing mud, blood, and Coach Paul, who taught two unforgettable clichés — "quitters never win" and "winners never quit," it's not about knock-downs, but get-ups that count.

Abruptly, a woman dashed into the shop wearing a bathrobe, sweater, and muddy slippers, nervously twisting her fingers. She saw Milo, and screamed, "Help me. I think my Jennifer fell into the creek."

Sharon rushed over to see about the fuss when Milo shouted. "Call the police. I'll see what I can do."

Milo and the frantic woman headed for the creek. Footprints and skid marks on the muddy bank told the story. The girl had slipped into the water and was trapped in the culvert. Milo ran to the bridge and peered into the foul darkness underneath. He called out, but heard only the rushing water. The thought of jumping into the roaring sluice terrified him.

He was powerless to marshal either his wits or demonstrate any level of valor, and precious moments rippled past with the spume. Sheer will finally wrenched him into action. Stripped down to shorts, shaking with fear and cold, Milo stood poised on the edge, summoning the courage to spring when suddenly he noticed paramedics and a scuba diver scrambled down the bank. Overcome with relief, an indelible thought fixed itself in his mind: the question of whether or not he would have acted; he'd never thought himself a coward.

A rough hand on his shoulder startled him, but the police sergeant spoke kindly. "We'll take it from here, son. You'd best get your clothes on or you'll be after catching your death. T'was a brave thing you tried to do."

Milo got dressed and waited nervously as they searched. Shortly, they brought her to the surface and placed her on a gurney. One of the paramedics tried to revive her, but to no avail. Ashen and blue-faced, her lifeless eyes brought back a familiar awareness to Milo and he knew she was dead. Her wailing mother filled him with sadness, guilt, and anger — with himself and God.

Mother and child left in the ambulance. It drove slowly away, siren silent, the silence of death. As if he could watch the light slowly die, he continued a descent into darkness.

~ ~ ~

CHAPTER THIRTEEN

Confession

Music, birds, and flowers were Milo's passions. Fresh growth sprouted everywhere. Multi-hued wild-flowers poked through patches of snow scattered across the meadow. Such a day normally put bounce into his step. Today it failed to lift his spirits. The sunny afternoon couldn't brighten the darkness in his heart or his coldness of soul.

Milo and Denise decided to picnic at a favorite child-hood hide-away, an upland meadow above Flask Pond. In love since first they met as sophomores, they'd been going steady for two years. As most teenagers of their genera-tion, they petted and necked, never going all the way. Denise always cooled things down. Milo respected that.

They hiked along the trail in silence. Usually talkative and outgoing, Milo was out of character. Denise wondered why.

At a pine grove high in the meadow on the bank of a winding creek, they made a bed of the needles and spread a blanket, the murmuring creek and echoing woodpecker the only sounds. They watched a pair of beaver construct a dam — he saw only a drowning child.

He uncorked a bottle of Nonno's wine, pouring for two. Denise placed an arm around his shoulders. "What's bugging you, Milo? Did I do something wrong?"

He brushed her cheek with his lips. Whenever he got quiet or angry, she always thought it was her fault. Denise knew nothing of Milo's involvement in the drowning. The newspaper made no mention of Milo nor had he discussed it until now.

"I feel bad about the little kid who drowned in Stoneridge Creek a few weeks ago."

Denise, squeezing his hand said, "It was so sad. She never should have been playing down there. Is that why you've been so quiet lately?"

"Yes. I guess so."

"Why is it bothering you so much?"

Denise had never seen him as angry or so sad. The transformation was jolting. Flushed and trembling, in a voice thick with self-loathing, he turned as if to vomit.

"I'm a fucking coward! That's why."

Denise sensed his need to get it out. Holding his shoulder, she gently pulled him around to face her. The tears she saw reflected his ache and culpability.

"What's going on, Milo?"

"I could have saved her."

Denise and Milo had always been inseparable. She felt betrayed. In a cutting tone, she said, "You were there? Why didn't you tell me?"

Milo lowered his head and spoke softly. "I haven't told anyone. I was at the coffee shop when the mother came for help. The kid slipped into the creek and got caught in the culvert under the bridge. The current was so strong. I was scared shitless. If I'd had the guts to go in after her, she'd be alive."

"Oh, Milo, I'm so sorry. Look, that doesn't make it your fault. You could've gotten caught and drowned yourself."

Denise hugged him tightly. He projected invincibility, but she knew otherwise. In her arms was a little boy, and like women through the ages, she wanted to make everything right for him.

"You're not a coward. Nobody can blame you."

They clung to each other in silence for several minutes. Milo felt better, but it didn't change the anger he felt towards himself.

Denise opened the basket and served lunch. They finished eating and shared another glass of wine.

"This is so good, a little strong, but I like it."

"Me and Nonno made it two years ago."

They stretched out in the softness of the pine needles. Milo drew near and kissed her tenderly. They caressed through clothing for a long while. Milo unbuttoned her sweater, fumbling to unsnap her bra.

Blushing, she whispered, "Wait."

Milo thought she'd decided to apply the brakes. He lay back with his hands behind his head looking at the clouds. Denise knelt over him and kissed him on the neck. Rippling sensations shot up the back of his neck. When he opened his eyes, she was hovering naked over him. Taking her in his arms, he kissed her breasts. Her taut nipples were reminiscent of the budding flowers in the meadow. This time, Denise was willing, eager. It seemed to him as if they were at the edge a pool of unknown depth, frightened, but ready to plunge. She rolled onto her back. With his lips he touched the velvet essence between her parted legs.

Almost without awareness, they'd lost control with no way to stop. He'd never felt her lips as hot, her body as yielding. She whimpered and wrapped her legs tightly about his waist. The warmth and wetness as he entered her erased any notion of dousing the fire. It would have taken more power than he possessed. Moving together only briefly, the fluid burst forth. They lay breathlessly locked in passion.

He looked at her for a long while. She lay on her side, hands together as if in prayer, cheek resting on the back of her hand. With silken hair lying loosely around her face, he likened her to an angel. He leaned to kiss her on the cheek. She rolled over and held him tightly.

"I love you, Milo."

"I love you, too. I'm sorry. I kept thinking you were going to . . ."

She placed her forefinger over his lips. "It's okay. I didn't want to stop."

"It's getting late. We'd better get going."

They dressed and headed down the trail. Milo wondered if she'd allowed it to happen out of sorrow. It changed nothing. According to his upbringing, he'd committed a sin and would have to confess. Father Flynn would surely recognize his voice. He decided he'd go to

Father Chechini instead. The penance would be more severe, but Chechini wouldn't know who did the confessing. He hoped Denise wasn't pregnant. He promised himself he'd be sure to use a condom the next time. With this thought, he realized he planned to sin again. No matter. Suffering the wrath of Father Chechini and a few prayers would erase it. Somehow, it didn't seem right, though.

Denise paused on the trail. "I almost forgot. Brandon asked if you could do his paper route tomorrow. He's sick."

"Sure. It's my day off. It'll be fun seeing some of my old customers."

~ ~ ~

Both Sebastian and Milo would savor the taste of romantic love early on. The result of Bach's experience was a joy defying words — for Milo, agony beyond belief.

~ ~ ~

CHAPTER FOURTEEN

I Puff My Pipe and Think of God

Sebastian's cousin, Johann Ernst, invited him to visit Hamburg. He had gotten an early start, hitching a ride a good part of the way on a wagon carrying fresh produce. He walked the remaining distance along the postal route, not as scenic but more direct, arriving late in the morning. Famished, and not shy about it, he wanted food. "Ernst, it's good to see you, but I can hardly see at all for my hunger!"

Ernst laughed at his younger cousin. "A true Bach, feed the stomach first and then the soul."

After devouring his meal in quick fashion, Sebastian leaned back in his chair and patted his belly. "Excellent, Cousin, thank you. I couldn't have gone another moment."

"Well, you can accompany me to market. There I shall refill my larder now that you've totally depleted it. And we can stop at St. Catherine's on the way."

"What is of interest there that I've not seen at Michaelisschule day in and day out?"

"Ah, my cousin, there you will see and perhaps play the most beautiful organ in all of North Germany. It has fifty-eight stops on four manuals and pedal."

Sebastian leapt from his chair. "What are we waiting for? Let's go!"

Ernst arranged for Bach to play and listened engrossed as the empty church overflowed with music. When he finished, Sebastian shook his head in admiration. "Wonderful! The pitch is perfect. She sings evenly and clearly right down to the lowest C. And, it doesn't have the hideous pedal noise you find with many organs. It's magnificent."

"Now, you've fed your soul."

"Yes, and now, I'm ready for supper!"

Ernst prepared a robust evening meal. Sebastian attacked the food voraciously, then washed it down with more wine than usual. He glanced about the room to keep from getting dizzy. The furniture looked as tired and content as he felt. A fire popped and crackled in the hearth. "This is a fine place you have here, Ernst."

"Yes. It's quite comfortable and the neighbors are most accommodating and tolerant of my late-night dalliances on the cello."

"Ah, that's most important."

"Tell me now, Cousin, how are things in Lüneburg?"

"Well, for one, I'm finished at Michaelisschule."

"What will you do now?"

"I haven't given it much thought. I suppose I must, though."

"Why don't you move here to Hamburg? I'm sure you'd find something rather quickly. I've plenty of room.

Besides, perhaps you could work with Reincken. He used to be the organist at St. Catherine's. I have a friend who might arrange for you to meet him."

"Oh my God, could you really?"

"I'll do my best. Now, let's enjoy a pipeful."

"I've never tried it."

"Well, now is as good a time as any. You may find it restful."

Sebastian coughed and wheezed at his first puff, but in short time learned to keep smoke out of his lungs. He slouched back in his chair, contentedly watching smoke swirls rise to the ceiling, enjoying the rich aroma. He grinned at Ernst and sang.

"On land, on sea, at home, abroad,

I puff my pipe and think of God."

Sebastian greatly admired Reincken's talent as an organist and composer. He studied Reincken's composi-tions in order to lay a base for his own writing, especially the principle of double counterpoint, the use of two musical voices, each of which could function as an upper or lower voice. With music hardwired in his genes, he had a built-in jump-start. Sebastian mastered the keyboard, gained first-hand technical knowledge of the organ, and laid a solid foundation for his future compositions. A master musician, he remained oblivious to his own genius.

Having accomplished what he'd set out to do in Hamburg, Sebastian returned to Ohrdruf, where he could be closer to his brother, Christoph. The seventeen-year-old virtuoso had begun the transition from adolescence to manhood. Music, daily life — everything reflected his passion. The urge to create set his blood to heat, discernible not only in his music; no wonder, he'd later sire twenty children. Christoph observed his younger brother's interest in the opposite sex with amusement. On the other hand, he wanted Sebastian to stay focused on music. One evening after supper, he spoke to Sebastian. "My brother, you have a wonderful future ahead. Girls are nice, but you mustn't let them distract you."

"What makes you think that will happen?"

"It's inevitable when one starts thinking with his tiny head instead of the one above one's shoulders!"

Sebastian thought for a second. His face grew pink and he smiled. "Nothing will distract me from my music, ever. I can do both!"

"You need to concentrate more."

"I'm working on an idea."

"Tell me what it is."

"It's only a seed now."

He sat at the organ and played. When he'd finished, Christoph nodded approvingly.

"That's quite good."

"Organ playing is nothing remarkable. All one has to do is hit the right notes at the right time and the instrument plays itself! Perhaps one day I will play it for Johann Adam Reincken."

~ ~ ~

Sebastian and Milo were separated in time by centuries. For Sebastian, the future held the promise of fame and fortune. Events would test the mettle and will of both. Each faced the challenges life presented in his own fashion. Bach became the guide, as Milo fumbled for answers.

~ ~ ~

CHAPTER FIFTEEN

The Favor

B randon, the thirteen-year-old brother of Milo's girlfriend, Denise, rarely sought the company of others of his age. Their mother's alcoholism and abusiveness traumatized Brandon, causing him to become withdrawn. After many years of trying to keep the family together, Brandon's father, who provided an emotional buffer against his wife's abuse, left the marriage. It devastated Brandon. Though not physically violent, yet her verbal assaults chipped away at Brandon's well-being. Increasingly depressed, he did poorly in school and his growing anger caused problems with students and teachers.

Milo liked him and related to his feelings concerning the loss of his father. He spent time with him whenever possible. They'd shoot baskets, toss a football, and plod through homework. A mediocre student, Brandon's grades soon improved with Milo's tutoring. After Milo got a better job, he turned his paper route over to Brandon. It turned out to be a good decision. Brandon proved reliable, and the ability to earn improved his outlook and attitude. Milo looked forward to covering the route.

On one of Brandon's off days, Milo rose early and drove to pick up the papers. He knew the routine. The *Boston Globe* and *Tybourne Times* were bundled with hemp twine. He would sort them, putting a *Globe* and *Times* together for customers receiving both, and singles for the others. The ritual took fifteen minutes or so. Usually able to finish the route by 7:30, it gave him time to grab breakfast and get to school. Proud he never missed a day, he was the only carrier to do so on foot, even during the heaviest storms.

Seeing Bill Parker still there surprised him. *He must be eighty-five or more by now,* he thought.

"Hi, Billy O."

Parker chuckled, smiling through the stogie always clamped between his tobacco-stained teeth. "Hey, Milo, what's going on? Want a paper route? You can earn some good Christmas money."

"Nah. I'm just doing Brandon Forbes's route today. He's sick."

"Oh? He's a good kid. How d'ya know Brandon?"

"He's my girlfriend's brother."

Bill grabbed the wet stogie out of his mouth. A piece of tobacco got caught in his throat. With a loud, raspy cough, he tried to clear it.

"Be careful there now, Billy. Don't give yourself a heart attack."

"It'll take more than a heart attack to put me under. Only the old die young. Anyway, I'm too mean to die."

Milo chuckled. "That's for sure."

"Are you rid'n or driv'n?"

"I was going to ride, but I don't have a carrier. Got one lying around?"

"Nope."

"Then I guess I'm driv'n. Brandon should be back tomorrow. If not, I will."

"Good ta see ya, Milo. By the way, great game on Thanksgiving. That offside cost ya a touchdown; the ref musta been blind. They was offside, not you guys. But that sixty-yard run ya uncorked was purty fancy step'n. Yup, it was a corker, surely was."

"Yeah, thanks."

Moving into the morning, Milo had no idea the hand of providence was about to demolish his newly won but fragile sense of self-worth with one cruel stroke.

~ ~ ~

CHAPTER SIXTEEN

The Accident

Changes had taken place on the route since he'd done it. Some houses were re-painted, and to Milo's dismay, the Carters had chopped down the ancient stately elm he loved. Just to make room for that ugly addition, he thought. Ever present within his being, Milo knew about emptiness. He saw at the Carter house a hole in the sky that would never again be filled.

As he tossed papers out the window, he realized that throwing from his bike had seemed more natural. Several times he missed the open window and had to go back, or the paper landed in a bad spot and had to be retrieved. *I'll use Brandon's bike if I do this again*, he thought.

The route ended on Lowell Street, where Denise and Brandon lived. Wooded on the left, this section of the street had a tract of houses on the right. Milo used to walk Denise home this way after a date. They'd stop in these woods to make out. Milo recalled a cold winter's night and how wonderful it felt to put his hands inside her jacket as they kissed, remembered the warm firmness of her breasts. He smiled at the thought.

Approaching the last house, four children, two on tri-cycles, were in the street to his right. As Milo tapped the horn and steered to the center of the road, he heard a loud thump. They threw something, he thought angrily. He stopped to check for damage. Lying motionless in the middle of the street was a little girl. She'd darted from the woods.

He screamed, "Oh my God, no!" White-faced and trembling, he knelt and saw blood pooled under her head. Remembering a first aid class, he didn't move her, but felt her neck for a pulse, relieved to find it strong. Frightened children stared.

Milo shouted to the oldest, "Go home and tell your mother to call an ambulance. Hurry!"

He turned to the others. "Do you know her?"

"Yes, she's Erin McIre."

"Where does she live?"

"Down the street."

"Go get her mother — run!"

He covered Erin with a blanket from his car and stroked her hand.

"Erin, can you hear me?" No response. Desperately, he spoke aloud to God. "Please not again. Please don't let her die. I'll do anything. Holy Mother, help me."

Erin's mother appeared, her face an ashen mask of anguish. Milo avoided her eyes.

"My God," she screamed. "What happened?"

"I thought one of the kids threw something. When I got out of the car, she was lying here."

The woman knelt. "Erin, do you hear me? It's Mommy."

No response. Milo wanted to be anywhere else, wished it were a nightmare from which he'd awake. The mother looked about, desperate and helpless. A distant siren sounded and an ambulance soon arrived.

The attendants rushed to them. "Everyone, get out of the way."

They moved as robots. When stabilized, Erin was placed on a gurney and into the ambulance. Milo stood awkwardly, surrounded by curious onlookers. The ambulance sped away, siren wailing. It left him with hope.

Police dispersed the crowd. Officer Bill Larsen, Milo's coach from the Police Athletic Baseball Program, walked towards him.

"What happened?"

Numb and cold, Milo struggled to gather his thoughts. He mumbled, "I never saw her. I tried to avoid some kids in the street and heard a thump. I thought one tossed something at the car. I never saw her."

"Relax, just take it easy. How fast were you going?"

No response. Milo wrung his hands. Disoriented and disconnected, mind blank, he stared dumbly through Larsen.

"I know it's tough, but I need to complete this report. How fast were you going?"

"About ten or fifteen miles an hour, I guess."

"Have you had any alcohol?"

"No."

"I didn't think so. You understand I had to ask. Would you consent to a test?"

"Yes."

Larsen appeared sympathetic, but Milo felt threatened.

"Calm down. This is routine. Have you moved your car since the accident?"

"No."

"I just need your license and registration, and we're done."

Milo got the documents.

Strobe lights bounced off gunmetal-hued clouds making the scene appear as if in slow motion. Jumbled voices crackled over radios, neighbors whispered and watched the goings-on. A bright spring turned bleak, lightning flashed. Chill winds moved the ominous clouds roiling in the distance. Milo shivered as cold rain struck his face.

Larsen's partner finished photographing the scene. He held a bloody blanket. "Is this yours?" Milo took it and thought he would vomit.

"We're finished. Look kid, don't worry. She'll be okay. We'll get hold of you if we need anything."

"Can I go now?"

"Whenever you want."

Milo didn't want to drive, but got behind the wheel. A last paper sat on the seat. He delivered it, and then drove to the hospital.

In a coma, Erin had sustained massive head injuries. Doctors were uncertain about the extent of damage and not optimistic. Only immediate family was allowed to see her. A pink-smocked, ruddy-faced woman at the reception desk smiled at Milo's approach.

"Can you tell me how Erin McIre is?"

"Spell that please."

"M-c-I-r-e, Erin."

"Oh, yes, of course, the little girl who was hit by a car."

His heart pounded a message — please say everything is all right, but the pit in his stomach said otherwise.

"Is she okay?"

"Unless you're a family member, I can't give out any information. I'm sorry."

Milo nodded.

Time seemed endless. He sat in the lobby and realized his life would never be the same. The thought made him feel ill. The receptionist waved him to the desk. "I never told you this."

Milo understood.

"She's stable, but critical, still in a coma. Poor thing, she's so young. I heard the doctors don't give her much of a chance. I'm sure her parents must be devastated, but accidents happen."

Milo fought back tears and went to the car to wait. Grief-stricken, he checked in hourly. At 3:30 in the morning, he decided to get an update and go home.

"I'm sorry. She passed on about fifteen minutes ago."

Overwhelming numbness failed to deaden Milo's shock and anguish. He managed to make the car before a primal wail, spawned in the depths of his soul, broke the night silence. After some time passed, his thoughts were of unanswered prayers and the worthiness of God's grace. He wished for sleep, saw lifeless eyes before him and shuddered, knowing they were his own.

~ ~ ~

CHAPTER SEVENTEEN

The Funeral

The early morning turned ugly on the day of the funeral. Dirty gray clouds shed a chilling drizzle over the solemnity of the occasion. The services were held at Saint Christopher's Catholic Church which served the diocese.

The funeral turned out to be one of the most highly attended ever in Tybourne. The entire community had been affected by the senseless death of a child. Saint Christopher's sat two hundred people. The stone church overflowed, with another hundred crowded into the narthex. More stood in the rain. The stolid presence of a granite crucifix dominated the entrance of the parking lot and cast its shadow over the assemblage.

Many generations of McIres proudly served Tybourne's fire department. Dress blue uniforms were sprinkled throughout the sea of mourners. The police chief, a close friend of the McIre's, provided a contingent of officers as pallbearers. Heads bowed, white-gloved, they sat near the casket. Incense swirled sorrowfully upward.

Father Flynn performed the mass. Milo had served him as an altar boy at Sunday mass a few years earlier. He'd assisted while his family proudly received communion. His grandparents took the host with tears of joy.

Milo beamed, with cowlick pointed skyward, in celebration of his first mass that day.

Today, Father Flynn gave communion to the mourners kneeling at the rail. An altar boy carried a gold cross slowly toward the casket. In unadorned vestments, Father Flynn followed. He had baptized Erin in this same place a few short years past, in a paradigm of priesthood.

The procession stopped at the casket. The creak of a pew, a muffled cough, mourners knelt, and then silence. Father Flynn made the sign of the cross.

"In nomine Patris, et Filii, et Spritus Sanctus. Amen. Introibo ad altare Dei."

The altar boy responded, *"Ad Deum, qui laetificat juventutem meam."*

Father Flynn began the forty-second Psalm, *"Judica me, Deus, Et discerne causim meam de gente non sancta: ab homine iniquo, et doloso erue me."*

Milo whispered the response, *"Quia tu es, Deus, fortitudo mea?"* He repeated the phrase in English. "For thou, God, art my strength, why hast thou forsaken me?" Milo prayed. "Why let this happen to me? Have you ever heard my prayers? I was a good altar boy, never miss mass, confess and do penance when I sin. What more do you expect? You let my father leave. I tried to protect my brothers and sister, cared for them like I promised, but they hate me and treat me like shit — why do you let them — punish me?"

Father Flynn continued, *Confiteor Deo omnipotenti, beafae Mariae semper Virgini."*

The altar boy responded, *"Mea culpa, mea culpa, mea maxima culpa."*

By habit, Milo struck his breast three times repeating the words of the Confiteor. "Through my fault, through my fault, through my most grievous fault." Milo spoke to God. "I think you're a hoax, the biggest joke ever played. You say, thou shalt not kill, but Christian soldiers kill heathen, Indian, witch. Fuck your brother's wife, go to confession, ten "Hail Marys," ten "Our Fathers," an act of contrition — bullshit. You let people die of hunger, disease. You don't obey your own fucking rules! It's like you pull the wings off flies and crush snails. Is it fun? You never show yourself. "Have faith," we're told. Do you hate us so much? You are worse than the worst of us. It makes more sense that humans are not different, but just like you — vain, jealous hypocrites, and killers."

"Credo in unum Deum, Patrem omnipotentem factorem coeli Et terrae visibilium omnium Et invisibilium."

Father Flynn began reciting the Nicene Creed. Milo continued his diatribe.

"Believe in God? Why the hell should I? I can't work, or eat, and I can't sleep. What about me? I feel like I'm losing it. I don't know what to do. You let her die. Why not me instead? If you're so freaking powerful, strike me down now. Let everyone see it happen. You can punish me in front of everyone right here. Come on, do it!"

The priest began the commemoration of the dead. *"Memento Etiam, Domine, famulorum famularumque tuarum Erin McIre, et, qui nos praecesserunt cum signo fidei, Et dormiunt in somno pacis."*

Milo looked at Erin lying in the casket. She looked to be sleeping. He whispered, "Where were you? Why couldn't I see you? Why didn't you see my car coming? I didn't mean to hurt you. I prayed so hard that you would live. Please don't hate me. I'd trade my life if you could be alive. I'm sorry. Please forgive me."

The priest ended the mass. *"Benedictat vos omnipotens Deus Pater, et Filius, et Spritu Sanctus."*

"Amen."

"Dominus vobiscum."

"Et cum spiritu tuo."

Flynn and the altar boy escorted the casket to the rear of the church. As it passed, Milo hunched in his pew and sobbed quietly. He remained until the church emptied. In the quiet, his eyes wandered over the Stations of the Cross, fourteen colorful, sixteenth-century depictions illuminated by candles. Spaced evenly around the church, each portrayed a stage of Christ's crucifixion, beginning with Christ's condemnation, through each event leading to death on the cross, ending with entombment.

Milo always lingered at the station where Christ met his mother. Now reminiscent of Erin's mother as she followed the casket into the drizzle, it captured the agony and sorrow in Mary's eyes.

Milo whispered bitterly, "You were crucified for nothing. Your Father did forsake you, just like mine did. God loved the world so much, He sacrificed his Son, let You die a cruel death to prove how much He loved us?

Right. If I were God, I could think of a thousand ways to prove my love, without killing my own son."

Milo rose slowly, "Why did you let her die? There is no God."

With that rejection, Milo felt he'd lost his soul. There'd be no more talking to God.

~ ~ ~

Chapter Eighteen

Phone Calls

Milo lay in bed, fighting sleep because of the nightmares it brought. His life without a father and his recent rejection of God fostered resentment towards both. Family and friends lacked the comprehension and ability to help him. In his perceived isolation, Milo had nowhere to turn but inward. He spoke to his inner voice.

"He didn't have to leave. I knew he wouldn't come back. I know he loved us. Why did he do it?"

"It doesn't matter. It happened, and you're stuck with it."

"Why did I have to get stuck taking care of the kids? They think I'm a bully, but I'm only doing what I promised. Those two little girls died because of me. What if they had been my brother or sister?"

"It would be the same. You'd feel just as badly, I suppose. Maybe there's a difference. You weren't responsible for taking care of the two little girls."

"But they died because of me. I'd like to find my father, to hurt him so he could know how I feel. And all that bullshit about God — I believed it. If there's no God, what now? Nobody understands. Poor Barnaby, he didn't deserve to die. At least I didn't cause that. He would help me."

"Did you want to kill Erin?"

"No, but she's still dead. Why? And that other little girl would be alive if I had any guts."

"Maybe, but you can't change what happened."

"How can I make the pain go away?"

"I don't know."

"I feel empty, all alone. Sometimes I want to die."

"Then kill yourself."

"I can't. I'm afraid."

Milo could not deliver himself from despair and isolation. In Tybourne, anonymity didn't exist. People looked away to avoid him, and darts of hostility from others felt as if they'd pierced his flesh.

To Milo, fear now seemed inseparable from life itself. Physical pain didn't deter him, but the emotional pain couldn't go away with an aspirin or an icepack. Milo had no answers — only continued existence, haunted by the bogeyman twins of pain and fear. He had learned about his first perception of fear and pain by asking his mother about it. The seeds of fear and pain were subliminally and indelibly implanted when Milo was two years old.

His memory had recorded a sweet, sickening taste that had elicited the vomit response. Panic-stricken, Milo had fought the restraints holding him to the operating table. Frantic, he shook his head to be free from the dreadful black mask. The odor of ether would be forever imbedded in his memory.

Milo had no understanding, only fear at its base level — survival. Gasping for air, only vile vapors entered his lungs. The anesthesia slowly took effect, dropping him into the center of a zebra-striped spiral, a slow spin to a pinpoint of oblivion.

On the voyage back to consciousness, the child sucked for air, but blood and mucus blocked his airways. Plastic tubes protruded from his nose and mouth. Ominous gurgling noises filled his ears. Muted voices spoke commands through surgical masks. Sedation brought welcomed sleep.

Milo's eyes opened to nothing recognizable, only the bars of a crib and a sense of horror. Soon he could move, but barely. Cotton plugs replaced tubes. The aftertaste of ether lingered; with it came nausea. Grasping the rail, he rose to his knees and wailed forlornly, looking for a familiar face. There stood his mother. Blissful eyes flashed as he grabbed through the bars, fingers extending and closing as to grasp her before she disappeared.

Milo always thought it had been a nightmare. Years later he discussed it with his mother. He'd had scarlet fever at a time when medical wisdom included the removal of tonsils and adenoids. His first memory of fear and pain had taken place as a two-year-old.

Tonight tears soaked the bedclothes, and relief came only periodically due to fitful sleep. A ringing phone jerked him into consciousness. Tiptoeing to the kitchen, he hoped it hadn't awakened anyone. "Hello," he whispered. "Hello, who's there?" Silence.

Three nights later, the voice on the line was like wind through a cracked window on a winter's night.

"This is Bobbi McIre."

Milo's stomach did a barrel roll. After a pause, she commanded, "Answer me." Her voice matched the eyes of Mary at St. Christopher's at the funeral. The gravity of those events struck him as a blow.

The words would barely escape his lips. "I'm here."

"My husband wants to kill you," she hissed with a staccato inflection. "God, I wish he would."

The phone went dead. The silence spoke. You drove the car — Erin died. God could no longer judge him, but Milo would be punished, a victim of his own perverted justice.

~ ~ ~

Bobbi was frightened when making the calls, careful not to wake her husband, Tom. She feared not for Milo, but of losing Tom. Cold and distant, his unyielding silence testified to her culpability. Bobbi blamed Milo for Erin's death and a deteriorating relationship with Tom. In a perversion of rationality, Milo became her support mechanism.

A week passed without a call. Relief came as if a gun pointed to his head had been lowered, only to be raised once more when a ring jarred him awake. Only the sound of a dial tone could be heard. Ten minutes later it rang again. After a moment of silence came Bobbi's muffled sobs. "Mrs. McIre, I need to hang up."

She threatened, "Don't you dare! If you do, I'll drown myself in Flask Pond. So help me, God, I will. Do you want two deaths on your soul? Damn you!"

Milo dropped to his knees and screamed. "Leave me alone! I can't take this anymore!"

"You'll pay, damn you."

The phone clicked dead. Frightened, Milo now believed her capable of suicide. Although the calls became unbearable, his inner voice told him to listen. Milo drifted into isolation, barely eating, trapped in a paradoxical cycle. Sleep came with exhaustion but brought nightmares. In weary wakefulness, Milo sought elucidation; in sleep, he fled from demons.

~ ~ ~

CHAPTER NINETEEN

Healing

In a bottomless void of helplessness, Milo groveled and was frightened as Bobbi took her vengeance. Each night he dreaded her call. Following her suicide threat, the calls became shorter.

Again, the phone rang. Milo said nothing, just listened to her breath. Unlike her previous calls, this time she spoke gently.

"Milo, I've had a chance to do a lot of thinking. What I've been doing to you is wrong. The accident wasn't your fault. These past months have been difficult for Tom and me. They must have been horrible for you."

Milo didn't trust her. He remained silent. "Have you spoken to anyone about the accident, Milo?"

"You're the only one I talk to about it."

"Well, that's not much help since I've been doing all the talking. Have you thought about talking with your family?"

"I can't. They avoid the subject or say stupid things."

"Like what?"

"Like, everything will be fine, or, it wasn't my fault. They really don't know what to say. They're only feeling sorry for me. I hate it. They have no idea what I feel."

"What do you feel, Milo?

Guilt and cowardice stuck like a fishbone in his throat. Milo swallowed his tears. "It was my fault, just like with the girl at Stoneridge Creek."

"I remember that. It was before Erin's accident. What do you mean? I don't get the connection."

"I was there when it happened. Her mother asked for help. The creek was running fast. I was afraid. If I had gone in after her, she would be alive. If I had taken Brandon's bike instead of driving, Erin would still be alive. If there were a God, they'd both still be alive. I'd rather be dead."

"Oh my God, I had no idea. It must be horrible. I know how terribly you must feel. Can we talk more when you're more up to it?"

Milo wept — silent, deep, and lengthily. He filled his lungs with breaths of relief, as if a boil had been lanced.

"I'm so tired."

"Get some sleep. I'll call tomorrow, okay?"

"Thank you. Good night."

~ ~ ~

As Bobbi hung up the phone, Tom stood glaring at her. "What in hell is going on? That son of a bitch killed our little girl."

"Tom, please. It's time to put this aside. It wasn't his fault."

"What! The fucker wasn't paying attention to where the hell he was going. That's what happened. I don't give a shit what they said at the hearing."

"Tom, the boy is suffering as much as we are."

Tom slammed his fist on the coffee table. Glass flew to the corners of the room. A vase fell and shattered. Swaying over her, he raised his hand as if to strike. Blood oozed from her cheek. Tom blinked in disbelief, and then felt the wetness on his hand. Tom's blood marked her face.

She reached for his hand. "Don't, I'll be fine."

"Let me help, you're bleeding."

"Leave me be. I'll take care of it. I'm sorry. You know I'd never lay my hand to you. God help me. My mind isn't right. I can't explain. I'm sick and scared — everything is screwed up. I feel like I'm going nuts. When I heard . . . How could you?"

She reached to touch his face. Gently, but firmly, he grabbed her wrist. "Don't."

"Tom, it's okay. I understand."

"You *don't* understand. How could you? I don't understand. I'm going to Canada to visit my brother in the morning. I need to think."

"All right, Tom. Maybe it's best."

Tom left without saying goodbye. Bobbi felt hollow and alone. The next day she plodded through her chores and afterwards collapsed in the maple rocker her father had made for her seventeenth birthday. She rocked in the darkness.

Evening came before she'd emptied her tears. Tom had to figure it out for himself, but Milo couldn't, she thought. How could he? He's not that much older than Erin. The boy needs consolation and forgiveness. Bobbi prayed for guidance and strength. She picked up the phone.

"Hello, Mrs. McIre."

"Hello, Milo. Are you feeling better?"

"Yes, thank you."

"Erin is an only child. Now she's gone, and nothing will bring her back, but we must go on. Your life is ahead of you. You must pray to God to give you the strength."

"You have no idea how much I've prayed. God never answered my prayers. How could God allow this to happen?"

"God works in ways beyond our understanding; you must have faith."

"Faith? Faith in what? In who?"

"Faith in God."

Bobbi sensed that she'd hit a wall. "Would you like to come to dinner? Tom is visiting his brother and we can talk more comfortably in person."

It seemed to Milo strange, somehow unsettling to be alone with Bobbi. "I don't know, Mrs. McIre. I work almost every night."

"Do you have a night off?"

"Well, next Sunday."

"Then, please come to dinner on Sunday evening. I'll cook a pot roast. It's time we talked face to face. Please come. Will you?"

"All right, Mrs. McIre. What time?"

"How about 7:00? Would that be all right?"

"Fine. Should I bring anything?"

"No, I look forward to seeing you then. Good night, Milo."

"Good night, Mrs. McIre."

During the week Milo thought about Bobbi, her cold eyes still vivid in his memory. He shivered walking the gravel path that seemed to crunch a message — "Turn back."

Three leaded panes formed a small arch at the top of the entry, allowing a welcome from the hearth within. With a timid knock, he hoped there'd be no answer. The door swung open.

Her eyes shone with the color of green moss agate, not what he'd seen in his nightmares. Candle-toned, blond hair fell about her face to her shoulders. She held a potholder. Milo stood awkwardly, uncomfortable, and speechless. This convivial, kindly person could not be the bitter, faceless witch of the agonizing telephone calls.

"Come on in. I was taking the roast out of the oven."

The warmth of the room drove winter from his soul. So good to feel warm, he thought.

Bobbi walked to the kitchen taking over her shoulder, "Would you like a glass of wine? It's on the table near the rocker. If you'll do the honors, I'll have one with you."

Milo didn't know about corks that couldn't be grabbed with your fingers, or how to use a corkscrew. Finally, he pushed it into the bottle, poured, and handed her a glass. Bobbi took a sip, removed a bit of cork from her mouth, and looked at him quizzically.

"Sorry, it broke off."

Bobbi stifled a smile, but Milo's face reflected his embarrassment. Bobbi eased the tension. "Not a problem.

It's delicious!"

Bobbi took obvious pride in her table setting. Atop the cherry wood Queen Ann table on ivory porcelain plates sat linen-wrapped silver. Between two candles, a crystal vase of fresh violets and jasmine blinked a reflection. Compared to the Italian-style country setting of chipped plates, mismatched utensils, and jelly glasses he usually dined with, Milo felt out of place.

Bobby brought out a feast: pot roast, potatoes, sautéed squash with carrots, and fresh garden salad. Within a wooden bowl, French rolls added fragrance to the savory aroma. Wine, olive oil, and vinegar were the only things familiar to him.

The sun went to bed for the night as they sat down to eat. Shadows danced in the candlelight, creating an atmosphere very unlike the earthy, casualness of suppertime at Nonno's.

She placed her hand on his, bowed her head, and closed her eyes. "Dear Lord, our faith, love, and trust in you carries us through our pain, thankful that Erin is in your loving care. Please give us strength. In the name of the Father, the Son and the Holy Ghost. Amen."

Right, he thought.

Milo picked at the food timidly. Bobbi tried to make him comfortable. "If you'd rather, I'm sure I have something else you might prefer."

"No, this is fine. I just haven't been very hungry."

"Have some wine; it will help your appetite."

She raised her glass and took a sip. Milo took a big

swig, and then another. "Be careful, you don't want to overdo."

"My grandfather's wine is a lot stronger. We make it every year."

"That must be interesting."

"It is. They used to crush the grapes with their feet in the old days, but now we have a machine."

Bobbi laughed. "That must have been fun, but sometimes machines can take all the joy out of things."

"Well, crushing grapes with smelly feet doesn't seem very sanitary."

"I'm sure people washed their feet first, don't you think? Besides, alcohol kills germs."

The wine loosened Milo up. Relaxed, he ate with relish. Embarrassed, he slowed himself down. "This is delicious. I guess I'm hungrier than I thought."

"Thank you. I'm glad you're enjoying it. There's plenty more where that came from. Tell me, what are your plans for the future?"

"I haven't thought about it much lately."

"I know these past months have been terrible for you, but you have an entire life ahead. What would you like to do?"

"Well, I've always wanted to be a pilot, but my grades aren't so great and I need two years of college."

"That's a good place to focus on."

"I can't seem to concentrate on anything right now."

"I know we've talked about this before, but you need to pray. God will help you."

"You don't know how much I've prayed. It never works. Look at what happened. I don't want to talk about that anymore."

"You need to get your mind somewhere else. What about your work?"

"I quit my job. Well, actually, I wasn't doing so well and got fired."

"Don't worry, you'll get another."

Milo carried the plates to the sink. "You don't have to do that."

"I don't mind. I help my grandmother all the time."

"How nice."

"If I didn't, Nonno would kill me."

"Your grandfather?"

"Yes, he's real strict, but I like to do it anyway."

"Do you live with your grandparents?"

"Yes, my father left us and they took us in."

"I'm sorry. You must be close to your mother. Why don't you talk with her? She will help you sort things out."

"She doesn't understand."

"I'm sure that's not true."

Milo went silent. Bobbi washed and Milo dried. When they were finished, she removed her apron and took him by the hand. Let's sit in the living room. Milo meekly followed. They sat on the sofa in the glow of the hearth. She squeezed Milo's hand.

"Erin used to help me with the dishes every night. Then we'd sit here just like this, our private time. She'd tell me her troubles and I'd comfort her."

Milo stiffened as Bobbi drew him near. She stroked his hair gently. "Relax, I'm not going to bite you." Her touch released his tears. Teardrops of anguish, guilt and gratitude flowed as if to drain and cleanse his being. Milo hugged her tightly, his body quaking with a suppurative force of sorrow. Bobbi laid her head on his and patted his back.

"I'm sorry I hurt you so, Milo. I couldn't help myself. I wasn't thinking of you at all. I prayed for strength and God answered."

Milo shuddered and sighed.

"I know you're angry with God right now, but he will forgive you."

Milo's body relaxed and he felt himself drifting in a dream of being snuggled in his mother's arms. Bobbi slowly pulled her blouse to the waist. Milo rested his head on her breast and began to dose. With a whimper, he took her nipple to his mouth. Bobbi drew him close. Milo suckled as would a child until his breathing told Bobbi he slept.

~ ~ ~

CHAPTER TWENTY

Monument

Several years earlier, Milo's grandfather, Joe, had sold the Ridgewood Monument Works and purchased a place in Tybourne. He wanted to be closer to Milo in order to insure the continuance of tradition. Joe called it the "new *Barraca*." It stood, appropriately, on Salem Street, across from Calvary Cemetery. Locals jokingly called Calvary, "the Citadel."

The graveyard was totally enclosed with eight-foot-high fieldstone walls, except where not practical. Those areas were fenced with eight-foot steel pickets, spaced four inches apart. North and south gates provided the only access. Unquestionably the grounds were a work of art, but since nobody was apt to escape, it seemed like overkill.

Milo sat in his grandfather's worn leather chair behind a battered walnut desk. It stood on ancient oak floors in need of oil. He felt safe there — everything covered with fine white dust and filled with familiar aromas he'd come to love. Milo found consolation in the continuity.

Tracings of artwork littered the draft bench with more tacked to the walls. On the desk, a photo of Tom, Bobbi, and Erin that Milo had clipped out of the obituary stared back at him. They look so happy, he thought, and pinned it to the table. With a fine pencil, he traced the photo to scale.

An idea came to Milo. Though the McIres had already placed a small marker at Erin's grave, he would expand it, replicating the photo on a granite headstone. The scrap piece of rose-colored granite lying unused in the yard would be perfect. For certain, his grandfather would help.

Milo had the knowledge of how to create it, but lacked the skills. He'd first need to sandblast the rendering into a raw hunk of stone and then carve it with an air chisel. He'd practice on a smaller stone until he got it down.

A sense of purpose made him eager to begin. Working nights and weekends, he figured a scale model would take about six weeks. The finished monument would require a couple of months or more. He'd talk with his grandfather about it on the weekend.

The week seemed endless, but on Saturday he rose early, anticipating the day. On the way to the *Barraca*, he took a shortcut through the cemetery, past Erin's grave, and surveyed the surroundings. A white, stately birch stood to the left of the site. A larger willow wept over the stone path directly behind. Milo visualized an understated monument framed by those trees.

The cheerful birdsong didn't break the spell in the quiet of morning. Milo strolled towards Salem Street at the south gate, two blocks from the *Barraca*. Sunlight bounding from the dew-covered markers lightened the somberness of their task. When Milo got to the *Barraca*, his grandfather gave him a hug and tousled his hair. Milo kissed him on the cheek.

"Morning, Grandpa."

"Buon giorno, Milo. You are here so early? Have some coffee. Your grandma, she made some biscotti to go with it."

"Thanks, Grandpa."

Sweet biscotti were perfect to temper the espresso. "What's on your mind, Milo? Your mood is serious this morning."

"I need help. I want to make a monument for Erin McIre."

"That's a good idea. What design you have in mind?"

Milo got the rough draft and spread it on the desk. "I want to use this photo to make a statue. Not real big, about waist high. What do you think?"

"It takes work, lots of work, but you can do it for sure."

"Thanks, Grandpa. I want to do it myself, but I need your advice. I was thinking of making a small one for prac- tice, and then use that piece of rose in the yard for the real one. I'll pay for it."

His grandfather pulled up a chair, took off his battered, dusty fedora and placed it on the desk. Legs apart, hands on his knees, he leaned towards his grandson and looked into his eyes.

"I was waiting for this day since you were born. My father, he was a *scalpellino*, and his father, and his grand- father. They did many fine stonework art pieces in Calabria, in Rome, all over. Me too. I worked on the Brooklyn Bridge stonework. Your uncle Remo, he never wanted to be *scalpellino*; he want to be bum. Your uncle Johnnie, your uncle Marko, they no want to be *scalpellini*. Your father, he was a dreamer. He want to be great conductor, like the Toscanini. So now, nobody left to keep the *scalpellino* tradition but you. I help you. Then you can take over the business when I die. It's what I want."

Dumbstruck, Milo didn't immediately know how to respond — knew if he said the wrong thing, he'd break his grandfather's heart.

"Thank you, Grandpa."

"You have a good idea. Do a small one first. You picked a good piece of stone, easier to work. It's very soft. I give it to you as a gift. It's a very good thing you're doing, Milo. If you put your soul in the work, a miracle will happen."

"Thanks, Grandpa. Do you have time to show me how to lay it out this morning?"

"Let me get uncle Johnnie to start on the new job, then you and me, we start. Finish your coffee now. I'll be back in awhile."

When his grandfather returned, they placed the scrap stone onto a platform of old railroad ties stacked waist high. They cleaned it with an acid and cemented a piece of rubber to its face. Joe showed how to rub the tracing, leaving the pencil marks on the rubber. Milo then cut and pulled out the pieces. They put the stone on wooden rollers and rolled it into the blasting room. Milo blasted the design into the stone, and then they brought it back to the shop. Milo peeled the rubber; it was ready to be carved.

"Good job, Milo. Now you take the air chisel and make all deep. Shape along here where line is, little by little, she's come. I show you a little bit, then you do. "Milo watched as his grandfather hammered into the stone with a wide-bladed chisel. He chipped along the blast line, rounding its face, making it look easy. Joe handed Milo the chisel.

"Okay? Now you do. Go nice and slow. Make it all even. Make all deep like so."

His grandfather observed and hinted as Milo worked. At first Milo took small cuts, but soon learned to use the grain of the stone to his advantage, and the work went faster.

"It's good. You got the idea now. Just do the whole thing like that, rough. Then I show you how to make a more detail finish."

Milo went to the *Barraca* every night, and each weekend after work. For two months he labored long into the night, slow and tedious work, as he mastered the fundamentals of stone carving. Proud of what his grandson accomplished, Joe offered advice and encouragement.

It took seven months to complete. Though not totally satisfied, Milo thought it a reasonable likeness. He'd managed to transfer the essence of the photograph to the rose granite. Milo told Bobbi about the project soon after he got the idea. She approved, thought it would bring him closure. She decided not to tell Tom until after it stood in place.

Joe inspected the work one last time. Milo made the minor adjustments suggested. Completed, they gave it a final acid wash. Joe blinked away tears, and put his arm around Milo's shoulders.

"This is a very good piece of work. I'm proud of your job."

"Thank you for the help, Grandpa. I couldn't have done it without you. Off the subject, I've wanted to ask you a question. Do you know where my father is?"

Sadness filled the old man's eyes. He sat wearily down on an unfinished grave marker, pulled a bandanna from his pants pocket, and wiped his brow. "Milo, you have to forget about him. You never gonna see him again. He's a bum. He doesn't give a shit about you."

"But, do you know where he is?"

"I don't know, but maybe you uncle Remo, the other bum, he knows. Do yourself a favor. Forget about your father."

Milo nodded, but decided to write once more. His uncle always answered the letters, but never the question. A festering urge to confront his father wouldn't be ignored.

Day dimmed toward dusk. Milo wanted to set the stone before dark. They levered it onto a dolly, and rolled it a short walk to the site through the south gate. They set the base behind the ground-level marker already there and positioned the statue. Milo stepped back to get a wider view. The dropping sun cast a peach-hued shadow over the statue. Milo turned to his grandfather. "It fits!" He grinned, and arm in arm they strolled back to the *Barraca*. When they arrived, he plunked himself deep into the old leather chair, exhausted.

"Grandpa, go on home. I'll clean and lock up."

"Why don't you come to have supper? Your grandma, she wants to see you. She has a special something you like to eat."

"Okay, Grandpa. I'll be about forty-five minutes."

It had been a long while since Milo felt happy enough, but he found himself whistling as he cleaned the shop. Finishing quickly, in anticipation of the feast his grandmother had prepared, a last detail remained.

"Hello, Bobbi. It's Milo."

"Milo! How are you?"

"Fine. I've got great news."

She sensed the levity in his voice. "Tell me."

"It's done. We just delivered it."

"Oh, Milo! That is good news. I'm looking forward to seeing it. Tom and I were planning to go to the cemetery on Sunday after church."

"I hope you like it."

"I'm certain we will. You've worked hard. I'm sure it's lovely. I'll call you on Sunday evening. Okay?"

"Thanks, Bobbi. Bye."

"Good night, Milo."

He locked the shop and headed for the cemetery for a last look. It made him edgy. Not that he believed in ghosts, but cemeteries spooked him, especially at night. After a short distance, a rustling stopped him short. Muscles in his legs quivered, and fine body hairs rose to attention. A sudden movement in the shadows prodded him to action. Probably a rabbit, he thought, and quickened his pace.

Tom had seen Milo walking through the cemetery on

several occasions and had been waiting for this opportunity. He'd locked the south gate after Milo had gone through, then drove to the other access, went inside and secured the gate there. When Milo got to it, he couldn't get out. What had started as jitters now leaned towards panic. Adrenalin put his danger mechanisms on red alert, and his reflexes were ready to launch. He ran back to the south gate. It wouldn't open.

Without a sound, but with his thumping heart banging in his ears, Milo scurried for cover in the willow near Erin's grave, each step seeming amplified by a thousand decibels. Branches poked his eyes. Struggling for breath, he fought panic. A loud voice echoed in the dark.

"I know you're there. You can't get away."

Milo shivered.

"You little bastard. You killed my daughter. You fucked my wife!"

"No! It wasn't like that. You don't understand!"

Tom walked towards the willow where Milo hid. The newly placed statue stopped him dead. He dropped to his knees and moaned. Bobbi had told him that what he had seen through the window that night was an act of comfort and healing. He hadn't believed her.

The *Barraca* was the only monument works in Tybourne. Tom knew Milo's grandfather owned it. He suddenly sensed that his actions might be misguided. My God, he thought, the boy must have had something to do with this. Bobbi would never betray me. He silently prayed. Lord Jesus, Erin is with you in heaven. Why, is beyond my understanding. Nothing will change it. I beg for courage and forgiveness. Tom rose to his feet and shouted. "I'll unlock the gate." He went home, filled with a new understanding and compassion.

Milo went to the *Barraca* where Joe snored in the old leather chair. Milo tried to take the coffee cup from his hand, but Joe snorted and rubbed his nose. "Milo, I was taking a nap. What happened? Your grandma, she's waiting."

"Sorry, Grandpa."

Joe poured a coffee and spiked it with a shot of brandy. "This will fix you up good. Drink slow, you don't want to be drunk, eh?"

"Thanks, I'm cold."

"You did a good job, Milo, but I been thinking. Your hands, they're not so good for being a *scalpellino*. Besides, the dust will ruin your lungs. I think you should be a pilot; it's better. You should forget to be a *scalpellino*, eh?" He winked. Milo smiled and hugged his grandfather. "Thanks, Grandpa. You go on home. Tell Grandma I'm on my way. I love you."

Milo sat at the desk, weary. He wondered if his father grieved for him, as Tom did Erin, or even thought about him. Loneliness and longing, devoid of anger, came to him like a tap on the shoulder. A wounded boy, he wanted his father. Milo picked up a pen and wrote: "Dear uncle Remo, I hope everything is fine with you. Grandpa told me you might know where my father is. If you do, please write and tell me. I need to know. With love, Milo"

Several days later, Bobbi called. She spoke gently. "Hello, Milo. Tom and I wondered if you would drop by this afternoon."

Milo understood. The moment to face Tom could not be avoided. "I'll be by after work."

Late on a tranquil afternoon, Milo approached the front door to the McIre's. The place where his car had struck Erin could be seen from the house where she would have grown up. He swallowed hard, but the lump of guilt wouldn't go down. Two towering maples, leaves dancing among embracing branches presented an impression, sentinels over the cozy Cape Cod-styled home, a safe place where a child could happily thrive.

Milo's finger hesitated. In obedience to a reluctant command, he pushed the bell. The door opened before he could turn and walk away. Bobbi embraced him. "Please come in."

With eyes embedded in wrinkled bags of sorrow, Tom sat on the sofa. The three struggled for words to begin. Tom rose and gestured towards a chair. "Please make yourself comfortable. Thank you for stopping by."

Bobbi gazed intently into Tom's eyes. Tom spoke through trembling lips. "This has been a difficult time for all of us. It was an unfortunate accident."

Milo's eyes remained glued to his shoes.

"I'm sorry I frightened you in the cemetery. God help me, it was a horrible thing to do. To lose a child is . . ."

Unable to continue, he wiped his own, then Bobbi's eyes, and took a breath. "Forgive me. Bobbi and I, we know how badly you must feel. Now it's time to move past this tragedy. We want to thank you for the lovely monument. Obviously, you put a lot of time and care into it and worked very hard."

Tom's words comforted Milo, but could not heal a shattered soul. Silent sobs wracked Milo's body. Bobbi took his hand, reached for Tom's, drew them near, and held them close.

~ ~ ~

Milo had rejected God and survived — shaken, but unbroken. Sebastian doubted, questioned, and wondered. Without God, from whence would his inspiration spring?

~ ~ ~

CHAPTER TWENTY-ONE

Girl in the Loft

S ebastian pursued an opportunity for employment in Weimar where his grandfather had worked sixty years earlier. He'd taken on tasks as a minor court musician to perform temporary duties without any prospect for permanent employment. A daring and innovative musician with superb scientific knowledge of the technical aspects of the organ, his reputation grew. The long nights of study, untold hours of tinker and experiment in the dust-covered bowels of the organ were about to pay off.

St. Boniface's Church in Arnstadt, the oldest town in Thuringia, had just been renovated. Despite his youth, town officials in Arnstadt hired eighteen-year-old Sebastian to assess the newly constructed organ there. His friend and former schoolmate, visiting on vacation, accompanied him. "Do you believe this, George?"

"No! I've never ridden in a private coach before."

"It's certainly much nicer than walking, though we did have a grand time on our travel to Lüneburg, didn't we?"

"Looking back on it, I suppose, but this is heaven."

"Can you believe they're paying me four taler, room and board, plus the expense of this coach, just to inspect the organ?"

"My God, Bach, how will you ever get your head out

the door of this carriage?"

Sebastian laughed, then went on with glee. "That's not the end of it. There's a very good chance I will be hired permanently as the organist."

"Uh oh, then I suppose you will only see me by appointment."

"I'll make an exception in your case. Do you know what this means, George? For the first time, a superb organ will be at my disposal at any time. All I must do is take faithful care of it, be industrious and reliable in my duties, and of course, appear promptly for divine services."

"Ah, I knew there'd be a caveat. You probably won't last a month!"

George would be proven wrong — however, not without incident. Many of the students with whom Sebastian had to work were older and harbored resentment towards him. Geyersbach, a bassoonist, rarely played in tempo and never in tune.

One day at rehearsal, Sebastian, who played first violin, suddenly bounded out of his chair. Within seconds, in intervals, the others stopped playing and turned toward Sebastian. He stood, eyes closed, hands covering his ears. When the ensuing disjointed cacophony ended, all eyes were focused on the person standing in a center of silence. Sebastian slowly lowered his hands. His eyes shot blistering darts at Geyersbach, and then fixed on a point at the apex of the hall ceiling. "Dear God, how could Thee create a being with not a pittance of rhythm, tone-deaf ears, and then give him a bassoon?"

He turned to Geyersbach, whose boiling blood by now had scorched his face. Their eyes met in a clash of fire. Neither blinked. "You, sir, are nothing more than a tinhorn bassoonist. May I suggest you pursue an occupation other than music, perhaps mucking stalls?" Sebastian stormed out of the hall in frustration.

Later, on his way home, huddled against the drizzle, he approached a small crowd gathered like storm clouds. From their midst bolted an infuriated Geyersbach. "Bach, you pompous dung heap, now you'll get your due."

He attacked with a stick. Sebastian went for a dagger he always carried, but never intended to use. Geyersbach tumbled into him and both fell to the ground grappling for body parts. Weapons gone, they fought, timidly protective of their hands, more like two girls wrestling in the mud than a death match. Once they'd sated their blood lust, the other students untangled them. But for a stray elbow to Sebastian's balls, and Geyersbach's bloodied nose, only pride and garments were the worse for the encounter.

Although the authorities found Geyersbach initiated the confrontation, they reprimanded Sebastian for his remark.

In another incident, Sebastian who'd let his hormones get the better of his judgment, invited a lovely young lady to make music in the choir loft, where females were traditionally excluded.

"Sebastian, we shouldn't be here. If we're found out, you could be out of a job and my reputation ruined."

"It's a small price to pay for a moment alone with you."

"Well, if it's more than talk you want, you'll not be getting it from me."

"Have no fear, Barbara, my intentions are honorable."

They were seen, and again Sebastian received a reprimand.

Sebastian became disenchanted with the lack of discipline in his fellow students and his lack of authority to correct it. A family friend informed him the town of Mühlhausen sought an organist. By then, he'd fallen in love with the girl in the loft, Maria Barbara, the daughter of his mother's cousin.

On April 24, Easter Sunday, Sebastian auditioned for a position at St. Blasius's in Mühlhausen. Negotiations took place with the town council.

"Your honorable sirs, if I were to take the position in question, what would be my duties?"

Cornelius Fink, secretary of the council spoke. "You will loyally serve the town authorities and show yourself willing to serve faithfully and industriously on Sundays, feast days, and other holy days. In addition, you will be responsible for the organ, its repairs and music. What would you ask as yearly recompense for such a position?"

Without hesitation, Sebastian replied, "Eighty-five florins, sir. In addition, since I must maintain my own household, I humbly request fifty-four bushels of grain, two cords of firewood, with six times three score kindling, delivered to my door. I would also respectfully request the assistance of a wagon and team to move my possessions."

"Very well, sir. Your request will be duly considered.

You will be advised of our decision.

Officially offered the post at the end of June, in the year 1707, Sebastian accepted. He began his duties the first of July, but his heart remained in Arnstadt. The new position required his full attention. Sebastian knew he wouldn't be able to do the job justice until a certain matter was attended to. He arranged for a short leave and returned to Arnstadt.

Maria Barbara stood in the church garden after the service. Her flaxen hair shimmered in the sunlight. The leaves had fulfilled their magical promise, warming her against a crisp autumn chill that put a blossom to her cheeks. Sebastian watched for a long moment and wondered how he could live without her. He decided he couldn't. He tiptoed up behind her and placed his fingers over her eyes. Not in the least startled, she turned and waited for him to speak. Sebastian gazed into her eyes, their color reminiscent of a transparent topaz. "You must say yes, or I'll surely be ready for a cold grave."

"And the question, Sebastian?"

"Will you be my wife?"

"Yes, my darling music-maker, I will."

"It means a move to Mühlhausen. Will you be happy there?"

"Only if there are plenty of little ones to occupy me."

"My dearest Barbara, that would delight me more than you can know."

Overjoyed, Sebastian could barely believe his good fortune. They decided to marry in Dornheim, a small town nearby.

Overwhelmed with the details of his decision, he sought the help of his boyhood friend, George Erdmann.

"George, as you know, in ancient times, men seeking a wife often had to capture the woman. A warrior friend was often employed to help. Thankfully, since you are totally lacking such physical skills, this will not be necessary. Nonetheless, you may be required to help me ward off other men who may wish to have her for themselves!"

George looked at him dumbly and scratched his head. "Get to the point, Bach. Is this some cryptic riddle?"

"I'm getting married, you idiot!"

"Ah, so. Am I expected to somehow save you from your doom?"

"Doom is hardly a word I'd use for a life with this fair maiden. The light of my good fortune cannot be dimmed by your lack of wit. You can, however, help me with the planning and, God forgive my loose use of the term, participate as my Best Man."

George smiled and shook his head. "I can see there's no talking sense to you. How may I assist?"

"For starters, let each of us make a list of what needs be attended to, and then compare them."

They each sat with pen and parchment. George wrote furiously, and Sebastian wondered how the thoughts were flying so quickly for George when he could hardly think at all. After a few moments, George grinned at him.

"I've written the invitation."

"Oh, I hadn't even thought about that. Read it to me."

"I bring you a nice greeting from the bride and groan.

They both request that you should be wedding guests. This coming (date to be inserted) is the celebration so set forth, dear guests.

"Bring along your knives and forks. There will be something to eat. An old sheep and a lame cow will certainly be there. A pig has suddenly been butchered which will certainly be taken. And seven hens and a rooster must all at one time be next. These are all so fat, like a dried-up wagon board.

"Our Aunt Alice, she bakes the cakes sour and sweet. She bakes them in her own way, like a wagon wheel. She has red hair and freckles. The food will taste awfully good.

"There will also be musicians who play *Hopsasa Trallalla*. With pines, violins and bagpipes there, one can dance with the time. On my cane, tie a ribbon to make it known to you.

"Blitz! Kreutz! I have forgotten something else — I'll keep entirely quiet from the brandy. In the cellar is a keg of beer. I am attracted to it. I haven't seen it myself. A little lying doesn't make any difference. Outside flies a sparrow. Give the wedding inviter a shot of whiskey."

Sebastian hunched over, his body convulsed with tears of mirth running down cheeks crinkled with laughter.

"Wherever did you come up with that?"

"It's what I can remember from a paper I wrote about old customs and rituals, which I borrowed directly from a book about old customs and rituals."

~ ~ ~

After a small wedding, the newlyweds settled into

their new home and he to work. To his surprise, Maria Barbara not only loved music, she took delight in the culinary arts. Eating held almost the same pleasure as music for Sebastian, and supper became a joy between joys.

Barbara finished cleaning the table. Sebastian lounged in his favorite chair. Eyes closed, he puffed on his pipe, conducting to an invisible rhythm. She removed her apron and plopped into his lap. He smiled and kissed her. "What is it, woman, can't you hear? I'm busy."

"Are you such as to have no time for tidings?"

"Well, get on with it then if you must."

"In a half-year and some, you're going to be a father."

Sebastian didn't blink. He spoke with all the somberness he could muster, through teeth clamped firmly on the stem of his pipe. "And who, may I ask, be the mother?"

Sebastian and Barbara were second cousins. They'd each received a windfall of fifty florins from the estate of his mother's brother, Tobias Lämmerhirt, who'd recently died. It helped, but Sebastian realized if they were to expand as a family, it would require more income than he presently earned. He tucked away the thought, but it was never far from his consciousness.

~ ~ ~

At approximately the same age, Sebastian followed a preordained vocation, but Milo couldn't get himself started on a path to his goal.

~ ~ ~

CHAPTER TWENTY-TWO

Ralph Bishop

Depression dogged Milo's every step in daily life. It interfered with almost every thought and action. For him, eating became something he had to do. Tonight he had an inexplicable urge for a Bishop's dinner. Milo felt drawn to Bishop's, because Ralph, the owner, made him laugh and cooked shrimp the only way he liked to eat it.

Fragrant, frying fish, and restaurateur Ralph's acerbic banter were a treat for the customers. The beating heart of Bishops was the prep room behind the deep fryers. Beneath lay a crypt-like cellar. There, well-defended secrets of his famous batter, tarter sauce, and coleslaw were prepared.

With flinty blue eyes, white hair, and a burgundy birthmark on his neck, Ralph spoke in a deep voice. The gap where the left forefinger used to be didn't interfere with skills of hand. His sharp, dark humor, often directed at the impatient clientele, usually got a laugh.

Ralph spotted Milo among the customers.

"Hey, Milo! How's it going? I'll take a break in a minute. Need a coffin nail. I want a word with you. Okay?"

Milo nodded his head, and Ralph pointed towards the cellar stairs.

In the crypt-like basement, Milo perched on a pine bench with the patina of an ancient pew, rubbing his hands mindlessly along its smooth edge. His life seemed to be filled with a murkiness he couldn't see his way through. The sound of nails driven into a lid turned out to be Ralph clumping down the stairs. He sat next to Milo, sighed, doffed his apron, pulled out a pack of Chesterfields, and took one. He handed the pack to Milo, lit Milo's, then his own. They sat quietly, enjoying the smell of freshly lit tobacco swirling around them.

"It was a tough break, hitting that little girl."

Milo cringed: another shovelful on his coffin.

"These things happen. Life goes on."

Milo tried to hide his filling eyes, but then cried out, "But why did it happen? Where the hell was God when I needed him?"

"If you mean God with the white beard, that's something I won't get into. I can tell you this. Don't be expecting him or anyone else to help. You got to do it yourself."

Milo reached a conclusion and spat, "There *is* no God." With that, his plunge was total. Ralph ignored the outburst.

"What do you want the rest of your life to be?"

Speaking in a flat tone, without affectation, he responded, "What does it matter?"

"It matters. Your life is just beginning."

"There's no way I can ever be a pilot now. My life's a mess. I have no job, and I just don't give a shit anymore."

"Listen, some things in life seem senseless, surer than shit, unfair. Later when you look back, if you're honest, you can see they shaped your life for the better. It depends on attitude."

He took a drag from the cigarette held between his thumb and second finger. Milo caught himself staring at the missing digit. Ralph squinted sidelong at him through the smoke.

"Tell you a story: when I was sixteen, I left home. Went south and ended up in a little hole in Louisiana. Morgan City. My family was from Quebec. A lot of those coon asses in Louisiana were descendants of French Canucks who'd mixed with Blacks and Indians. I was cozy there, but they were a rough, hard-drinking bunch and full of hell. We were hitting the bottle and whorehouses pretty regular.

"There was one old guy, the coon ass king, Pierre Labois, a nasty fuck. One night, old Labois was drunk out of his skull. On a dare from some asshole, I took a solid gold earring out of his ear. Next day, two of his bravos surprised me, and dragged me to Labois's dive.

"Labois never said a word. His boys dragged me over to this big chopping block. I started kicking and screaming. They held my hand down. One of the guys says to me, 'By God, boy, be still there. It is better to lose one finger than the whole hand. That be for sure, boy.'

"Labois came over and looked me straight in the eye, and offed my finger. I stared at it doing a little jig all by itself on that chopping block. I couldn't believe it. I screamed. They cauterized my stump with a hot coal from the grill and bandaged my hand. When they finished, Labois came over and said, 'Nobody steal from Labois.' Then he gives me a job in his joint. I was there for three years. He gave me the recipes I use here."

Ralph ground out his cigarette and put his hand on Milo's shoulder. "One thing's for sure, life's going to throw some shit at you from time to time. Try to keep this in mind. Bend, but don't break. Got it?" Milo nodded.

Ralph grabbed an apron from the counter, tossed it to him and said, "I can use an extra hand around this dump. Put it on and get to work on that basket of spuds."

"Thanks, Ralph."

He nodded and clomped up the stairs. Milo put on the apron and started peeling. It felt good.

As he lay in bed that night, instead of prayer, he discovered a renewed feeling of self-affirmation. "I will bend, but not break. I will get back up. I will fly."

~ ~ ~

Milo fell fast asleep without nightmares for the first time in months. Perhaps now he could begin to put the puzzle of his life together. He'd learned some things that may even have helped Sebastian, but time machines exist only in fiction.

~ ~ ~

CHAPTER TWENTY-THREE

Off To Weimar

S ebastian engaged in his work with intensity. In short order, he managed to persuade the staid parish authorities to renovate the organ, no easy task for the upstart twenty-three-year old. He'd been able to impress them with suggestions, such as having the one-hundred-fifty-year-old stops replaced with new longer ones, to provide more varied sounds with special effects, including glockenspiels.

Proud of their new organist's initiative, imagination, and technical expertise, the town council awarded two hundred fifty talers for the project. Sebastian then composed a cantata. It awed those in the loft- and gallery-filled audience of the four hundred-year-old church, his first triumph.

A short time later, Sebastian surprisingly received a post from Duke Wilhelm Ernst of Weimar, not far from Dornheim where he and Barbara were married. "Barbara, I can't believe it. They want me to perform in Weimar, and then to inspect the organ."

"You're becoming quite famous, sir. How long will you be away?"

"Less than a fortnight I presume."

Sebastian's performance beset the duke. At a reception

afterwards, he summoned Sebastian to a private room. They were alone. Sebastian sipped his wine and waited politely for Ernst to speak. "Bach, your performance was deeply moving; extraordinary, in fact. It spoke of facility and knowledge far beyond your years."

Sebastian bowed graciously. "Thank you, most honorable sir. You are too kind."

"No sense bandying about, I'll come directly to the point. Effner, organist to the court here, is tired and old, ready for well-deserved retirement. I'm prepared to offer one hundred fifty florins as a salary, plus whatever you receive in grain and firewood now. In addition, expenses to move your family, housing assistance, and thirty pails of beer to assume the position. You will have assistance in the performance of your duties, which will allow adequate opportunity for you to create new music."

Stunned, Sebastian swallowed hard and took a moment to fashion a response. *I suppose I'll need to acquire a taste for brew,* he mused. In as unflustered a voice as he could manage, he replied, "Most noble, honored, most distinguished sir — your obedient and obliged servant, I humbly accept."

Ernst smiled and raised his wine glass. Sebastian did likewise. They shook hands to seal the pact. The moment of elation faded somewhat. Sebastian wanted to leave Mühlhausen on good terms, but in a flash decision he'd put his family first.

After being at the post only a short time, he'd committed the authorities to a major organ renovation. He decided to officially resign the post with a promise to help find a replacement to oversee the project. The town council accepted his resignation with regret.

He and Barbara were off to Weimar. "You never cease to amaze me, Sebastian, but I hope we can stay in one place long enough to raise a family."

"Thank you, Barbara. How could I refuse such an offer if I'm to support the future Bachs? You made me promise. Remember?"

"Yes, my darling. You've done us well, and we'll now have ample time to create both children and musical masterworks!"

"I don't create masterworks. They come from God. I'm but his humble servant."

Yes, Sebastian, but God didn't muck around on the inside of grimy organs and didn't spend endless hours practicing scales and studying. You did that all by yourself."

"Ah, yes, my dear wife, but to what purpose without inspiration from the Creator?"

Nonetheless, his wife's words struck a chord. His musical ideas were far different than that of the Church, and he despised the compromises he'd have to make. Somehow, God's plans didn't seem to synchronize with Sebastian's, and it chaffed. He remembered his father's words about having faith, but doubts about where to place it simmered beneath the surface of his psyche.

Although Sebastian's pay increased to an annual two hundred florins, aside from added benefits, it remained unchanged for the duration of his employment in Weimer.

~ ~ ~

A kernel of doubt had sprouted for Sebastian. The spring of hope had begun to flow for Milo, but only one could help the other.

~ ~ ~

CHAPTER TWENTY-FOUR

Flight School

Even as a child, birds and their ability to fly had charmed Milo. He would climb into the cockpit, an old leather chair, and with a pair of goggles and a cut-off broomstick between his legs, fly high into the sky. So vivid were these flights of fancy, they terrified and thrilled him. He concluded that birds flew unafraid and he, too, would one day fly like an eagle! Now he thought it would never be possible. *Everything had gone wrong; my life's blown apart. He spoke to his inner voice:*

"Will I ever fly? I didn't realize how tough it would be. A lot of shit has happened. My father skips, my best friend dies, had to watch the freaking kids all the time — then, the two girls. How can I do it? I can't think straight."

"Did you expect a cakewalk?"

"My grades suck."

"So, fix them. Bishop gave you good advice and a job, so get off your ass. Remember, you will bend, but not break. You will get back up. You will fly."

"I will fly."

Confronted with the reality of improving his grades in order to qualify for military flight training, Milo became determined. He worked nights, pumping gas in order to attend barber school, which would allow him to earn more by cutting hair. He attended prep school nights and improved his grades enough to meet the military flight training requirements. He applied for the Naval Aviation Program.

Milo loved the sea and reasoned that flying jets off carriers would be ideal. He talked with a recruiter and arranged to take the exam. Given in parts, the applicants were graded after completing each and allowed to take the next only if they passed. He breezed through the first four sections. To his great disappointment, he failed the flight aptitude section. The testing officer tried to encourage him.

"Sorry, son. Don't let it discourage you. If you haven't had flight experience, it can be difficult. You can take the exam again in six months. It might be a good idea to take some flight lessons. I'm sure you'll make it. You didn't miss by much."

Milo couldn't contain his disappointment. "Six months? Geez! That's a long time."

"Sorry. Those are the regulations."

Neil Adams, the captain of the football team and a good friend, knew how badly Milo wanted to fly. That weekend, after their regular Sunday flag football game, Milo told him what had happened.

"Hey, I've got an idea. My brother Chuck is an ex-Navy pilot. When he got out, he wanted to keep flying, so he joined an Army National Guard aviation battalion in Fitchfield.

"Why did he join an Army unit?

"The Navy doesn't have any guard units close by.

Chuck took me up once on a weekend drill. It sucked. I got sick as a dog." Milo laughed.

"Call Chuck. Maybe he can help you out."

Neil gave Milo his brother's telephone number.

"Thanks, Neil. I appreciate it. Nice block on Coot. I thought he had my ass for sure."

"Yeah, same old shit. If it wasn't for me, you'd never score."

"Fuck you."

"Up yours. I'll see you next Sunday."

Chuck looked anything but a Navy fighter pilot. He wore an ill-fitting, olive green flight suit. Quiet-spoken, unassuming, he reminded Milo of an accountant as he filled out the flight plan. Once in the air, he became Superman. Chuck pointed to the barf bag and smiled. The intercom crackled to life. "Don't mess up my airplane."

Milo fumbled for the microphone button. "Don't worry, I won't.

He didn't, but still managed to fill the bag.

Milo's confidence grew, but the struggle to succeed had just begun. Nothing came easy, but it served to make him more resolute. He didn't want to wait another six months. He flew almost every weekend. Chuck advised him to join the aviation battalion, which he did. Milo applied for active duty and OCS (Officers' Candidate School). The demanding course took its toll physically. For the first several weeks, cadets washed out on a daily basis. Milo managed to hang on with determination and fitness.

The drill sergeant leaned over Milo, shouting so close

that spittle sprayed Milo's burning ears. His drums throbbed under the high-decibel barrage.

"Don't you know how to do a proper fucking pushup, asshole? My mother can do a proper pushup and she's ninety-four, so why the fuck can't you? You're more than pathetic. You're a pussy!"

Milo had enjoyed football boot camp, but it didn't compare. He grumbled under his breath. This is ridiculous. I must've done a fucking million pushups already.

"That'll be twenty more, asshole!"

Fuck you, he thought defiantly. I can do as many as you can dish out, dipshit.

By graduation, the luster of Milo's confidence matched the newly won bars on his shoulders.

Once commissioned, Milo reported to Fort Gordon, Georgia, where he completed the Signal Officers' Training Course, then applied for flight training. Thanks to Chuck's tutoring, he passed the exams easily. He expected a posting to Fort Rucker, Alabama for fixed-wing training, but orders changed at the last moment to Fort Walters, Texas, the primary helicopter training school.

Helicopters! They're nothing but a bitchy bucket of bolts and blades. At least they were based on theories by another wop, Leonardo Da Vinci. Wop, wop, he thought, and smiled. The little knowledge he had said, theoretically, choppers weren't supposed to fly. After an orientation flight, all disillusionment vanished. It would be real flying. Unlike an airplane, helicopters couldn't be flown without hands on the controls every second. It seemed that Milo and helicopters were destined for each other.

Flight training turned out to be a nightmare. Because of his academic inadequacies, the demanding courses kept Milo studying late into the night in order to keep his grades at an acceptable level. Fatigue affected his flying — that, and incompatibility with his flight instructor. They didn't like each other.

Jim Peal had a reputation for washing out students. Constantly on the edge of failure, Milo remained determined, but grew worried as he approached the maximum number of flight hours allowed before a solo flight.

Today Milo would reach the limit. He brought the helicopter smoothly to a hover. Without warning, Peal cut the power. Milo reacted, applying sufficient pedal to counteract the loss of torque, he quickly reduced the pitch of the rotor blades and at the proper moment rapidly increased the pitch, creating lift in the blades. The helicopter came to a soft landing. Peal opened his door, got out, and walked over to Milo's side. He shouted above the noise of the lapping blades.

"Take it around the pattern three times."

Milo was filled with relief, fear, and elation. "Roger."

He called the tower. "Billings tower, this is Romeo Four-Two Echo. Over."

"Billings tower — go ahead Four-Two Echo."

"Roger. Four-Two Echo requesting permission for takeoff. I'll be staying in the pattern for three takeoffs and landings. Over."

"Roger, Four-Two Echo. Congratulations. Left-hand

pattern approved. Wind is south-southwest at eight knots, gusting to fifteen. Altimeter is at two niner niner zero. You are cleared for take-off."

"Roger. Four-Two Echo lifting off."

It seemed to Milo that the pounding in his chest was louder than the rotor noise. His palms were sweaty. He brought the helicopter to a hover and made a smooth take-off. The radio mike switch was on the cyclic stick, which controlled the attitude of the helicopter. Milo got to pattern altitude and was on the downwind leg. He couldn't contain himself, "I'm a fucking eagle!"

Whereupon came the unexpected response, "Yeah, well, keep your eagle eyes outside the cockpit, or you'll find yourself fucking buzzard bait!"

Milo's face flushed. In his excitement he had triggered the radio mike.

Milo soloed, but his ordeal continued. His academic grades were acceptable, his flying borderline. Peal busted Milo on his final check ride. Given six more hours of training and three more of solo, another pink slip and he'd be washed out. During his solo time, he practiced his deficiencies. The time for his check arrived, finding him confident yet scared.

Peal, in a sour mood, curtly asked Milo to complete a series of maneuvers. The instructor could suddenly cut the power at any time and at any altitude. Milo's last take-off, while practicing pinnacle operations, Peal chopped the power at about three hundred feet. Prick, Milo muttered to himself, but he was already in an immediate 180-degree turn and made a perfect autorotation onto the pinnacle. The check ride over, Milo began to relax as they turned towards Billings. Peal turned to Milo and smiled.

"Not bad. You could use a little work on . . ."

Suddenly Peal cut the power. There were two choices — on the right, a steep approach into a confined area surrounded by tall trees — ahead, a large open field seemed best. Milo chose it. He made a perfect approach and a soft touchdown. Peal looked over and said, "I've got it."

Milo responded, "You've got it."

Peal took the controls and flew back to Billings. When they reached the ready room for the debriefing, Peal said nothing. He put his feet up on the table, smiled at Milo, and handed him a pink slip. Milo was stunned. He had failed the check ride. He looked at Peal in disbelief.

"Why the hell did you bust me?"

"You made a downwind autorotation."

Peal smiled grimly and walked out.

Milo slumped in his chair. He couldn't believe he'd been busted. His self-assurance faded along with his hope. He wouldn't be able to face his family. They thought him a dreamer, and he'd always thought himself a failure. Now they'd both be proven right.

Milo spent a sleepless weekend evaluating his options. He realized for whatever reason, Peal had been trying to discourage him from the start. Milo's fragile self-confidence bred insecurity, exacerbating matters. Peal had looked for an excuse to bust him — and found one. Milo spoke to his inner voice.

"Now what?"

"It's about the wind."

"What?"

"You're a runner and a pilot, man. You know about the wind. Use what you know."

"It's always riddles with you."

"When you're running into a brisk, thirty-knot wind, it's more difficult. Right?"

"Yeah, so what?"

"Well, flying is like that. Life is like that. If you use the wind you will soar. If you're only willing to ride down-wind, then your destiny is at the whim of the wind."

That night in bed he whispered to himself. "I will bend, but not break. I will fly." Milo refused to accept failure.

On Monday morning Milo received devastating news. First, two weeks leave and then an order to report to his former signal corps company for further assignment. He requested an appointment with Colonel Zack Ridgewood, the commanding officer of flight training operations.

The next morning Milo reported to Ridgewood's office. He sat nervously, waiting to be called, trying to marshal his thoughts. The colonel's aide beckoned him. He walked to the front of the desk, came to attention, and snapped a brisk salute.

"Lieutenant Damiani reporting, sir."

"At ease, Lieutenant. Have a seat. What can I do for you?"

"Thank you, sir."

Ridgewood interrupted. "Where in the Boston area are you from?"

"From Tybourne, sir."

"Ah. You guys had a hell of a ballplayer there. Joe Casti, I believe. He ran over me several times between '51 and '53. I was a linebacker for Winthrop."

Milo smiled. It must be my accent, he thought. He looked directly into Ridgeway's eyes and knew he would get a fair hearing. He relaxed. "Casti was before my time. He's still a hometown hero. His records still stand."

Ridgeway went to the point. "I see here that you busted two check rides, Lieutenant. It's not the worst thing in the world. Not everyone is cut out for flying. It won't reflect negatively in your service record."

"Sir, with all due respect, I *am* cut out for flying. I busted the first check clean, but the second was almost perfect."

Ridgewood handed Milo Peal's evaluation. Milo looked at it and next to the Emergency Procedures block, Peal had scribbled in red "dangerous and unsatisfactory autorotation."

"If you can't do autrotations, it's serious business, Lieutenant. It can cost your life and others."

"Sir, during the check ride I made a good autorotation to a pinnacle. I thought the check ride was over. On the way home, Peal chopped my power again and. . . ."

Ridgeway scowled and interrupted. "So what? It's his prerogative. Peal is one of our finest instructors. He washes out a lot of students, but the marginal ones don't get by."

"Sir, I made a perfectly safe autorotation the second time as well."

"Are you calling Peal a liar, Lieutenant?"

"No, sir. When he chopped my power, there were two places to land. One was a confined area, the other an open field. I made a perfect landing to the open field."

"I don't understand. Am I missing something?"

"Yes sir. I made a downwind landing. But since the wind was negligible, I thought it the better of my options. The landing was totally safe. A downwind autorotation can be dangerous, but in those conditions it was superior to a steep approach over high obstacles into a confined area."

The colonel studied Milo's eyes long and closely. Milo kept contact and said nothing. "Technically, Peal is correct. However, I admire your judgment. It was instinctive. Instinct cannot be taught. I'm going to grant you five hours of solo. You can fly them all in one day or split them however you please. Be at the flight line at Billings next Friday morning at 8:00. I will give you your final check ride. Stay relaxed. Have some fun with your flight time."

Euphoric, Milo wanted to jump over the desk and kiss him. He saluted. "Thank you, sir."

Ridgewood smiled. "You're dismissed, Lieutenant. I'll see you Friday morning."

Milo decided to fly an hour and fifteen minutes each day. He did exactly what Ridgeway suggested. He had fun and for the first time experienced the joy of flying he'd only dreamed of. The sky became his playground. On the first morning, it was CAVU (ceiling and visibility unlimited).

After a careful pre-flight, Milo got clearance from the tower and headed due west to an area clear of training sites. He tuned to a Dallas classical music station and made a slow climb to ten thousand feet. He'd never been higher than five thousand feet, solo or otherwise. At that altitude, the earth seemed partitioned into a variety of shapes, shades of color, shadow and relief. Control movements were amplified. He seemed to be tottering on a sphere. Exhilarated and afraid, at ten thousand feet he cut the power. Lowering the pitch, he began to freefall in graceful 360-degree turns as he'd watched eagles do. He had never experienced such freedom — or icy fear. He turned up the radio and shouted at the top of his voice. "I'm a fucking eagle"

"Roger that, Four-Two Echo. If you don't keep your head up and locked, you'll be buzzard bait."

Milo laughed and muttered. I fucking did it again.

On Friday morning, relaxed and confident, Milo arrived at the flight line forty-five minutes early. He'd completed his pre-flight when Colonel Ridgeway walked up. His soft, wrinkled, leather flight jacket spoke of countless hours. His gleaming boots shot off beams of highlights. The hills skirting the flight line reflected in Ridgeway's Ray Bans. On his face he carried a wide smile.

Milo came to attention and saluted. Ridgeway casually returned it and said, "Stand at ease, Milo. Good morning."

"Good morning, sir. Would you like me to start my

pre-flight again?"

"No, run'er up and get started."

Milo completed the cockpit checklist and radioed the tower. Cleared for take-off, he brought the helicopter to a hover, then did a clearing turn. Ridgeway chopped the power. Milo brought the helicopter smoothly to the ground. Ridgeway turned to him, flashed a grin and keyed the mike.

"Let's go."

"Roger."

The check ride consisted of nothing but autorotations. They did them from varying altitudes into every conceivable type of area, into the wind, crosswind and downwind. All of them terminated in a landing rather than a simulation to a hover. Milo performed flawlessly. When Ridgeway was satisfied, they returned to Billings. Milo shut down and tied the blades. Ridgeway walked over and placed a hand on Milo's shoulder. "Good job, Lieutenant. You've earned it."

"Thank you, sir." He received orders to Fort Rucker, Alabama for instrument training. Having almost washed out in primary, Milo wanted to do well, but that persistent fear of failure impeded his progress. Providence intervened. Sandy Peters, also an Army aviator, completed the WOC (Warrant Officer Candidate Course).

During the Vietnam era, the Army, facing a shortage of helicopter pilots, initiated the program. It allowed qualified enlisted men to enroll in the aviation program, graduating as warrant officer pilots. They were required to complete a difficult boot camp, similar to OCS as they simultaneously learned to fly.

Designed specifically to eliminate all but the cream, the grueling program had an extremely high washout rate. Many failed, others quit of their own volition, usually in the boot-camp phase. Hazed day and night, they were pushed to the limits of their physical, mental, and emotional endurance.

Milo, in flight training as a commissioned officer, greatly admired the WOCs. He watched them work late of an evening as he enjoyed a cold beer. He wondered if he could have cut it. He found flight school sufficiently taxing without the added stress they had to contend with. Sandy had breezed through. He qualified expert in every weapon. He graduated first in his class both academically and on the flight line, a fact that never went unmentioned by him at every opportunity.

In the instrument flight phase, Milo had difficulty with orientation. He decided to spend every spare moment under the hood to overcome it. Unlike a fixed wing aircraft, which tended to self-recover from unusual attitudes, a helicopter would not. This inherent instability could prove fatal when flying in the blind. Without reference to the horizon, a pilot had to trust his instruments, not his sensations. The senses might indicate level flight when the aircraft was actually in a dive or turn. The opposite is also true. This condition is known as vertigo. Milo experienced it the day he first met Sandy.

The simulator, an ugly pod from which protruded

wires, tubes and pistons, hung in the air like a giant khaki cocoon. It didn't look at all like a helicopter except for its color. The simulator gyrated wildly, pistons hissing, dipping up then down, right, left, and every direction in between. It suddenly groaned to a halt.

"Fuck!"

Milo exited the pod. There stood Sandy smiling.

"Why the shit-eating grin, Warrant?"

"You turned that muthafucka every way but loose."

Milo laughed. "No shit. Ugly, wasn't it?"

"Could've been worse; you might've been a warm pile of ash at the end of a sudden stop. Don't worry about it. I get vertigo sleepwalking, f'crissake."

"I'm Milo Damiani. Who the fuck would you be?"

"Sandy Peters, the hottest pilot on base, if I must say so."

"Got any words of wisdom, hotshot?"

"It's a mental thing. They pound you all the time to trust your instruments. I look at it this way. I don't trust what my body tells me. You keep the old eyeballs glued to that green globe with the white line, scan the instrument panel, and pray the gauges are right."

"It isn't that simple when shit starts going south."

"That's what happens when you make those gross control movements. Sure as zits on a thirteen-year-old, you wouldn't do it flying visual. So in the dark, make incremental corrections. Then you can track tendencies. You're more apt to get vertigo when the fucker is flying like a dragonfly on LSD."

Milo laughed. Sandy made sense.

"How about working with me for a few nights? The beer and pretzels are on me."

"Throw in dinner and you're on."

Milo grinned. "Fuck you." They shook hands.

Milo got through instrument training, Sandy got his dinner, and they parted ways.

Crisp and clear, the morning of graduation set a sparkling table as thirty-two new aviators and their families waited for the ceremonies to begin. Milo sat next to his mother, flanked by his brothers and sister. His mother could barely contain her pride as she squeezed his hand. I'm not just a dreamer any more, he thought. One by one the aviators were called to the podium to receive their diplomas and wings. After the ceremony, his mother fastened them above the pocket near his heart with shaking hands and mist-glazed eyes.

"I'm so proud."

He felt as if he could fly with the wings she'd just pinned to his chest.

"I'm an eagle, Ma."

At last he'd achieved a life-long milestone, overcoming all obstacles, and without the help of any god. He'd answered his own prayers. The satisfaction of accomplishment lifted his spirits, but a downside of reality made it short-lived. Milo had earned his wings; now the price had to be paid, perhaps in blood.

Milo fingered the letter in his shirt pocket. He had thirty days leave and a mission. The voice over the loud speaker blared, "British Airways Flight 1056 to London is now ready for boarding." He waited until most of the passengers were boarded, then took his seat in first class, just aft of the cockpit. Traveling in uniform had its advantages.

The senior flight attendant had upgraded him from coach. The 747 turned onto the active runway. The flight attendant opposite him buckled in and triggered the intercom. "Passengers, prepare for take-off." Now that he'd earned his wings, he didn't fancy flying in an airplane any more than being a passenger in a car. The turbines screamed as the pilot thrust forward on the throttle. Milo closed his eyes and imagined the yoke in his hands. He felt the aircraft getting light on its gear. In anticipation of lift-off speed, he pulled back on the controls and the monster aircraft lumbered airborne. He smiled and thought, nailed it!

When the aircraft reached cruising altitude, the "fasten seatbelt" sign turned green and the flight attendant approached him smiling. "Nice take-off, Lieutenant. Milo blushed and squinted uncomfortably, partially hiding hazel eyes that flashed a hue of sea green, depending on the light. Women were sometimes transfixed, looking at them intently as if they were separate from his body. He hadn't figured out how to handle his unease when it happened. Savvy to his discomfort, she let him off the hook. "I didn't mean to stare."

"It's okay, he stammered. He reached for his wallet. "Can I have a scotch, please?"

"It's on the house in first class. Do you want ice or

straight up?"

"Straight up. Thanks." He usually diluted it with water.

Caught between anger and longing, Milo wanted a quick buzz to ease the confusion and stress he felt about the upcoming confrontation.

For whatever reason, his uncle Remo had relented and sent Milo his father's address. Milo sent a telegram the day before his flight. It simply said: ARRIVING HEATHROW TOMORROW ON BRITISH AIRWAYS FLIGHT 1056, 11:20 A.M. — MILO.

He could only imagine his father's reaction and only hope he'd be at the airport. Milo reclined his seat, put the puny pillow under his head, and spoke to his inner voice: "What the hell am I going to say?"

"Say what's on your mind."

"I don't know why in hell I'm doing this."

"That's bullshit.

"I'm so angry. I'm afraid I'll smack him one."

"I don't think so."

Milo brushed the side of his face with his fingertips. "I can still feel the sting of my mother's slap the day he left. I want him to feel it."

"What will that solve?"

"It will make me feel so fucking good!"

"Is that what you want out of this?"

"I don't know what I want."

"I suggest you figure it out because in three and a half hours or so, he may just be there when you walk off this airplane."

"You're no fucking help."

Sweat stained the armpits of Milo's shirt. The sight of food set his stomach in motion. He couldn't eat, but the Chardonnay calmed him. Whatever the outcome, he wouldn't be prepared. His heartbeat quickened as the pilot announced touchdown in forty-five minutes — the longest forty-five minutes of his life. It seemed an entire day had gone by when the voice came over the intercom. "Flight attendants, prepare for arrival."

A rush of warm stale air met him as he walked into the terminal. He'd waited almost twelve years for this day, almost half his lifetime. He looked into the mass of faces milling beyond the roped-off area. None were recognizable. Disappointment crept over him — his hunched shoulders, lowered head, and downcast eyes a body meltdown of sorts. It passed as he took the moving escalator stairs two at a time down to baggage claim.

First to deplane and last to get his bag, he thought, as the endless stream of luggage floated by. At last the ugly, green duffel-bag crept towards him. He reached for it. "I've got it." His heart jumped a beat. He knew the voice. "Pop, I thought you weren't going to show."

They embraced and touched as if lost in a wasteland, clutching at a mirage. The familiar body odor drifted to his nostrils. He buried his face in the crook of his father's neck, again a little boy.

There would not be a more appropriate moment than now. Tears welled in his eyes and flowed with the words. "Why did you leave us?" His father's contorted face showed terrible pain and anguish. Milo barely heard the softly spoken words through his father's silent weeping.

"I had a choice between music and my family. Music is my life. God help me, I chose my life."

Milo looked deep into his father's eyes. He had become skilled at reading eyes. He saw something in its reflection and recognized truth.

"Can you forgive me, Milo?"

Milo held his father close. He suddenly realized that nobody could forgive ones sins, not even God.

"Pop, I love you. There's nothing to forgive." Filled with a feeling of completeness, Milo just realized that an end and a beginning could occupy the same point in time. It had just been proven. But, it didn't resolve the question still lingering — who then to forgive him?

~ ~ ~

Milo had unanswered questions and no God to provide answers. Sebastian had God, but faced the same quandary.

~ ~ ~

CHAPTER TWENTY-FIVE

Freidlina

The Duchy of Weimer had a population of about 5000, a third of which were in some way employed by the court. Sebastian and Barbara moved into one of several apartments reserved for employees of the Court. The freyhause (free house) located in the market square of Weimer delighted them. From their apartment they could see beautiful St. Peter and Paul's Church dominating the square. They also took delight in watching the hustle and bustle below, partaking in the wonderful aromas of freshly baked goods, and listening to the buzz and barter of exchange. Only a five-minute walk to the Wilhelmsburg Ducal Palace and Sebastian's work, it couldn't have been more convenient. They settled into the routine of Weimar. Sebastian sensed Barbara's anxiety about the arrival of their firstborn. He approached his wife with a smile and twinkle in his eye.

"Why don't you invite your sister to help with the baby? I'm sure the old spinster would be delighted."

"Don't poke fun. She hasn't married because no man has yet to meet her standards."

"More likely because she's a cross between a parrot and a cow!"

"Sebastian, be nice!"

"I suppose I can always play forte over her squawking chatter for a short while."

"Thank you, She will be a great help."

Barbara invited her elder sister, Freidlina, to move in and help with the baby. She would remain in the Bach household until her death twenty-one years later.

Sebastian composed many of his greatest works for organ in Weimar. He also wrote a simple but lovely Aria of note to celebrate the 52nd birthday of his patron, Duke Wilhelm Ernst von Sachsen. While at a performance of local artists, a Weimar poet, Johann Anton Mylius, struck up a conversation with Sebastian. "Herr Bach, your music was quite stunning!"

"Thank you kind sir, but please call me Sebastian, lest we sound as if we speak to ourselves, since we share the name Johann. May I address you as Anton?"

"The pleasure is mine Sebastian."

"I'm honored Anton, and I too much enjoyed your poetry. Would you be willing to collaborate with me on a gift to my patron, the good Duke, which I shall compose for his birthday?"

"What do you have in mind, Sebastian?"

"I'm thinking of an aria for soprano, with strings and basso continuo."

"Most interesting, what would be the theme?"

I thought we'd use the Duke's motto, 'Alles mit Gott und nichts ohn' ihn.—'everything with God and nothing without him.'

'How many stanzas would you require?"

"That's your department Anton, you end when you've said everything you want, and I'll let my music be the background for your thoughts on the matter."

"Done, Sebastian and with pleasure! Do you have a soprano in mind?"

"I'm pleased! No, I hadn't yet considered a soprano, why do you ask?"

"I' know of an extraordinary and quite lovely young lady. She is visiting from Cöthen. I had an opportunity to hear her at the conservatory. Her voice is crystalline. Her name is Ana Magdalena Wilcke."

"What do you mean by young?"

"She's eleven years old."

Sebastian didn't blink. He knew a gift from God could come at birth.

"Thank you, Anton; I trust your judgment. Let her parents be assured she will be well chaperoned if she is willing and they allow her to perform."

In October of 1713, Ana Magdalena Wilcke sang Anton's poem, to Sebastian's Music. After the performance, Duke Wilhelm spoke with Sebastian. "My dear Sebastian, what a heavenly surprise, the music was superb."

"Thank you, my most gracious lord."

"And if I were you, Herr Bach, I would keep my eye on the lady Wilcke. She is most talented. She will go far."

"Indeed, my lord, I couldn't agree more."

Ironically, Sebastian would spend more than a month in jail at the hands of Duke Wilhelm. No mistaking,

Sebastian was stubborn and often angry. His unyielding obstinacy rarely stemmed from ego, but rather when pushed to compromise on principal and especially his musical ideas, which were often radical and contrary to the status quo. A rare exception occurred when the Duke refused to let Sebastian resign from his duties. He lost his temper and angered Wilhelm who had him imprisoned. The crime was not that Sebastian wanted to leave, but that he forced the issue. It turned out to be time well spent. It was during this short incarceration Sebastian began composition of the *Well-Tempered Clavier*.

In addition to his normal duties, he also had ten pupils, including two, Schubart and Volger, who had followed him from Mühlhausen. Through years of study on the keyboard, Sebastian realized that total control over each finger movement was essential, and some fingers were dominant. He developed a detailed plan to equalize all of his fingers, including the thumb, rarely used by even the greatest organists of his day. This enabled him to play clear, connected and independent melody lines in the base and harmony of the music. He developed pedal technique to perfection. His students marveled at his effortless command of both. Sebastian had given them exercises that required months upon months of practice. One day a discouraged Volger threw up his hands in disgust and lamented, "Maestro, this is impossible."

Sebastian sat on the bench next to his student. He took Volger's hands in his own and examined them closely.

"Hmm . . . Volger, it looks as if you have five fingers

on each hand just as healthy as mine. My conclusion is that you should just practice diligently and you will do very well."

That attitude endeared him to them, earned their lasting love, gratitude, and respect. Well thought-of by his students and the duke, his first child soon to be born, the twenty-four-year-old experienced a period of time when all seemed to be in harmony, illustrated by his innovative and stunning compositions.

On the day after Christmas, Sebastian nervously paced the hall outside the bedchamber. He heard the door open behind him, turned and hurried towards it. Freidlina bustled out of the room to refill a water pan and Sebastian stumbled into her, causing it to spill. She stood drenched and flustered.

"Sebastian, you clumsy oaf. Look at what you've done. I'm soaked."

"What's taking so long? Has something gone wrong?"

"Calm down, everything is fine. This often happens with a first child."

"But, it's been almost the whole day."

"Fretting about it isn't going to make it happen any faster, and you're driving me absolutely mad."

Sebastian's eyes lit up. They looked at each other and smiled as the wailing infant signaled its arrival. "Go and have a pint. When your wife and child are presentable, I'll summon you."

Sebastian looked at her with wonder in his eyes. "I'm a father."

A short time later he sat at Barbara's bedside clumsily holding his daughter. He'd never been happier. Barbara spoke weakly. "We shall name her Catherina Dorothea."

"Yes, a lovely name, as beautiful as she. "Oh no" he exclaimed, holding his daughter at arm's length. "She's leaking!"

Barbara laughed. He looked at her adoringly. "My dear wife, I thank you for giving me this precious gift. I love you more than life itself."

"Thank you my dear Sebastian. I can't imagine life without you."

The preceding months had been blissful. Sebastian adored his first child and delighted in spending as much time with her as possible. He held his year-and-a-half-old daughter in his lap. She watched mesmerized as his hands flew over the keyboard. When he would finish, she'd look at him quizzically as if she'd witnessed a miracle. He placed her hands gently on the keys. "Now it's your turn, Dorothea." She gleefully began pounding the keys while he proudly looked on.

Barbara came into the room and sat beside them on the bench. "Supper will be ready soon, my dears."

"Did you hear, Daughter? The only thing as good as music — food is coming!"

Barbara smiled teasingly. "Not quite the only thing. It seems Dorothea will have a sibling within the year."

Sebastian looked at her lovingly and hugged her to his chest. "It's no wonder. You drive me mad with passion. This time, it will be a boy. Of that I'm certain."

Six months later, to Sebastian's great joy, their son Wilhelm Friedemann raucously arrived. It seemed he would wail forever. Freidlina did her utmost to quiet the child, but to no avail. Sebastian, unperturbed, spoke over the noise. "A good sign, he can already sing better than most of the choir!"

The future seemed bright, but it appeared God had other plans. Everything looked cast in gray on a snowy February morning three years later. With Dorothea fidgeting between them and holding both of their hands, Sebastian and Maria Barbara fixed sightless eyes upon two miniature caskets. They appeared toy-like, unnatural. Wilhelm Friedemann, unusually quiet, sucked his thumb and nestled in the crook of Freidlina's shoulder. The bells of St. Peter and Paul's Church chimed dolefully in the distance. Perched on a branch of a stately maple, bereft of its leaves, a lone chaffinch sang. Sebastian glanced upward. Its song had long been locked in his memory. In his sorrow, he felt the weight of his heart and fury at the yoke of his faith.

He prayed in silence. "Heavenly Father, Thou art the creator of all that is goodness and just. Give me wisdom to understand why Thou hast taken my children, and strength to bear the pain of their loss. Forgive my anger and doubt. Keep in heaven these purest of angels whose lives Thou hast chosen to tear away from Thy humble servants."

The caskets were slowly lowered into the frost-hardened earth. Barbara's wailful sobs of anguish were the only sounds to break the silence but for the chaffinch. The senseless hand of death had smote again to snuff the candlelight of life. The twins, Maria Sophia and Johann Christoph, fourth and fifth children of Sebastian and Maria Barbara were buried that day.

Three more children were born to them. The first, Carl Phillip Emanuel, was born almost a year to the day of the twin's death, Johann Gottfried Bernhard in May of 1715, then Leopold Augustus in November of 1718.

"Dear Lord, of what crime, what trespass am I guilty to deserve Your wrath? I create music to Your glory although the closed-minded clergy may not see it as such. Your humble and faithful servant, I prostrate myself at Thy feet to beg Your lenience and forgiveness. And if Thy wish is to punish me, strike the fingers from me, Lord God, but spare my beloved and innocent wife Thy hand."

Sebastian sank into a pit of depression and guilt. Somehow, he thought, the blame for the senseless, meaningless deaths must lay with him. Had he done everything possible to protect them? Had he given them the love and attention they required during their short lives? Did his music deflect him from his fatherly duties and responsibilities? The torment of the questions added to the immensity of his bereavement.

~ ~ ~

In an oddity of fate, Sebastian and Milo were both tested — one armed with bullets, the other with creed — and neither with cast-iron ammunition.

~ ~ ~

CHAPTER TWENTY-SIX

Vietnam

When Milo finished instrument flight training, he received orders to fly the Cobra, the Army's new attack helicopter. Not happy with its purpose, he nonetheless loved its sleek lines, speed, and maneuverability. He suffered mixed emotions. The Army had given him the opportunity to realize his dream, but the military was not concerned with dreams. He wanted no part of their mission to destroy the enemy, however after a month's leave, he received orders to Vietnam.

The Army's status in Vietnam, supposedly advisory at that time, didn't prevent covert operations daily. That meant many combat deaths were officially listed as accidental. In Vietnam, there were two types of American warriors — the drafted, mostly reluctant, and the volunteers. Each had its misfits. In addition to Colonel Ridgeway, men from both categories would resolve Milo's dilemma.

Some of them were only part hip. Hippies were into free love, drugs, and against war. Others took the drugs and free love and went to war to become legalized killers. They were addicts at home and took advantage of the easily available drugs in Vietnam. They were happy to do the killing. The war became their reason to live and to die.

Later, he would rescue many shattered in both body and mind.

Upon reporting, he found to his surprise that Colonel Ridgeway had been transferred and now commanded the Air Assault Unit to which he had been assigned.

The colonel sat with feet propped on the desk, brow furrowed, deep in thought. He looked up and smiled. Milo noticed the familiar flight jacket, but saw a troubled face, not unlike the well-worn leather.

"Lieutenant Damiani reporting for duty, sir."

"Good morning, Milo. Welcome aboard."

He rose to shake his hand.

"Take a load off your feet." He poured two mugs of coffee, handing one to Milo. "Cream and sugar?"

"Black is fine. Thank you, sir."

"I see you did well at Rucker, great check rides and tops academically. Good work."

"Thank you, sir."

"You will be replacing one of my Cobra pilots. Poor bastard took a tail rotor hit and burned it in."

"Sir, I've got a problem with that."

"Damn it. I have enough fucking problems. What is it this time, Lieutenant?"

"I'm not going to fly a gun ship, sir."

Ridgeway turned red, put his hands on the desk and leaned forward, incredulously. "What?" He slammed his fist on the desk and dropped into his chair, exasperated.

"You're in fucking dangerous territory young man. We are at war. Do you understand?"

"Yes, sir."

"Do you know that you can be court-martialed for what you just said?"

"Yes, sir."

"Is that what you're looking for, a way out?"

"No, sir."

"Well, damn it, that's what you're toying with here. You've got a promising career ahead of you. Don't blow it. I'm going to forget what I just heard. Now, I advise you to get your ass out that door and report to Captain Jethro so I can get back to work."

"I can't do that, sir."

Ridgeway rubbed both hands through his hair and leaned back in the chair. He glared at Milo, eyes on fire.

"I'm at the end of my patience with you, Lieutenant. You've got thirty seconds to explain before I have you dragged off to the fucking stockade. Understood?"

"Yes, sir."

"Get on with it then."

"I joined the Army, not out of patriotism, but because it was the only way I could ever fly. I don't believe in this war."

"Your ass belongs to Uncle Sam now, young man. It doesn't matter what you think about the war. You had a choice. You could have gone to Canada, for Christ's sake."

"That was not an option. I wanted to fly so bad that I didn't think about the possibility of having to kill anyone. This wasn't supposed to be a war. I thought we were just advisors."

"Shit happens. We have been called to serve America. Where is your sense of honor?"

"I understand my duty, sir. I am honor bound to serve, but not to kill."

Ridgeway took in a breath and slowly exhaled. His demeanor softened, and he spoke quietly.

"Milo, let's make sure we're on the same page here. What you're telling me is you prefer another assignment. You did not, and are not refusing to fly a gunship. Isn't that correct?"

Milo caught the drift of the question, especially the nuance between prefer and refuse, emphasized by the forceful tap of pencil to desk. Relieved, Milo knew his answer would defuse the confrontation.

"Oh yes, sir. This is a request, not a refusal to fly the Cobra."

Tension escaped the room like air from a pricked balloon. "Good, I'll assign you to Medevac. It solves both our problems. I figure there are more than enough cowboys to do the killing. They will need all the help they can get. Now get the hell out of here."

"Thank you, sir."

"Good luck, Lieutenant. May God watch your back and keep you safe."

Milo thought, *Right. I'm not counting on it.* If there were a God, we wouldn't be standing here, now would we? He said, "You saved my ass again, sir."

Ridgeway smiled and they shook hands. Milo snapped a salute, did an about-face, and constrained himself from doing a jig out the door.

Milo thought about what Ridgeway had said. Am I looking for a way out? Am I a coward, afraid to die? Dead-eyed, soulless zombies with flags of skull and cross bones marched through his field of cerebral vision in a parade of death. His rational mind denied it.

It was the last time Milo would speak with Ridgeway. Three weeks later, while relieving a fatigued Cobra pilot, Ridgeway bought it. Stunned, Milo knew he owed a dream, and maybe his life to the colonel. He would always be grateful.

Assigned to Duster, the Forty-ninth Medical Detachment Helicopter Ambulance Unit, Milo knew this wouldn't be a picnic. The Forty-ninth had arrived in Vietnam in 1962. Then, pilots customarily communicated on any available vacant radio frequency. Oddly, the Navy controlled all communication call words in Vietnam. They allowed the Forty-ninth to adopt the call sign "Duster," which appropriately described what happened when landing helicopters propelled dust, and anything else not tied down, all over the troops on the ground.

Milo joined an elite group. During the Second World War, it took an average of ten hours before a wounded soldier reached a hospital. In the Korean conflict, the introduction of helicopters allowed the evacuation of about twenty thousand wounded. It cut the mortality rate in half.

Duster used the Bell UH-1 that allowed the wounded to be carried inside, allowing for treatment en route. With reduction in transport time to one hour, Duster reduced mortality to one-fourth the rate of the Second World War. By 1967, Duster pilots had rescued more than ninety thousand injured, and by the end of the conflict almost a million.

Determined to do his share, Milo got the opportunity. Sixteen months later, now Captain Damiani became a short-timer. He was training a new pilot, Lieutenant Seymour "Skip" Beasley. An easygoing fellow, Beasley chewed tobacco and always had a wad in his cheek. This proved to be a burdensome habit, out the window being the only place to spit while flying. It meant the fuselage of whatever helicopter he flew became sullied with splats of brown juice and tobacco bits. He was obliged to clean the fuselage each day, a task he bitched to the crew chief was far beneath the dignity of a helicopter pilot. "What, me worry?" was tattooed in red on his right forearm. He rolled only his right sleeve up to prominently display it.

Milo discovered a peculiar idiosyncrasy of Skip's he was delighted to exploit. Allergic to mustard, Skip's throat would constrict and he'd begin to wheeze at the mere thought of mustard. A few days after learning of it, Milo ended a training flight. Skip called the tower for clearance to land. Between instructions from the tower, they bantered over the intercom about the mission.

"Know what, rookie? You can't fly worth shit, man."

Skip accentuating his Alabama drawl warped by the wad in his cheek, replied, "Well, fuck, pardner, we done survav'd another day, didn't we?"

"Yeah, but barely. I'm about ready for an iced beer. How's about you?"

"It sounds lak a plan, pardner."

The tower: "Duster Four-Niner X-ray cleared for final. Over."

Before Skip had a chance to respond, Milo keyed the intercom.

"Hey, Skip, you buy the beer, and I'll take care of the dogs . . . with . . . mustard!"

Skip gasped as he tried to respond to the tower. Milo restrained his laughter.

Tower: "Duster Four Niner X-ray: Do you hear me? Four Niner X-ray? Are you with me?"

Milo keyed the transmitter.

"Roger, Four Niner X-ray. Cleared for final. Out."

Skip groaned, "You muthafucka!" They burst into laughter.

At the hot sticky day's end, they headed for the poor-excuse-for-a-pilot's lounge located at the far end of the corrugated maintenance hanger. It's only redeeming feature — the ice cooler kept filled with soft drinks and beer. Milo muttered, "We shoulda joined the Air Force." Skip liberated his mouth of tobacco sap. "Yeah, they don't treat pilots like fuckin' truck jocks."

Milo opened a pair of cold Schlitz, tossed one to Skip and plunked down on the lump-ridden chaise. He drained half the can and lit a Chesterfield. Milo's mail had finally caught up with him. His hands shook as he opened the first of two wires from London written by his stepmother.

The first, dated ten days prior said: "DEAR MILO FATHER SCHEDULED FRIDAY NEXT TO CORRECT HEART CONDITION. CERTAIN ALL WILL BE WELL LOVE MIRIAM"

Milo relaxed, grabbed a handful of stale popcorn and opened the second, dated yesterday. It read: "DEAR MILO DEEPLY SADDENED TO INFORM YOUR FATHER HAS PASSED ON FUNERAL SATURDAY, THE 5TH TERRIBLY SORRY LOVE MIRIAM"

"Shit," he mumbled. He put his head between his knees and took a moment to gather himself.

"What's up, Milo?"

"My old man died."

"Sorry, pardner. Were you close?"

"It's a long story, dude. The funeral's in London on Saturday."

"Holy shit, Milo, two days. It can be done, but we gotta crack. You go arrange leave. I'll check out Air Force flights."

With persistence and luck, Skip managed to cop Milo a transport to the airbase at Giebelstadt, Germany. An Air Force captain in Dispatch got him booked on a commercial flight from there to London.

Haggard and saddened, he watched the clouds drift silently past. Even in a war zone, everything seemed peaceful and orderly from this altitude, he thought. He spoke to his inner voice.

"Isn't this the shits? What the fuck?"

"Well, you can't blame God for this one."

"Shut the fuck up!"

"My, aren't we testy."

"Yeah, I know. It's just part of life. Shit."

"You got it."

"So what? That doesn't change the pain."

"You got that right."

Miriam's family was Welsh. To a one, the clan had clearly adored Milo's father. Singing is as natural to the Welsh as to the birds that dwell in the woodlands of Wales. With voices filled with sorrow, deep and dark as the coal mines in which they and their ancestors had sweated, bled, and died, they sang: "Each lonely place shall him restore, for him the tear be duly shed. Beloved, till life can charm no more, and mourned till pity's self be dead."

Milo glanced down at his half-siblings, a seven-year-old brother and six-year-old sister. Miriam held her two-year-old son. Mournfully they watched the earth swallow the casket. They cast their flowers into the grave. Milo knelt and gathered the children to his chest. That he could but make their pain his own, he wished. Miriam placed her hand on his shoulder.

"I'm so pleased you had a chance to see your father before he died, Milo. For many years he suffered, tried to strike the memory of you and your family from his mind. He never could, nor find courage to stir up the mud. His months after your visit were peaceful and happy. For that, I'm grateful."

"We're family, Miriam. These kids are my brothers and sister. Nothing will ever change that."

Despite sadness, Milo felt serenity on the trip back to

Vietnam, a peace that would last mere hours before being blown to bits, scattered as fragments of memory in a hell-hole of war.

The hot smelly deuce and a half jounced down the shell-pocked road. In a surreal scene, jade-hued mist rose eerily around the villagers working the rice paddies in the valley below. He thought, they live their lives as if the barrage pummeling the countryside, less than a half-hour's walk away, held no concern. Didn't they feel the earth tremble, or notice the billowing smoke mixed with cinders and ashes of death? Didn't they hear the screams of terror as limbs were blown away and torsos spilled their guts? Didn't they see the river of tears shed in sorrow?

Death — would he never escape the sense of its breath on his neck except in his own death? A stream of sightless eyes paraded through his mind. He'd seen them countless times, knew he couldn't bear the thought of being one of them, but knew he would. He spoke to his inner voice:

"What about in between?"

"That's called life."

"What kind of life is waiting to die?"

"Uh, no kind, if you're standing around waiting to die!"

"Very funny, asshole. What in hell is that supposed to mean? Is that what I'm doing?"

"I don't know. Is it?" Maybe living and dying is the same thing."

"Now there's a cool concept."

"Well, it seems dying is a process that began the day

you were born. It's a good indication you're still alive. Life appears to be what goes on during that process, doesn't it?"

"That's deep shit, something to think about."

The next day, he and Skip flew a mission to a field hospital near the Cambodian border. They were to airlift a couple of troops who'd been ambushed while on patrol. Though not critical, the wounds they'd suffered would likely be a ticket home. Skip flew. Milo listened to music.

"I'm really sorry 'bout your father, pardner."

Milo looked at him. "That's life, dude."

The radio squawked loudly, the voice calm and matter-of-fact. "Mayday, Mayday, Cobra Four-Two. Zulu going down with a dry turbine. Over."

Milo scribbled the coordinates, then checked his map.

"Roger, Four-Two. Zulu, this is Duster Three-Three Whisky Tango. You're about forty kilometers west. We're on the way. Hold tight. Over."

"Roger, Whisky Tango. It's hot, but you'll have cover fire. Over."

"Roger Four-Two, Zulu. Whisky Tango out."

Skip was about to lose his cherry. Just past dusk, Milo could still see smoke drifting laterally across the battle zone. Three Cobras circled their downed flight leader. Their guns spit blistering fusillades to keep Mr. Charles at bay, an awesome sight. Thank Christ I'm not on the wrong end of it, he thought as he keyed the intercom.

"I've got it, Skip."

"Roger. You've got it."

Milo had the Huey pegged at redline. He skimmed the

treetops trying hard not to be an easy target. Charlie had no qualms about using a Red Cross for target practice. The downed gunship came into view. He pushed down on the pitch and pulled the Huey into a flare. The loaded blades forced him into his seat.

Dust swirled around them obscuring his view. Gun smoke and jet fuel exhaust drifted into the cockpit. He put down fifty feet from the Cobra and kept his machine at the ready, light on its skids. He turned to Skip, only to see his face explode into fragments of tissue, bone and plasma. Milo's helmet got spattered with globules of flesh and misted with blood. He gagged at the taste of it. Partially blinded, he swiped it with his left hand and almost lost control of the chopper. Milo put it on the ground and screamed into the intercom.

"Beasley's dead. Get him the fuck outta here."

Two of the crew hurried forward and pulled the nearly decapitated body into the cargo bay. Milo opened his door and wretched. Tracers streaked from all directions. He spotted movement to his left. At first, he thought it was the downed pilot. It wasn't. Charlie charged with what appeared to be a tomahawk in his hand. Milo reached for the .45 strapped to his boot. Before he could pull, the man flew backwards, hit just below the mouth. A bullet tore away his jaw and collarbone. Milo glanced towards where the shot had come from. The Cobra pilot nodded and flipped him a salute.

The deadly look of him, like a warrior who'd just taken a scalp, evoked in Milo the unnerving sensation of a spider tiptoeing up his spine. Maybe a misfit had saved his ass or prevented him from killing, he thought. In that desperate moment, he wanted out of the madness with all of his parts, and not in a body bag.

After six mind-deadening months on autopilot, his tour ended. Reenlistment never occurred to him. At first, nothing else made much sense either. There's always music, he mused. He loved the guitar. The sound of it warmed him. Its sensual curves were comforting. He wished someday to play the *Chaconne* on it. He'd heard of a luthier in Japan who constructed magnificent guitars. If he were to play the *Chaconne*, he wanted the best. The timing seemed right. He decided to take a break, a holiday in Japan.

~ ~ ~

In a quest to mend a war-shredded spirit, Milo would seek healing through Bach's *Chaconne*. In the sacred language of music, Sebastian had constructed an inspiring road map for the restoration of his own ravaged soul . . . and Milo's.

~ ~ ~

CHAPTER TWENTY-SEVEN

Again the Chaffinch Sang

In desperate need of a respite, Sebastian sought refuge and solace in his music. He sat at the harpsichord trying to resolve a melody. Barbara entered the room waving an envelope.

"Sebastian, you've a post from Cöthen." He looked up and smiled. *How fortunate I am to have this wonderful woman for a wife,* he thought. "Whatever can it be?" She handed him the letter.

"It looks quite official and important."

"Perhaps an invitation to perform," he replied. He broke the seal and read the letter. "I've been commissioned by the authorities."

"Are you to perform?"

"No, I'm to travel to Berlin to acquire a new harpsichord for the princely court. It will pay me more than a few talers, plus expenses. Perhaps I will have the opportunity to make contact and perform for the Prussian court."

"That will be wonderful, Sebastian. How long will you be away?"

"Not more than ten days, I presume. Too long to be away from you and the children; however, it will do me good to put this elusive piece of music aside for a while. I'm tired of the fighting and disagreements between Ernst

August and his brother. It's a ridiculous situation having co-reigning dukes in the first place. Ernst has been a supporter, but his cousin is a donkey's ass! I need a bit of fresh air. The trip will do me good, and perhaps I can make a useful trip to Berlin as well. Thank you for understanding."

Bach did indeed make a trip to Berlin, where he met Margrave Christian Ludwig of Brandenburg, brother of the deceased king, and Grand Elector, Friedrich Wilhelm of Prussia, contacts that would later prove beneficial.

More importantly, as a result of Sebastian's acquisition of a superb new harpsichord, and his admiration for Sebastian, Prince Leopold offered him the position of Kapellmeister to the court of Cöthen. It would be a more complicated matter moving his growing family to Cöthen than it had been to Weimar. Maria Barbara had added to their furnishings. He'd acquired many instruments, including several harpsichords, expanded his library, and his own voluminous works had grown. In addition, they'd made many friends and contacts. In the end, he decided it would be worthwhile and accepted. The prince considered the hiring of Sebastian a personal triumph.

Now that he'd made the decision, Sebastian became enthusiastic about it. Upon his return home, he gathered the family about him.

"I've made a difficult decision, but it is in the best interests of all. Prince Leopold has offered me the position of Kapellmeister in Cöthen, and I've accepted."

To his relief, the children held hands and danced

around their father. They considered it an adventure. Maria Barbara and Freidlina took it in stride.

"My dear husband, it is a wonderful opportunity. Don't you think so, Freidlina?"

"Yes, of course. And we will be close to Hamburg and shopping."

"Indeed, my sister. I hadn't even thought of that."

"I suppose any raise in my earnings as Kapellmeister will quickly evaporate when you two get to Hamburg. In any case, as an added benefit, perhaps Freidlina will finally meet a man crazy enough to marry her!"

Their elation would be short-lived. Within a short time after their move to Cöthen, it became clear to Sebastian and Barbara that their last-born, Leopold, would not be with them long. Weak and sickly from birth, the doctors were puzzled as to his illness. He succumbed within a year of his birth. Sebastian's prayers for his son had been for naught. On September 28, 1719, again the church bells tolled; again the chaffinch sang. The casket containing their son, Leopold Augustus, inch-by-inch descended.

In July of 1720, Sebastian had been invited by Prince Leopold of Prussia to visit Carlsbad, a health and resort area located 130 miles north of Cöthen. There he would participate in a summer festival for the performing arts.

The series of life's misfortunes that had beset him left Sebastian appearing and feeling more than his thirty-five years. His hair had begun to thin and turn gray. His eyesight worsened almost daily. A spirit as broad as his shoulders allowed him to bear his burdens and pursue his genius, but not without pain. Maria Barbara anchored his ship.

"My dear wife, I hesitate leaving you for this travel. I'd rather not."

"Of course you must go, Sebastian. You cannot refuse the prince without damage to your career. Freidlina will help with the children. We will be fine."

He looked adoringly at his wife. Color had come to her cheeks and her high spirit returned. She had blossomed as a summer rose. He couldn't bear to leave her again, but he knew she well understood his dilemma. He enfolded her in his embrace, tenderly touching his lips to hers.

"Almighty God has given me two gifts, neither of which I can live without. He then always presents a wretched choice between them."

On the day of his departure, they strolled in the garden. Suddenly, Sebastian stopped and hushed her. Just above them a Chaffinch sang. They shared a warm embrace. Barbara stroked his face and looked deeply into her husband's saddened eyes.

"Despite unbearable sorrow, you have made my life a joy and my grief bearable, Sebastian."

"And you, my love, have made my life bliss. I cannot fathom what plan of God it could be to bring us such suffering. He gives with one hand and takes with the other. Thankfully, he has given me you, or I surely would have gone mad. Our thirteen years together have been the happiest, though the saddest."

"I love you, Sebastian. God carry you safely."

"I miss you desperately, and I haven't yet departed."

After a hard day's travel, Sebastian reached Carlsbad, his second trip there at the behest of Margrave Ludwig. Despite his yearning to be home, his performance at the festival did not suffer. He astounded a sophisticated audience with his musical wizardry. At a reception after the recital, Sebastian and Margrave Ludwig enjoyed a glass of wine. Couples bedecked in finest fashion circled the room in a stately dance played by an ensemble of stringed instruments.

"Congratulations on a brilliant performance."

"Thank you most honorable and elegant sir."

"Mind you, Sebastian, I do not share this view; however, some in the audience have said your music is strange and frivolous, and even a sacrilege."

Sebastian smiled and made a sweeping gesture as to encompass the room. "To those who cannot hear the music, the dancers must seem mad."

Gone only five days, an exuberant Sebastian arrived home and burst through the door as if it had been five months. He shouted in delight and anticipation, "Barbara, children, where are you?" Only silence met him.

~ ~ ~

In the music of *Chaconne*, Milo sensed a deeply spiritual union between a man and a woman, one shattered by death. He would experience a similar connection, not crushed by loss, but one shrouded in wonder and mystery.

~ ~ ~

CHAPTER TWENTY-EIGHT

Chado

Upon his arrival in Japan, Milo went to Hamamatsu to see Isuro Khono, the luthier. His family had been making stringed instruments for six hundred years. Khono had become interested in Spanish guitars and spent five years in Spain with a master, learning their construction. Returned to Japan, he added this knowledge to that of his ancestors, and produced guitars of exceptional sound and beauty. Milo wanted to buy one.

In Hamamatsu, it took almost three hours to find the luthier. Neither sign nor number identified his shop at the end of a narrow cobbled lane. By going door to door, pretending to strum a guitar, he found an elderly woman. She nodded rapidly and beckoned him to follow. When they reached the shop, she politely knocked and spoke quietly in Japanese. She turned and ushered him through the door. Smiling broadly, she bowed and departed.

Khono, a scholarly-looking man with a long, wispy white moustache, had a tall, wiry frame supporting shoulders bent as if burdened. When he extended his hand, Milo felt strength and softness in his fingers. His eyes were black and bright, and his smile infectious.

Guitars hung from the exposed rafters. There were stacks of rosewood used for the back and sides, spruce and pine for the tops, and ebony for the fret boards. The luthier's tools were arrayed above his bench like samurai ready to battle the wood. Hundreds of years of tradition permeated the place. At once, Milo knew he would purchase his guitar here. When he saw her gleaming on the bench, he knew which one.

He spoke in Spanish.

"I'll take that one."

Also in Spanish, Khono asked, "Would you not like to play her first?"

"No. That's the one I want."

"Very well then, but the price is . . ."

"It doesn't matter."

Khono nodded knowingly, and proceeded to apply some final touches, then placed the guitar in its case. Milo paid, feeling fortunate at its low price. To him, it was priceless. Afterwards, Milo pulled a bottle of sake from his carry-on bag and presented it to the surprised luthier. Khono bowed.

"This is very fine sake, indeed. Mr. Jihei Kanoh, the founder of the house of Hakutsuru, was a lumber dealer. My family bought wood for our instruments from him and his ancestors until he began the production of Hakutsuru Sake in 1743. Their motto "To friendship for all time" is quite appropriate for this occasion."

He left momentarily, then returned with two elegant porcelain cups. He handed one to Milo, then bowed and thanked him for the gift. He poured the sake and recited a Haiku: "*Ki no moto ni tsuyu mo namasu mo sakura ka na."* (Under the tree with drink and food, not only the cherry, blossoms.)

Milo's flight to Madrid wouldn't depart until the following day. On a whim, he decided to ride the train to its final destination, the Japanese gardens at the Ryotanjii Temple in the mountains.

Hamamatsu is surrounded by tree-draped rivers, lush forests, mist-shrouded mountains, and the Pacific Ocean. The bustling city, halfway between Tokyo and Osaka, belies the breathtaking natural beauty around it. Milo boarded the train at the station near his hotel. As the scenery flashed past, he fell in love with the landscape. Distaste of the food, and disinterest in the language aside, Milo thought Japan a most mysterious country. With business finished there, he looked forward to Spain.

Not only did he think the food and wines far superior, he was starved for conversation. On his visits there he sought conversation with the elderly in order to gather insights about Spanish history, lore, and culture.

Milo closed his eyes, giving himself up to the moment, and the rhythmic motion of the train, letting his body move from side to side. He usually felt like a fly in a beehive when he rode the crowded trains in Japan, but there were only five other people in the coach — three of them men in casual European clothes, and an older couple in traditional dress, all of them somber-faced. The pitch of the wheels told him they were approaching the next stop. In choreographic unison, everyone's motion shifted from side-to-side to back-and-forth, as the engineer intermittently applied the brakes. With a sudden forward lurch the train screeched and hissed to a halt.

Milo opened his eyes to see a beautiful Japanese woman glide onto the train and sit diagonally across from him two seats away. Her satin hair flowed delicately over her shoulders, splashing onto her kimono. Her slender fingers held an unadorned fan. It concealed the lower part of her face, but showed her dazzling ebony eyes, discreetly lowered. Milo stared as would a child. An uncomfortable interval of time passed before his eyes obeyed and turned away, leaving him flushed and feeling foolish.

She had noticed his stare, and though the fan hid her mouth, her eyes told Milo she was smiling. He imagined her firmly bound in tradition, destined for a loveless marriage.

At the next stop, two of the men in western clothes got off. Milo found it difficult to be discreet; his eyes kept wandering to the woman. She appeared to be in her early twenties and stunning. He wished he could speak Japanese.

The train stopped again, and this time, the last man in western dress left, leaving only the old couple, the young woman, and Milo in the car. The older couple looked at him, smiling broadly and nodding their heads, the man jabbering something in Japanese. Milo had no idea what they were saying, but smiled and waved. The young woman kept her eyes lowered, pretending not to notice. She swayed to and fro, as if moving to the song of a gentle spring breeze.

At another stop the couple got off, leaving Milo and the woman, she with lowered eyes, he with pounding heart. Then in a moment of inspiration, he shyly spoke to her.

"Good afternoon, Miss."

She raised her eyes, bowed her head, appearing not to know what he had said, but an obvious greeting. She answered in Japanese. He didn't know what else to say. They rode the rest of the way in silence. When the train stopped, they both exited. It was a short walk to the temple through the gardens and he tried to stay a reasonable distance behind so as not to make the woman uncomfortable.

The gardens were tranquil and in bloom, bursting with colors and fragrances and birdsong. A pair of swans surrounded by a dozen bobbing cygnets preening in the pond beneath the wooden bridge hurriedly paddled away at the hollow sound of footsteps, continuing their grooming a short distance away. He followed the woman into the temple, admiring its simplicity and serenity. She beckoned to him shyly. He walked over and stood before her. She bowed and spoke in Japanese. From her gestures, he gathered Seisai was her name.

Clumsily, he returned the bow, saying, "I'm Milo."

She walked away and turned as if to see if he were following, whereupon she guided him on a tour of the temple. They spent the better part of three hours enjoying the artifacts and architecture. They communicated with inflection, expressions, gestures, and the esoteric idiom known only to lovers.

Finishing the tour, she turned to him, smiled and said questioningly in Japanese, "*Chado*?"

He didn't understand, but assumed it an invitation and bowed saying, "Yes. Thank you."

She understood. Delighted, he'd no idea he had been invited to the Way of Tea. Milo had no understanding of *Chado*. Only later, after hours of reflection, would its full significance be revealed. When they reached the station, the train was there.

In Japan, the tea ceremony is a sacred ritual. Japanese æsthetic correlates with concepts of Zen Buddhism. At its core is the consideration and contemplation of existence and interrelatedness of all things. Sen Rikyu, a fifteenth-century tea master who transformed *Chado* into a metaphor of life, said,

Holding a bowl of tea whisked to a fine froth.

Such a simple thing yet filled with a spirit

That reaches back more than a thousand years.

Milo would later realize the ritual of *Chado*, much like the *Chaconne*, had many variations on a theme and a resolution, its theme — enjoyment of tea. Seisai would perform the ritual steps to a resolution. It would be as a dance.

When they arrived at the station where she had boarded, they got off. The sounds of the train faded, leaving only the silence of the rural village. As they walked, the restful gardens held him spellbound in the setting sun.

They walked till they arrived at a dirt path, and after a

short distance came upon a small pine structure. The faded, worm-holed wood gave it an appearance of great age. Milo followed her to it. They removed their shoes and entered a bathhouse. A steaming wooden tub stood in the center of it. Eucalyptus-scented vapors filled the room. The aromatic mist, barely allowing them to see each other, filled their eyes with tears and cleansed their lungs. She indicated he must bathe.

Her fingers lightly touched his skin as she bashfully helped him out of his clothes and he shivered. Feeling vulnerable in his nakedness, he stepped into the tub, but it was so hot it was several minutes before he could submerge to his neck. Seisai lit an oil lamp and he watched the wavering shadows encircle her as she bowed and left the bathhouse. He sat, steeping in the dimness. It seemed a dream. Would he wake on the train to find her gone, he wondered.

While awaiting Seisai's return, he experienced a moment of insight. His life experiences, his decisions and choices, many fraught with disappointment and rejection, had led him to this convergence of time and place. He had been thrust into a spiritual interlude as an honored guest.

After they entered the garden of the teahouse, he sensed a reverence and solemnity not unlike a religious observance. He fervently hoped he would not defile the sanctity of the moment or unwittingly dishonor her.

The dying rays of the sun cast a spectrum of shimmering color onto the floor as she entered, then disappeared as she closed the door behind her. Holding a large white towel and a silk robe, she beckoned him to her, and dried him. Through its softness he felt the strength of her gentle hands. He had not been touched by a woman or felt the comfort it brought for a long time.

Overwhelmed and unable to stem his tears, he was thankful for the mist to hide them, but it did not and she traced a tear down his cheek with her fingertip, wiping it away, and then laid her head in the crook of his neck for a moment. She dried his body and held the robe for him, then tied the *obi* around his waist in a loose knot. Snuffing the lamp, she led him into the cool of the evening.

After a short distance they entered a garden, this one flowerless, the *Roji*. They followed a winding, moss-covered stone path, intended to induce one to shed the filth of the profane world before entering the teahouse. Seisai whispered a verse in Japanese. The lilt in her voice indicated it was verse, but he could not appreciate the meaning of the lyric: "Since the dewy path is a way that lies outside this most impure world, shall we not on entering it cleanse our hearts from the earthly mire?"

All around them were pine and cypress of differing heights, adding fragrance to the air. Willows with graceful branches drooped protectively over the miniature mimosa and oak. The sensation was that of walking in a wooded glen. No birdsong broke the spell.

At the end of the *Roji* stood the *Cha-shitsu* in all its antique simplicity, a spare wooden structure devoid of decoration, existing solely for appreciating tea. Seisai opened the medieval gate, which had a thatched, helmet-shaped roof. Turning to Milo, she humbly bowed, waiting for him to pass through into a tranquil waiting arbor. Hanging from its rafters was a wooden gong to announce the arrival of guests. She indicated he should strike the gong once with the heel of his hand, a purely ceremonial gesture, since no hostess was awaiting a guest in the tea-house as would usually be the case. The reverberating tone excited a sympathetic oscillation, rousing the hairs on the back of his neck.

They stopped before a small water basin. To its left was a lantern of uncut stone. A small cypress behind it with one branch hanging over its top cast back the dancing flame of its wick. She bade him wash, a symbolic ablution to remove the dust of the world, making him fit to partake of *Chado* in a state of purity. He picked up the delicate dipper, pouring fresh water onto his hands. The corners of her mouth dimpled as she tried to suppress a smile at his clumsiness. Pulling a white napkin from the thin *obi* wrapped around her waist, she handed it to him. A flush rose to his cheeks and he smiled shyly.

Stepping out of her sandals, she placed her hands, thumbs crossed, pointing upward at mid-chest, bowed and entered the small waiting area. Milo removed his shoes and stood, awkwardly waiting. She turned and bowed in formal greeting, inviting him to enter the tearoom. In an alcove, a shelf held a fluted vase with a single white chrysanthemum.

Smoke from the incense burning nearby drifted upwards, permeating the air with the aroma of sandalwood. She indicated he should sit on the mat on the floor opposite her. He noted her elegance as she sat loosely clad in her kimono. With willowy grace, she began the "making of the fire."

When the coals began to glow, she dusted the hearth with a feather brush. She then added two pastilles of incense to the burner placed on her right.

He enjoyed her every motion. She stood, bowed, and left the room. She returned with an enameled tray bearing rice, clear broth, broiled fish, and two bowls of vegetables, softly speaking the name of each dish. The food was simply prepared and served with sake. He had some difficulty manipulating the chopsticks. Seisai remained solemn, leaving him smiling and unconvinced of her earnestness.

They consumed the meal without conversation. When they finished, she placed the bowls and utensils on the tray and left him sipping the last bit of sake from his cup. He felt light-headed, but at peace, and pure of soul.

Seisai returned with a water jug, tea bowl, teaspoon and tea caddy, an empty bowl, a hot water ladle, and a bamboo tea whisk, making a separate trip for each. Every movement artful and flowing, he saw the rhythm and grace of the ritual.

Removing the lid from the kettle, she ladled in a cupful of fresh water. When the *cha* finished brewing, she whisked it into froth. She poured the tea, filling his cup halfway. Taking the steaming cup in her right hand, and then shifting it to her left hand, she presented it to him.

Milo bowed his head, accepting the tea. The green liquid was delicately flavored and a perfect temperature. He sipped slowly, savoring the taste and sensation it created in his mouth.

Everything had been accomplished in complete silence, but for three sounds. The first, as she placed the lid on the kettle producing a deliberate clinking sound. Then, while preparing the tea, she tapped the tea bowl on the mat three times. Finally, there were delicate bell-like tones, reminiscent of his guitar, as she struck the tea bowl with the teaspoon. Drinking the tea ended the ceremony. Milo was moved and honored. Sitting quietly, reflecting in the tranquil ambience of the teahouse, he felt complete.

When he finished, Seisai slowly came around the table on hands and knees. When she reached Milo, she sat before him. With her head bowed, and holding it lowered, she reached for his hands. He placed them in hers, feeling her strong fingers and soft palms, and their warmth crept to his heart. He closed his eyes and wished the feel of them could be with him always.

In her fingertips, he felt her pulse lightly beating. He could hear her quiet breathing and without conscious effort, they began to breathe in unison. Milo felt as if his body were getting lighter and would at any moment levitate.

Her heart began to hurry, and so did his. Their breathing became more rapid as their hearts beat faster. The pulse in her fingers became a forceful throb, and he could feel and hear it throughout his body. She raised her hands and keeping his firmly in her grasp, gently pushed him backwards, and then opened his robe.

Her soft and trembling lips were upon his chest and her hands caressed his face. He let out his breath in small gasps and shivered. Holding his face, she kissed his forehead and her tears rolled onto his lips where he tasted them. In his last rational moment, he thought he'd been drugged, but it didn't matter. Overcome, he could but succumb.

An exquisite moistness surrounded him. He could not tell where his own flesh ended and hers began. He trembled. Their accelerated breathing resonated in the room. At first almost imperceptibly, her movements above him became rhythmic and subtle. Involuntary spasms overcame him, and sounds he had never before uttered escaped his lips. Seisai's breathing came in subdued gasps and then softly in an impassioned monadic song.

Immersed in her scent, submerged in the liquid fire of their unity and waves of contractions, a cresting comber swept over him, and he spent himself. Their ardor gave way to bliss. They clung, stroking each other, whispering endearments. Their lips touched, tasting of each other's tears.

He awoke to the patter of raindrops striking the thatched roof. As sleep lifted, he reached for her. He bolted upright and looked about the room. There remained only her lingering perfume. He reached for his clothes and found a note written in English. It said, "My virtue dwells alone with thee, as does yours alone with me. Dishonor there will never be."

Milo stared into the garden at a weeping willow. It held his gaze. He shook his head. She knew English. She seduced me just as the guitar had. Fighting an impulse to find her, Milo would not be distracted. *I'll take a short break in Spain and then go home and sort out my life, but, how will I ever play guitar without thinking of Seisai, Chado . . . and Sebastian.* He smiled.

After a short visit to Spain, he thought it marvelous — the food, wine, and most of all the people and their culture. He felt at home. One day perhaps he'd return. Now, he needed time to think, to find peace and a way to fulfillment.

~ ~ ~

If the timetables of life could be reversed, perhaps Milo could have helped Sebastian through his ordeal, but alas the universe permits no such proviso.

~ ~ ~

CHAPTER TWENTY-NINE

The Death of Maria Barbara

A lthough mid-summer, cold penetrated his bones as if it were the dead of winter. Sebastian shivered. The children ran to surround him. Carl Phillip, the youngest, grabbed his leg and held on tight. Catherina Dorothea, the eldest at twelve, and Wilhelm raised their solemn faces, hands stiffly at their sides. Sebastian squatted, and gathered them to him.

"What is it? He looked at his daughter. "Catherina, where is your mother? Where is your aunt?"

Clad in black, head lowered, Freidlina walked slowly into the room, as if to the rhythm of a dirge. Hunched forward, slumped-shouldered, hands pressed to her stomach, tears flowed down her pallid cheeks. She could scarcely speak.

"Maria Barbara is gone."

"Gone? Gone where?"

"She is dead and buried."

The floor seemed to crumble beneath Sebastian. Falling to his knees, face buried in his hands, and through choked sobs, he cried, "No! Oh my God, no."

The bewildered children hugged their father. They'd

never seen him weep. They cried in chorus, as much for him as the loss of their mother. Sebastian could not fathom his wife's sudden demise. She'd been in perfect health and recovering from her grief. He dared not think she could have taken her own life. Sebastian composed himself and rose. "Please put the children to bed and then we can speak."

Freidlina embraced him. She returned composed, the words flowed freely, as had her tears.

"I'm so sorry, Sebastian. It is a mystery. It began the day of your departure. Maria Barbara asked me to prepare supper for the children. You know how much she loved doing it herself. I thought it odd but attributed it to fatigue. I did get concerned when she refused to eat and then went straight off to bed. I immediately dispatched Catherina to fetch Doctor Hauptman. He arrived within the hour. Nothing could be found amiss, yet she failed to respond to any of his questions. She never opened her eyes nor did she appear to be in any discomfort. He suggested we allow her to rest. After I had fed the children and put them to bed, I thought she might enjoy some hot soup, which I prepared and took to her. I tried to wake her, to no avail.

Doctor Hauptman returned and told me she'd perished, just like that. Since we had no idea when you'd return, he, for reasons of sanitation, suggested we bury her. The next day, with the help of your assistants, I arranged a service. They were very cooperative and sympathetic and took care of the preparations. We found a lovely plot for her close to the twins and Gottfried."

Sebastian said nothing. He went to his study and locked the door. At dusk, he lit candles, sat at his desk, and wept.

As the sun rose over the cemetery, Sebastian looked in disbelief at the simple granite headstone. Morning sun condensed the evening moisture to droplets of dew. It sparkled on every surface, became one with Sebastian's tears. In the silence of the cemetery came the trill of a chaffinch. Sebastian refused to pray, but simply whispered, "Goodbye, dear wife."

He isolated himself in the study, leaving to bathe, but only when Freidlina and the children slept. Freidlina understood. She never entered the room, leaving food and drink at the door. She explained to the children their father needed solitude. Repeatedly, Sebastian tried to discharge, express his feelings in thought, but to no avail. They were like festering pus.

How could I ever have thought to leave her, even if only for days? Had I not, I may have somehow saved her. I would not have let her die. And what of my poor children, left without a father to console and comfort them through such horrible trauma? I've failed my beloved family. How can I seek forgiveness from a jealous and vengeful God? How cruel that heaven and hell are not abstract, but reality here on earth.

Sebastian then knew he must liberate himself with music. At that moment, his memory recalled the haunting warble of the chaffinch. He sat at his desk, reflecting upon the tools of his craft, a stack of dark brown paper and the copper-gallic ink powder to be dissolved in inkpots of distilled water. He selected a raven quill pen from its brass container, which he carefully sharpened. Selecting a rastral, he meticulously ruled the staff lines. Blowing the parchment to dry it a bit, he sprinkled the ink with fine sand to blot it. Satisfied, he put the notes to paper in sequence. For the first time in many nights, he slept soundly.

Awake at dawn, Sebastian decided to compose a work in memory of his beloved. He fetched the breakfast Freidlina left at his door, bolted down the newly baked bread and washed it down with a goblet of milk. He placed a parchment on the desk and dipped his pen. Five carefully drawn horizontal lines connected on the left with a treble clef, appeared on the blank brown page.

The burnished violin shone with endless hours and ages of loving touch. Sebastian held it to his chest and gently patted the arc of its back as if inducing an infant to expel an air bubble and spoke.

"Yes, my beauty, I know. That confounded contrivance of pipes, bellows, and pedals has intrigued me so, I've been neglectful. But now, I shall write for you. Through your sweet voice, the melody shall flow as a meandering brook. It shall be a dance, a dance of life and of death. A chaffinch gifted me a melody of eloquence some twenty years past, but I knew not why, then. From it we shall create a sequence of chords upon which to build a cathedral of music."

Sebastian placed the violin under his chin and took

bow to strings. The melody of the chaffinch rang forth with rich and vibrant clarity, as if from the depth of the instrument's ancient soul. As he wrote, he spoke to his beloved wife.

"You were a flower always in bloom. How I miss the feel of your body close to mine in slumber, your silken hair upon my face and the scent of it. I can scarcely bear the acknowledgment of never again knowing your tender touch upon my brow, your breath of angels on my face. How shall I live without you?"

First hours, then days flew by. Often by candlelight, Sebastian labored through the night, slept when exhausted, ate when hungry, and didn't bother to bathe. He wrote and mourned and spoke so only he could hear.

"Our poor children! I know too well their pain. I'm thankful of your forethought that brought Freidlina to our household. It would be most difficult to raise them alone. Did you know you'd leave us? My dearest, my life, even the stars could not fill the emptiness I now feel in my being. How could God punish us so? Why has God continued to rebuke me? Have I not dedicated my life to His magnificence? Have I not availed myself of His bestowal and heaped glory upon His holy name? Can God possibly believe my music, inspired by Him, is blasphemous? I remember clearly my father's words. 'You are a Bach. Music is sacred. It comes from God. You are blessed. God shall punish you if His calling is not heeded.' Have I not done such? Why then has He inflicted unbearable anguish upon this faithful and humble servant?"

Sebastian angrily threw his quill in disgust. Red ink spattered the score, rendering it hopelessly illegible. He crumpled it into a ball and hurled it into the glowing embers of the hearth. It sprang to flame, the room bathed in its glow. Slowly through a palette of crimson hues, it dwindled as the sun ending a summer's day. He laid his head on the desk and wept, then drifted off to sleep. It became a cycle of existence: he wrote, wept, and slept. Despite a former passion for food, he ate only to carry on.

"Dearest Barbara, in the vast nothingness of my existence without you, to reduce the memories and emotion of our life onto so few pages seems an unachievable task. And yet, I'm compelled to try. Forgive me, the children are in need of my attention, but would they have but a modicum of it until my task is done? I think not. My God, torment me if it is Thy will, but comfort my children."

Spent of his anger at God, he contemplated the seeds of doubt planted in early childhood.

How did I dare question God's plan? How did I allow my faith to erode in the face of ordeal and human suffering, which pale in contrast to that of Christ our Savior? Is it no wonder I've been punished so? I must repent, and shall in this memoriam to my beloved.

Reflecting carefully upon the numerous chorales he'd composed during his years in Cöthen, Sebastian selected those with tonalities adaptable to the melody of the chaffinch; there were eight. He dipped his quill and listed the text titles: "*Christ lag in Todesbanden*" ("Christ in bonds of death was laid"); "*Dein will gescheh*" ("Thy will be done"); "*Befiehl Du Define Wege, Jesu Meine Freude*" ("Jesus my Joy"); "*Auf Meinen Lieben Gott*" ("To my dear Lord"); "*Jesu Dein Passion*" ("Jesus your passion"); "*In Meins Herzens Grunde*, Nun Lob' *mein Seel Den Harren*" ("Now paradise my soul awaits").

Sebastian would use the music from these chorales in the *Chaconne* and would write his repentance from the sacred text titles.

With courage, he brought the full ferocity of thoughts and feelings to the surface, note by note — almost thirty-two hundred of them — in the language of music.

Sebastian contrived more than seventy repetitions of the chord progression and multiple variations, a daunting task on a non-chorded instrument.

"Ah ha! And now begins the mischief. We must be bold, audacious. Here we must transpose from D minor to major."

As Sebastian penned the notes, emotions surged forth, flowing free. Not a bound-up bubble tangle of confused insensibilities. No, they were lucid and reasoned. He relived the ardent love of the woman who gave him refuge from sorrow and death. He evoked their passionate love-making, her nurturing care, the pain of her loss. He expressed his anger at God, questioned his faith, and finally accepted her death and his repentance.

Through endless days and sleepless nights, Sebastian wrote and spoke so only he could hear.

"Now the time has come to say goodbye, dearest wife. I'd like to believe we shall be rejoined in heaven, but how can it be? Heaven already existed for us on earth. How difficult it is to know I will not ever see, touch, or hold you near again. Rest well, my love. My memory of you shall breathe in the music and in the chaffinch song."

Sebastian placed the parchment on which he'd written the sacred text titles, and wrote, "My Lord and Savior, now my wife, in bonds of death is laid. Thy will be done. Jesus, my joy, from the bottom of my heart, with all Your passion, I beg forgiveness. Now, praise my soul, paradise awaits me."

Sebastian put down the pen, secured the bow, lay his head upon the desk, and wept.

Sebastian's *Chaconne* would come to be considered by many the greatest piece of music ever composed. To achieve it at all required consummate skill — to pull it off without ennui, sublime genius.

The next morning, Sebastian sat in his favorite chair before the hearth, enjoyed a pipe, and awaited the children. Wilhelm saw him first. He rubbed his eyes and smiled, then flung himself into his father's lap. "Phillip, Dorothea, Papa is better."

~ ~ ~

Lessons Milo learned from Sebastian through his music remained stored in a potent intellectual arsenal to combat life's adversity. They would serve him well.

~ ~ ~

CHAPTER THIRTY

Chiara

Milo struggled to keep from falling to his knees. The pain in his gonads couldn't have been more excruciating had a karate master kicked him. And all because of *her*. He'd recently been through an intense, life-changing period of personal reassessment. He now had purpose. Women had not been a priority, until he met Chiara. The pain came from the vernacular "lover's nuts."

The path of a directionless existence had disheartened him, left him with an emptiness echoing with confused inner voices. Keeping his life, a blur of loss, pain and fear, together, seemed like holding on to a runaway horse, unable to get on and afraid to let go. He had to gather and find a means to reassemble it in a sensible form. He remembered a math teacher who always harped "simplify." He quit his job and planned an escape from familiar surroundings, family, and friends. He loaded his car for a long camping trip, packing only essentials, and aimed it north.

The vastness, rhythm, sounds, variety of life forms, and scent of the sea were a magnet. They drew him to the coast. For days he drove the coastal route through Massachusetts, New Hampshire, and now, Maine. He rose early, the morning still draped in darkness. He grabbed a quick coffee, and hit the road. He rolled down the window and drew a deep breath, thinking if there were a better blend than tangy sea breeze and the jolt of fresh java, he couldn't imagine it. In Lubec on the Bay of Fundy, dawn crawled out of the dark like a lazy groundhog. Known as "down East," the locals say, "There America greets the day."

With majesty, the sun seemed to swell from the ocean floor to the raucous welcome of gulls. On a cliff above the hammering sea, the candy-striped East Quoddy Head Lighthouse emerged ghostlike from the rolling fog. He wondered at the color of the towering spruce blanketing Campobello Island. Out of the mist, they emerged as peaks with the hue of an African emerald. Natives in the region where they're mined believe the emerald to bring the body, mind, and emotions into balance. A good omen, he thought.

The sun burned the fog to steamy wisps above the tides in the narrows, reminiscent of a boiling lobster pot. A bald eagle circled, looking for breakfast. This is the place, he thought. He found an abandoned cabin on the island, and settled in. It seemed a paradise, a perfect place to set a new course, only this time with a favorable wind in his sails.

He lived monastic months of profound introspection. The cathartic ebb and flow of the sea bathed him in its healing powers. At first, he simply enjoyed his surround-ings, exploring the island, swimming in the frigid ocean, and fishing. Milo's only contacts with the outside were trips for supplies.

Each fading night set in motion the following morning, one of those *Glory Halleluiah!* mornings — the kind you think is the best you've ever experienced until the next comes along. The warm sun, soft sea breeze, and bedewed foliage brought forth the exclamations that sprang to his lips.

What a way to begin his first day in this paradise, he thought. As he hiked inland along a winding path softened by layers of spruce needles, movement ahead looked at first to be a field mouse. Instead, a recently hatched wood dove fluttered its featherless wings as it floundered, helplessly grounded. Milo picked up the bird, and scoured the trees to find its nest, to no avail. Milo cradled it in his hands to keep it warm. It immediately opened its mouth wide, noiselessly waiting to be fed. "Well, little guy, it's just you and me."

What will I feed it, he thought. He smiled at the thought of motherhood. "Okay, little fella. Let's go home." Using a cardboard box, he made a nest of pine needles and dried grass. "That's the best I can do, guy"

Having raised pigeons as a boy, he remembered the regurgitated mixture they were fed by the hens. It seemed like ground corn mush. Cornflakes and powdered milk would have to do. He mixed a batch, put some on the end of his finger and poked it into the wide-open hungry beak. Sure enough, it disappeared. He fed the dove until it appeared satiated. "That's it for now, little guy. It's bedtime."

The dove thrived. It learned to let him know when it wanted food, which seemed like always. Soon the naked body was covered, at first with down, then pinfeathers. He knew he'd have to set it free some day soon and tried not to get attached, but it didn't work. He'd been trying to teach it how to use its wings. Perched on his finger, the dove would frantically flap as Milo dropped his hand, but it held his finger in a death grip. Soon its wings became strong enough, but so did its hold on Milo's finger. At that point, he decided to toss him into the air and it worked. The dove took a short flight with a rough landing.

That afternoon as he sat reading by the fireplace, the dove landed on his shoulder at the crook of his neck and settled in. From then on, he knew it would be difficult to set him free. The dove now had the run of the place. The few droppings here and there were no bother. Soon it made its first foray into the world, and found the leftovers from the bird feeder Milo had hung on a nearby limb. Each night though, it returned to the cabin.

One morning as the dove was feeding, Milo saw the flashing tan body dive for the bird. He screamed a warning, but too late. He managed to frighten off the cat, but the damage had been done. In the dove's croup, a gaping gash oozed blood. He took the bird inside and washed the wound with hydrogen peroxide; then, with great difficulty, sutured it using a needle and thread from his sewing kit.

For the first few days it seemed as if the dove would live. On the morning of the third day, Milo found its cold body. It couldn't have been worse if it had been a person.

Milo remembered the unforgettably beautiful morning he'd found the orphan. Now he'd always remember the day it died. He realized another dichotomy. Life is sometimes grand and sometimes not. The dove had taught him much about patience, compassion, and unconditional love. Milo had taught it how to fly, but he couldn't teach it about cats. Only a real mother could have done that, he thought.

He got back to reviewing the unpleasant pain and fears in his life. The lessons he'd learned were clear. Yet, he felt like flotsam trapped in the narrows, at the mercy of the tides. He knew to break free he'd need a new course. He spoke to his inner voice:

"I'm lost."

"No, you're right here."

"Right here. What a great help that is."

"What are you doing here?"

"Trying to figure out what's next."

"What's so hard about that? Tell me something. What is it that you've always wanted to do, for as long as you can remember?"

"Lots of things."

"That's sort of vague. Tell me something more specific."

"To play the *Chaconne* on the guitar."

"Well, what's stopped you?

"Life — it's always something. I've never had time."

"You speak as if you don't have any control over what you do."

"I hadn't thought about it in that way."

"That's bullshit! Who decided to go to flight school?"

"That's different. I can make money flying."

"So, are you going to let money define your choices? Is time to be defined as the time between gas fill-ups of your fancy car? Is space what you need to keep all the things you buy? Is everything you want, wish, desire, an actual need?"

"A great deal of it is."

"Think small here. What you need is food, clothing, and shelter. Everything else is one of those other things."

"That's a good point. Hadn't thought about it that way before."

"Well, you bought a guitar. Seems like a good starting point. Or, is it just another toy to fill your space?"

Milo decided his purpose would be best served through music, but as an avocation. He'd do what he'd always aspired to, but had never found the time. A name popped into his head, Turan Mirza Avicenna. An acquaintance, a guitarist, had studied with him. Milo had met Ana Lisa at a party a few days before his trip up the coast. Their mutual love of the guitar gave them instant rapport. Milo half-heartedly tried a lesson with her. They never made it past a short demonstration of her skills. Clothing flew in all directions. Drenched in body fluids, they lay gasping for air.

Tall and sensuous, Ana Lisa had short, raven-colored hair, large innocent eyes, and lips that he would rather suck than kiss. She also had the most beautifully shaped breasts he'd ever laid eyes on. Both recognized it as pure lust, but felt comfortable enough to spend the night. In the morning they shared a coffee.

Five minutes earlier she'd been sleeping soundly. Amazingly, one wouldn't know it. High cheekbones shone with a natural glow. The natural color of her sensuous lips could never be duplicated with lipstick; even her short-cropped hair fell naturally into place. If she threw on an evening gown, I could take her anywhere — not many women can do that, he mused. Ana Lisa interrupted the thought.

"Good morning and thank you."

"For what?"

"Well, love is all well and good, but there's a lot to be said for pure fucking."

Milo sprayed a mouthful of coffee on her tee shirt, most of it striking her in the chest. The wet cotton cloth clung to her breast, bringing to eminence an erect nipple. They both stared at it and laughed.

"For sure, I'm not destined to teach you guitar, but I do know a fellow you might try. He's rather eccentric, but a fabulous guitarist. I'd be happy to at least get you an intro. He may work with you as long as he's in the area; he lives an hour's drive from Boston."

"What's his name?"

"A mouthful, Turan Mirza Avicenna."

"Where does he live?"

"He's laying low in New Hampshire right now, but normally lives on the West Coast, in Santa Barbara."

"Hiding? From what?"

"I'm not sure. His father is from Uzbekistan. I think

he's involved with the CIA somehow. Turan had a concert scheduled at the university there, and it had to be canceled because of a threat against his life."

"Right now I need to get my head straight. I'm heading up the coast for a while, but I'll call you when I'm ready. Thanks, I appreciate it."

Weeks later, Milo drove south, refreshed from the sabbatical, and ready to go forward with a plan to study the guitar. Amazing how things seem to fall in place sometimes. This is a good time to visit Turan, thought Milo He'd just crossed the Maine border into New Hampshire and needed gas. While the attendant filled his tank, he called Ana Lisa.

"This is Ana Lisa."

"Hi, it's Milo."

"Nice to hear from you. Thought you'd pulled a Casper."

"Kind of, I spent some time up north on Campobello Island, trying to get my head screwed on straight. I'm in New Hampshire and thought you might arrange a meeting with your guitar friend, Turan."

"Oh, I thought you wanted to fuck!"

"Not a bad idea."

"I'll give you the phone number, but I want to talk with Turan first. I'll let him know you plan to call. Don't be put off; he's a great guy."

Ana Lisa rattled off the telephone number in a husky flirting tone. Just talking to her got a rise out of him. Milo let it pass.

"I'll call him in a day or so."

"Thanks, I appreciate it."

"Good luck, Milo. Let me know when you're in the area again. We can have breakfast, but . . . after desert." She laughed.

Eccentric turned out to be an accurate description. Milo arrived in a secluded wooded area after a long drive down a rutted dirt way. When he ran out of road, he found himself at a well-hidden cabin and turned off the headlights. A square of luminosity broke the darkness. In the doorway loomed a man wielding a shotgun. A German shepherd, hackles at attention, eyed Milo, licked its chops and sounded a guttural warning. Turan glared at the dog and growled an order. "Calma te hombre, siéntese ahora."

The dog whined and sat. Milo had a second thought, but decided, what the hell. Turan used the gun to wave him inside. Black eyes gleamed between the antlers of a magnificent buck's head that hung over the fireplace. On the wall to the right, a boar snarled through purple-lipped, white fangs.

Turan looked a Tartar to the core — flowing moustache with a full beard and a hint of slant to his dark intelligent eyes. The dagger in his belt caught Milo's eye. Turan held out his hand. The large thick fingers looked unsuitable for guitar playing, but Milo felt their strength and sensitivity.

"Welcome, Damiani. Be at home. Have you eaten?"

"No, I've been driving all day and haven't had a chance."

"Good, I'm about to grill some venison. Ever had it?"

"No, but I like steak."

"It's much better if it's properly cured."

He handed Milo a goblet and filled it. "Compañía Vitivinícola Aragonesa, Barbastro. Spanish wine, one of the world's best-kept secrets. This one is from Áragon."

He went to the pantry and returned with a platter. "Pata Negra, Jamon Iberico, Spanish ham. The cheese is El Trigal, Manchego."

Milo put a bit of each on a cracker, took a bite followed with a sip of wine. "Unbelievable! Delicious! I've never tasted anything quite like it."

"Ana Lisa tells me you want to study guitar."

"Well, I do, but mainly to play a particular piece of music, not as a profession."

"Interesting, what music?"

"Bach's *Chaconne*."

Turan looked at Milo and smiled. "Hombre, you've only chosen the most difficult piece of music ever composed. It was written for violin."

Yes, my father played it for me when I was a child."

"My impression is you're serious about this."

"Yes, it's something I've always wanted to do."

"Let's discuss it after supper."

"Ana Lisa tells me your life was threatened and your last concert had to be canceled."

"True, but in any case, I'm finished performing. It was my father's dream, not mine. Let's eat."

After supper, Turan got his guitar, tuned it and handed

it to Milo. "Play something."

Milo's hands shook as he fumbled through an exercise. Turan raised his hand. "Stop. My friend, I can see you lack even a minimal foundation. Before we go any further, if you want to play the *Chaconne*, it will require more than you can imagine. You must first master the guitar, one of the most difficult instruments. Then you must know Bach, not a part-time job. You must give this pursuit your life, the difference between a want-to-be or a will-be. Will you give up your career, your life to the music? Are you willing to go to Spain to study? These are difficult questions only you can answer, and the most difficult is why. I can't help you, but if you decide you want to pursue your crazy idea, I know someone who will. His name is Antonio Ortega. He lives in Madrid. Ortega was my teacher. I will give you a letter of introduction if you wish."

It gave Milo a lot to think about. On the way back to Boston, he heard a radio announcement. Andres Segovia, acknowledged as the greatest classical guitarist of his generation, would perform there. Emerging refreshed from nearly a year of seclusion, and energized by his decision, Milo thought a concert would be an appropriate way to end his isolation.

Hushed murmuring of the audience bounced between the acoustically tuned walls of the auditorium. People were still filing to their seats, when came the soft chimes of the warning bell. The lights dimmed. In the semi-darkness, a young woman struggled to get to her seat.

"Ouch", he whispered.

"Oh, excuse me. I'm sorry." She laughed nervously, taking the seat on Milo's right.

"What's so funny?" he whispered, slightly annoyed.

"I'm so clumsy."

She wasn't whispering. Hearing the echo of her own voice, she lowered it.

"Sorry."

The red velvet curtains parted. An amber glow lit the stage, framing the lone chair in soft shadow. The hall fell silent, except for her cough. Shit, he thought.

"Sorry," she whispered. So am I, he thought.

An explosion of applause broke the silence. Andres Segovia ambled slowly towards the chair. His large, rounded shoulders made the ill-fitting dinner jacket appear comfortable. Polished rosewood found a home in his large hands and thick fingers. The ebony fret board made a perfect backdrop for the six gleaming strings.

Segovia sat and adjusted the footstool. Pushing his precariously perched glasses to a firmer grip on his nose, he bowed his head in humble greeting. He ran his fingers through his sparse white hair, stared at the audience, and waited for silence. Not a whisper. Not a cough. He began.

Effortlessly stroked with the fingers of his right hand, the exquisite sound strings reverberated throughout the hall. The audience was captivated by the richness and poetry of Bach's *Chaconne*. Milo had heard his father play it on the violin when he was a boy. Later, he'd listened to Segovia's recording. He'd been waiting to hear him live ever since. He listened raptly.

At intermission, Milo noticed her eyes. He saw in them her inner beauty and sadness. He walked over to her and smiled.

"My name is Milo. What's yours?"

She switched her drink to the other, extending her right. "I'm Chiara."

He grasped it lightly, feeling a tremble within its softness.

"It's nice to meet you, Chiara."

She blushed. "Nice to meet you, too."

They listened to the rest of the concert in silence. Afterwards, he invited her for coffee, and they exchanged telephone numbers. Milo thought himself too jaded to feel as he did, and being smitten triggered an alert. I will not be coerced into changing my plans, he thought. I'm going to Spain no matter how attractive she is.

He didn't call, but two weeks later she did, inviting him to dinner. He accepted, resolving to tell her that she was not included in his plans, but wondered if she even cared. Her apartment had immediate appeal to him. Its simple elegance matched her personality. Two watercolors almost hidden in an alcove intrigued him. One was of a windmill, the other of a pelican. Executed in delicate strokes, both bore her signature without flourish in the bottom right corner.

Tension tortured his testicles. Milo grimaced and looked into her eyes. They were of such a blue that anyone who saw them would know why they defied description. Her hair was the color of beach sand, the contour of her lips sensuous. Chiara reached for him. Her brows, furrowed around her delicately aquiline nose, mirrored his pain.

"What's wrong?"

Not knowing what to tell her, he lied. "Just cramps."

"Something you ate?"

"Wish it were."

He smiled at the private joke. "I'll be fine in a bit."

Concerned, Chiara had no idea she'd caused the distress. The ache eased. It doesn't matter how nuts I am about her. Nothing is going to stop me from going to Spain, he thought.

"Listen . . ."

She interrupted before he could continue.

"Are you sure you're all right?"

"Yes, I'm fine now. Listen. If you had come into my life at any other time, things might be different, but in three weeks, I'm leaving for Spain."

It would have broken his heart if she'd shown indifference.

"Oh? How exciting. A vacation?"

"No. I'm going there to study."

She lowered her head and stared blankly at her hands folded in her lap. "How long will you be gone?"

"Two, maybe three years, perhaps more. I don't know."

Like a projectile, the pain of her disappointment struck. She spoke through trembling lips.

"Oh well. Just my luck to finally meet a guy, someone who makes me feel something new and wonderful, for the first time in my life . . ." Her voice trailed off. "I'm sorry, never mind."

Chiara's lashes tried, but couldn't contain the brimming moistness that made her eyes sparkle like the shifting colors of an opal.

"You could come with me!" Seemingly devoid of volition, the words leapt from Milo's mouth, directly from the gut, without rationale. Milo was as surprised as Chiara. Her eyes widened, and for several pounding heartbeats, both stopped breathing.

She threw her arms around him. "Yes."

Milo held her tightly. The realization of what he'd done struck him. He took a deep breath. His heart slowed. He'd made an impulsive decision, but did not regret it. He looked directly into her unforgettable eyes.

"I really don't want children. Big house, fancy car, none of that stuff is in my plans. I'm opting out of the rat race. Understand?"

"Yes. And anyway, I can't have children."

He could barely fathom his good fortune.

"Can you live with it, a simple uncomplicated life?"

She looked directly into his eyes.

"Yes."

"Then marry me."

Chiara paused and smiled shyly, "With one condition."

Milo smiled back and thought, oh shit, here it comes.

"I don't want children either. Besides, it would be dangerous for me to conceive. But if ever I changed my mind, would you consider adoption?"

Milo thought, help me. I'll never be able to say no to her. He looked into her eyes. Without fear, doubt, or hesitation. "Yes."

They fell into each other's arms. Chiara's lips were like velvet magnets. She healed Milo's pain, most of it.

After a small wedding, they left for Spain, landing in Madrid in dead of winter. They had backpacks and pooled savings, enough money for two years, without working. Chiara had majored in Spanish and was fluent. Milo knew none, but spoke some Italian. Language would not be a barrier.

They cabbed from the airport and found a small pensíon (bed and breakfast) in the heart of Madrid. They took an immediate liking to the proprietors, Felipe and Vicenza, deciding to stay with them until they found a flat. Milo presented his letter from Turan and made arrangements to study with Ortega. Before he could begin, he and Chiara had to find a home. In a month he would meet Antonio for a first lesson, not much time to get settled.

After two weeks exploring the city, they found a suitable neighborhood on Cuesta De San Vicente, a small *barrio* between the Plaza España and the Palacio del Rey. They scoured the area asking neighbors if they knew of an empty flat nearby, but had little success.

As they strolled, trying to encourage each other, they came upon an overweight elderly woman struggling with an overfilled shopping bag. Milo offered to carry it and she gratefully accepted. Chiara engaged her in Spanish, and from the bits he could understand, he knew her name was Julia. He wondered why she asked most of the questions as if she were interviewing prospects. She finally divulged a *piso*, next door to hers, had been unoccupied for many years. Until now, she'd preferred it that way, but she liked them. Julia gave them the name of the owner, and encouraged them to see him.

Don Federico politely told them the apartment was uninhabitable, and he too busy to make it so. Milo fibbed, telling him that he'd much more construction experience than he had, and begged to see it. With a smile and a negative shake of his head, Don Federico gave Milo the key.

The moment they opened the door to the *piso*, they recognized it as home. Walls and ceilings were chalky with peeling paint. A terrazzo floor, covered with dirt and rodent droppings, managed to show its hidden beauty. Stray cats had used the patio adjacent the kitchen as a toilet. Because of the kitchen, they knew it would be home. The opalescent light beaming in reminded him of Chiara's eyes. Via stained glass, only sunlight would pass uninvited through the heavy wooden doors. With the look of antiquity, the stone hearth seemed a welcoming embrace.

They looked at each other and smiled. They felt safe. Milo asked Don Federico to install a new refrigerator, pay for materials, and he and Chiara would provide the labor. After many questions and six months rent in advance, he agreed.

It was a bone-aching task. They cleaned and painted the bedroom first. Camping in it, they completed the work on the rest of the flat. It required removing what seemed like centuries of crud. It took four weeks from dawn to dusk, but when finished, Don Federico was impressed. He offered them a perk — they could drop their laundry at the hotel one morning a week to be washed and pressed by evening. Otherwise, it would've been a washboard and elbow grease.

For furniture, they went to the Rastro, a Saturday street sale covering fifteen or more blocks. Almost everything and anything could be purchased, but there were no fixed prices, and Milo loved the haggling despite the language barrier. Speaking a bastard combination of Italian, Spanish, and English with gestures, he had little trouble being understood and never felt cheated. It was an adventure. Within a short time they'd furnished their home.

Milo couldn't bear the stench of cat urine and feces in the patio. He spent three days disposing of it, and then washed the patio with disinfectant. This endeared him to all their neighbors, and with slingshot and pinto beans he discouraged the cats' return, harming nothing but their pride. There would be no dead cats. To the delight of the other tenants, the patio, unusable for years, was now clean, sanitary, and relatively free of felines.

Chiara decided to take a job with a computer company and had left for work. Antonio would arrive shortly to begin a program of study he'd outlined for Milo. Their only contact had been indirectly through Chiara by mail because Antonio spoke no English. Milo didn't know what to expect, but it wasn't the dapper Dan who walked through the door.

Barely topping five feet, Ortega wore a brown fedora,

a calf-length brown, woolen overcoat, and tapioca-colored scarf. His stiletto-thin moustache seemed pasted on, and rather hastily at that. At first glance Milo couldn't determine whether it was the moustache or his upper lip that was crooked. They shook hands, leaving Milo to wonder how he could play the guitar at all with such small fingers, and crooked to boot. It turned out he couldn't. His long years of practice and study, along with a performing career were dashed by the onset of arthritis. Undaunted, he'd devoted himself to teaching, and developed a reputation as an excellent professor.

The language barrier proved difficult for both. Until Milo learned to speak Spanish, it would be mime, as Ortega was not about to learn English. Milo told Ortega about a goal to play the *Chaconne*, who also knew it was one of the most difficult pieces to play on guitar, requiring a high level of technique. To his credit, he took Milo seriously.

Milo began with several handicaps. He'd started at a later age, and finger dexterity had been established for less delicate tasks. Guitar technique requires that each finger move independently in a fluid, but strong stroke. As a pilot, Milo's fingers were conditioned to collectively grasp a control mechanism in each hand. Independent finger movements are rarely required. Additionally, he'd broken the thumb and one finger on his right hand and the carpel bones and two fingers on the other. Oblivious to these obstacles, he later thought that had he known the difficulty, he wouldn't have tried. He soon discovered it is more difficult to unlearn than to learn anew, an added value lesson. Milo realized some things were applicable to all aspects of life.

Five hours a day, he practiced the exercises and scales given him. To move a digit without another moving with it proved frustrating. In the limited space between strings, it created chaos. Milo invented. He'd tape small fishing weights to each finger to add resistance and created exercises to isolate and retrain the broken ones. His fingers moved as if rusty and no amount of oil would free them.

With almost imperceptible progress, Milo would have quit, but the *Chaconne* and his will would not permit it. He knew he'd play it one day. He focused on the journey rather than the destination. He didn't know it would be twenty years before he could play it with any semblance of coherence and fluidity.

Though Chiara had captured Milo's heart, no person had yet been able to breach the emotional fortress that housed his spirit. A succinct encounter at a luthier's shop changed that. Early one morning during a break from the guitar and teaching English, Milo strolled through the winding, narrow, cobbled streets of old Madrid towards Carrera's guitar shop. He watched the *porteros* (janitors) scrub and hose the sidewalks in front of their buildings, a daily routine he considered a good idea, given the propensity of older men to urinate on any handy building when the need arose. Casually accepted, nobody seemed to think it odd or crass.

As Milo approached a bakery, the irresistible aroma led him by the nose directly to the front door. He bought a barra, broke off a chunk, and then put the still-warm bread under his sweater. It felt good against the early morning chill. Canaries sang in chorus from sunny windows all along the street in delightful contrast to the morning traffic horns and motor revs.

Manolo Carrera had a shop a short walk from the Palacio del Rey. It drew guitarists from all parts of the world. Carrera guitars, superbly handcrafted of the finest woods, were valued for their exceptional beauty and tonal quality. Unlike many luthiers, Carrera's signature on the label guaranteed that he, not an apprentice, had made the instrument.

Wood, glue, and varnish combined to fill the air with an atmosphere that said: this is the stuff your guitar is made of. Manolo brought life to guitars as Geppetto had to Pinocchio. Manolo spoke to the one he worked on, and didn't hear Milo enter. Absorbed in the music that floated from the back of the shop, Milo didn't even notice Manolo, and walked past him towards the superb sound. There sat a young man not yet rid of his baby fat, but the music emanated from an ancient soul. Milo waited until he'd finished the piece, extended his hand, and introduced himself in halting Spanish. "Hola. Soy Milo."

"Nice to meet you. My name is Juan Miguel. Do you play the guitar?"

"Yes, badly, but I'm a student of Antonio Ortega."

"I know of him! My teacher and he studied together under the same master. You are American?"

"Yes. I'm teaching English here."

"Fantastico."

"Do you play Bach?"

"Of course. He is my favorite composer in all of music."

"Would you play something for me?"

"Sure, of course. I will be happy to."

Juan Miguel spent a few seconds tuning the guitar, and then brushed unruly chestnut-shaded strands of hair away from onyx-tinted eyes. Milo noticed how they shimmered with passion just before they closed and he stroked the strings. Slender fingers seemed to scarcely move to the opening bars of Bach's *Chaconne*. Milo could scarcely believe the feast. When Juan Miguel finished, joy filled both their eyes. Neither spoke, not wanting to interrupt an extraordinary moment, and then they embraced. In that instant, a lasting fraternal bond had been created. From then forward, they referred to each other as brother.

~ ~ ~

In Juan Miguel, Milo found not only a fellow lover of Bach's music, but one qualified to help him in the difficult undertaking he'd made his mission — to play Sebastian's *Chaconne*.

~ ~ ~

CHAPTER THIRTY-ONE

Johann Adam Reincken

In February of the following year, the hand of death struck again. Sebastian received the news that his brother, Johann Christoph, had passed on at the age of forty-nine. More a father, Christoph had been an inspiration to Sebastian. Two people closest to him were now gone. He must now depend heavily on Freidlina to help care for the children. Strangely enough, during this horrific period, Sebastian composed some of his greatest works, including the Brandenburg concertos.

An anguished Sebastian spoke to God. "What is it that You want from your humble servant? What transgression have I committed to be so deserving of Your wrath? Have You no mercy or compassion? Death has followed me closer than my own skin. Will You take everyone I love from me? You are the God of death, vengeance, and pain and yet without You, from whence shall my music spring?"

In a respite from despair, his long-time idol, Johann Adam Reincken invited him to perform at St. Catharine's Church in Hamburg. Sebastian couldn't believe the stroke of good fortune in the midst of his desolation. By that time, Reincken had reached the age of ninety-seven. After the recital, they had a chance to speak.

"Honorable sir, thank you for inviting me to perform. It has been my greatest pleasure to play for you."

The tired old man sat hunched over his cane. His bright eyes were buried in folds of wrinkles and unkempt white brows. His beard reached to the bottom of his neck. Sebastian took his hand. It shook almost in sync with his voice.

"My dear Bach, the Wasserflüssen *Babylon* was truly magnificent. I thought this art was dead, but I see in you it still lives."

Sebastian had kept his promise to his brother, Christoph. He bowed politely. "Most cordial, genial, and most gracious sir, I'm deeply privileged and honored."

He returned to Cöthen confused and lonely, but providence intervened. He had the good fortune to meet once again the young girl who had now come into flower as a fine woman, Ana Magdalena Wilcke, a soprano chamber musician to the court, its first woman and highest salaried employee. Although he yearned for Maria Barbara, he knew he must get on with his life. Ana would help with the musical education of his children and lift his flagging spirits. Sebastian would be pressed to keep pace with a woman sixteen years his junior. His enormous energy proved equal to the task.

Since they both had careers to attend, the help of Freidlina would prove to be invaluable. Perhaps the memories associated with Cöthen, or the wishes for a fresh start were motivations. Nonetheless, Sebastian traveled to Leipzig to audition for the position of cantor at St. Thomas

School, and musical director for the city's four churches. In an ironic cynicism, the Leipzig City Council noted in the minutes, "Since the best men are not available, mediocre musicians must be considered."

Offered the position, he now faced the proposition of obtaining his release from Prince Leopold. Sebastian arranged an appointment.

"Most honorable sir, it is with deep regret that I seek your release from my employment. You have been most supportive in my tenure here. However, it is my wish to leave Cöthen and begin anew in Leipzig, where I have been offered a position. I humbly petition your grace to accept my leave."

"My dear Bach, we have at all times been well content with the discharge of your duties here. It is with deep regret that I grant you a most gracious dismissal, with my highest recommendation for service elsewhere. God bless you in your new duties."

"Always a humble servant, your honorable grace, you have my sincere thanks and lasting admiration."

With that, Sebastian prepared to move his family and began the last phase of his life. They packed four wagons with possessions, boarded the family in two carriages, and departed for Leipzig. They arrived on May 22, 1723. Approaching forty years of age, Sebastian would use the remainder of his life to build a legacy.

Town Councilor Lehmann, chair of the St. Thomas school board, formally presented Sebastian to the student body in the upper auditorium.

"My dear Herr Bach, it is my immense pleasure to introduce you as Kapellmeister and musical director. I'm certain you will industriously discharge your duties of the office and show respect and willingness to the authorities. In addition, it is my hope you will cultivate good relations and friendship with your colleagues. I'm certain you will conscientiously instruct the students in the fear of God and other useful studies, and will thus keep the school in good repute. As for you, students, you will give obedience and show respect for the newly appointed cantor. God bless the school of St. Thomas."

"Most honorable councilor, I am most graciously pleased to accept the office which has been conferred upon me. It is my promise to serve with fidelity and zeal, and conduct myself in a manner that my greatest devotion should always be observed."

Sebastian and Ana Magdalena maintained an affectionate relationship. She became his confidante, assistant and partner. They also performed together regularly. With all of that, Sebastian and Ana would add thirteen children to the family, but the curse persisted. To an endless thump of coffin lids, the litany of death continued like a conveyor belt of caskets: Christiana Sophia, three years old, in 1726; Christian Gottlieb, two and a half years old, in 1728; Ernestus Andreas, one month old, in 1727; Christiana Benedicta, three days, in 1730; Christiana Dorothea, two and a half years, in 1732; and within seven months of each other, Regina Joanna, five years, and Johann August, one day old, in 1733. Words were not enough for Sebastian to describe the depth of his pain and sorrow, but they were manifest in his glorious music.

Freidlina, who had moved in to help with Maria Barbara's first child, remained in the Bach household for twenty-one years in all, serving Ana Magdalena with the same loyalty and devotion as she had for her own sister. On July 30, 1729, she passed on at age fifty-five. The emotional impact of the cruel tragedies spanning his lifetime may have overwhelmed an ordinary person, even in those difficult times, yet Sebastian bore his burden with dignity and courage. His vision of God, however, began to change.

~ ~ ~

An invisible thread spanning centuries connected Sebastian to Milo. More than teaching and inspiring, it worked in a similar way to the magnetic compass on an instrument panel in stormy weather. The pilot had to trust it, but Milo wondered about Sebastian's relationship with God. Even though the Church and the court paid him to compose, Sebastian's music seemed to be jazz in disguise. Unquestionably, Sebastian appeared to be deeply religious and baptized all of his children. On God and religion, Milo refused to be swayed by Sebastian, but did make a concession.

~ ~ ~

CHAPTER THIRTY-TWO

Adoption

Chiara and Milo had been in Spain a year. Milo progressed with his studies, and had six private English students. Things couldn't have been better for him, but he worried about Chiara. She seemed perplexed. He waited to see if she'd discuss it. She didn't.

As she readied for work, he poured a glass of juice, smiled, and gave it to her. "What's wrong, honey? You've been preoccupied for a week. Something's bothering you."

"Not really." Their expressions said neither believed it. She took his hand. "No, that's not true. Remember you said if I changed my mind about having children, you'd consider adoption?"

He tried to keep his composure, almost choking on his toast. Things were going too well. Here's the fan, he thought. Now comes the shit. "Of course, I remember. I thought *you* wouldn't. Just kidding. What brought this on?"

Animated, the words blew out of her mouth in one lungful of air. "Maybe it's just hormones or something. My friend Núria is having a baby. She looks so happy. It's all she talks about. It got me thinking. If we don't do it now, we may miss the chance. Besides, it'll be easier to adopt in Spain, won't it?"

Right, he thought. He knew he'd be unable to refuse her anything. "It will mean a lot of responsibility. Kids are worse than pets. You can't take them to the pound when you get sick of them. You're sure about this now, are you?"

"Yes. It's all I've been thinking about lately, but are you?"

"No." He tugged at his ear and tried to keep the mood serious. He could not. He rolled his eyes and threw his arms up in surrender. "If you're happy, I'm happy."

Though blindsided by the unexpected, and not keen about the distraction and responsibility, he would keep his word. The next morning he talked with the local parish priest, who put him in contact with the Church's internal adoption agency. He made an appointment and submitted an application. After two extensive interviews, they were told of a two-week-old child awaiting adoption in India. They were also informed that the coordination of the Indian, Spanish and American governments would be tedious, and patience would be required.

The bureaucratic nightmare could not be imagined. The paperwork was daunting. Two years passed without a decision or indication of when it might be forthcoming. Not wanting a child over two, they became discouraged and abandoned the adoption. He was secretly relieved, she depressed. The sadness in her eyes when they'd met had returned.

~ ~ ~

Isabél García Contreras, thirty-four years old and four

months pregnant, came from the Galician coast of Spain and now wandered the streets of Madrid, not wanting her family to know her condition. Her religious beliefs forbade abortion, so she entered a Catholic home for unwed mothers. Isabél agonized over giving up her child, but was determined to be involved in the selection of its future parents. Today, the Mother Superior had said that was forbidden.

Isabél left the home. Desperate, with little money, she found herself in front of a small pensíon, the one in which Chiara and Milo had stayed when they arrived in town. She took a room, and locked herself inside.

Felipe and Vicenza, owners of the pensíon, had become friends with Milo and Chiara. Felipe raised canaries as a hobby and when he found out Milo's love of birds, he'd given him a pair. Felipe and Vicenza had sponsored them in the aborted adoption process.

Isabél had been in her room for almost two days. Vicenza became concerned. She knocked lightly on the door of Isabél's room.

"Miss, is everything all right?"

Vicente put her ear to the door and heard Isabél weeping. She called softly, "Please. May I come in?"

Isabél opened the door. Vicenza wondered where she had seen eyes the color of the saddened one's that were fixed on her own. Vicenza's heart opened. She spoke reassuringly.

"What's the matter, my child? Tell me."

Isabél saw her situation as hopeless. Her shoulders

slumped. She covered her face with her hands and through her sobbing, tearfully told her tale.

"I'm with child. I'm not certain who the father is, but he'll never marry me anyway. My family knows nothing. I told them I was coming here for work."

"Dios mios, you can go to a home. There's one nearby. I'll go with you and speak with the monsignor."

"I was there. I left and came here."

"But, why?"

"I wanted to be sure that the child would have good parents."

"Surely it will have, Isabél. They will find a good Catholic family for it. You must go back."

"No, they won't allow me to choose them."

"Is it that important?"

"Yes."

"Very well then. Rest now. I will bring you something to eat. You must think of the child. I will speak with Felipe. We will think of something. Do not worry."

Isabél felt safe. For the first time in days she slept soundly. Vicenza told Felipe the story. He said nothing and went about his work. Vicenza brought Isabél dinner and reassured her that all would be well. She had faith in her husband and God. Vicenza set the table, and called Felipe to dinner.

"What can we do to help this poor woman? What about Milo and Chiara?"

"Milo was not disappointed when their adoption was unsuccessful; you must never tell Chiara."

"Of course, but Chiara was. Perhaps he will change his mind. Why don't you invite them to eat with us on Saturday? I will prepare something special."

Felipe called and extended the invitation. Milo and Chiara accepted. They had no idea that their lives would be forever changed. Milo burst through the door with his usual verve. He embraced Felipe, and handed him a bottle of Hernanderos Del Marques De Rascal Rioja. Felipe peered at the label over his bifocals. He nodded approvingly.

"This is much too fine for the humble meal Vicenza has prepared. On the other hand, it will no longer be humble."

Milo then wrapped Vicenza in a bear hug and kissed her cheek. Beaming, she wiped her hands on her apron, held his face between her hands and kissed him on both cheeks.

"Come to the table. I have prepared your favorite."

Vicenza had prepared a feast. First she served gazpacho, a soup made of crushed fresh tomatoes blended with cucumber, garlic, olive oil, and salt, and served cold. Paella, a rice dish containing sausage, chicken, and a variety of fish and shellfish, then followed. Barbecued over an open hearth and seasoned with saffron, it took on a glorious golden hue. The shellfish were positioned in a circle around the pan, intermingled with strips of pimento and wedges of lemon. It was beautiful to behold, and delectable to the palate. Afterwards, Chiara and Vicenza served espresso and tartas de plátano, a scrumptious banana tart.

Felipe had decided it would be best to speak with Milo first, to safeguard against any disappointment for Chiara. While the women were cleaning up, Felipe invited Milo to a brandy and a smoke. They went out on the balcony and lit up.

"Milo, there is a woman from Galicia, who several days ago came to us in great distress. Her name is Isabél She is with child. She came to Madrid to give up the child to the Catholic home for unwed mothers. They told her that she would not be able to know the adoptive parents, so she left and came here. I thought you and Chiara might want to meet her."

Panic almost caused Milo to choke on his cigar. He'd thought adoption a concluded issue.

"You haven't said anything to Chiara, have you?"

"Of course not. Why don't you give it a few days, and think about it? If you decide against it, the matter will be dropped. We will try to convince her to go back to the home."

In the days that followed, Milo stayed aware of Chiara's sadness and disappointment. Fuck it! I promised, he thought. We'll give it a last shot. On his way home, he stopped at the market to buy flowers. Chiara hadn't yet arrived so he decided to prepare something special for dinner. She was fond of gazpacho and the tomatoes were perfect. He'd surprise her. He hummed to himself as he peeled the potatoes for the tortilla, which she enjoyed. He lit the candles, uncorked a bottle of wine, and poured himself a glass. He smiled in anticipation of her reaction to the news.

When she walked through the door he greeted her with a hug. Revealing the flowers hidden behind his back, he bowed and presented them.

She smiled in delight. "What's the occasion?"

"It's Tuesday."

She laughed. It had been weeks since he'd heard her laugh or seen her smile. He poured her a glass of wine.

"I don't want to get your hopes up, but there's a possibility for us to adopt a baby." She was shocked.

"What? How?"

"There's a woman staying at Felipe's. Vicenza found out she had come to Madrid to a home for unwed mothers. She hadn't wanted her family to know. She left the place because she wanted to meet the potential adoptive parents, and they wouldn't allow it."

Chiara was speechless.

"If she likes us, we can file adoption papers. I don't want you to be disappointed if it doesn't work out."

She grabbed his hands and looked intently into his eyes. "It will work out."

There was no denying his feelings about it, but it would be anguish to see her let down again.

He called Felipe, and arranged for them to meet Isabél. Chiara was on a cloud; Milo under one.

Isabél sat nervously, hands in her lap. Worn in a bun, her brown hair looked sun-damaged. Her hazy blue eyes seemed not to match the ruddy complexion of her face. A stocky frame barely revealed the life growing within. Of sturdy, country stock, she could have been taken for Irish; her ancestors may well have been. Within a few moments they were all excited. The confluence of events seemed ordained. Chiara's joy told Milo he'd made a good decision. They spoke for hours. She told them of her background and her wishes for the child.

It was decided Isabél would stay with Felipe and Vicenza. Milo and Chiara would pay her living and medical expenses. Later, a sum of money would be given her to return to Galicia with expenses for six months after that. She requested not to see the child after its birth. All agreed to no further contact after she left the hospital. Everything was perfect, they thought.

Felipe recommended an attorney. The next day Milo made the call. Nothing could have prepared him for what followed. After the situation was discussed, it turned out it was illegal for foreigners to adopt Spanish children. How would he tell Chiara? She'd be inconsolable, he thought.

That proved true. For days she didn't eat or talk. He didn't know how to console her, and it caused him intolerable pain. He walked to the Plaza España, found an empty bench, and wept. The answer came as swiftly as a cobra strike.

Pain gone, he ran the four blocks home, and burst through the door. Chiara was in bed puffy-eyed and doleful. He knelt and took her hand. "Honey, we're going to have a baby!"

She bolted upright in bewilderment and pulled the

wisps of hair from her eyes. She spoke hoarsely. "What did you say?"

"We're going to have a baby."

"Are you joking? How?"

"I'm going to claim paternity."

Light jumped into her eyes. She flung herself into his arms and wept. He held her close, gently rocking till her tears subsided.

The following day they met Isabél, and he explained the plan.

She said, "Certainly the child is a boy. He is special. God has chosen you and Chiara to be his parents."

He had a cynical thought, but instead said, "Thank you, Isabél. He will be loved and cared for."

He made an appointment with a pediatrician at the British-American hospital. A portly, jovial man, Dr. Miguel Juan Cimarosa was almost a comic figure, every movement slow and deliberately executed at a snail's pace. He seemed strangled by his own tie. It appeared not to bother him. More likely a rooster would lay an egg, than the sparse hairs be able to hide the doctor's gleaming dome. Milo liked him immediately.

"Before you examine my . . . my girlfriend, I'd like to ask a question."

The doctor spoke passable English. In a deep bass voice, heavily accented, he responded, "Of course. How can I be of assistance?"

"We have an unusual situation. Isabél and I do not plan marriage. She doesn't want the child. An abortion is out of the question."

Cimarosa looked uncertain. "Is it absolutely out of the question? Is that your question?"

Milo smiled. "No, sir. It's just . . . since I'm responsible I think it best for me to take the child."

"And so . . . what?"

"What do I do?"

Amused, Cimarosa scratched his chin. "What do you do? What do you do? What kind of question is that? You keep it of course."

"Just keep it? Don't I have to go through some procedure or something?"

Cimarosa, a mischievous twinkle in his eye, spoke seriously.

"Yes. It's quite complicated. You see... there is this paper. Here in Spain, we call it a certification of birth. There is a line where you must sign your name. You do write, don't you? In any case, you can make an 'X.' Yes?"

Milo laughed. Cimarosa shook his head slowly and chuckled.

"You Americans, you complicate even the simplest of matters." He reached out and shook Milo's hand. "If your question is now answered, please allow me to proceed with the examination."

~ ~ ~

CHAPTER THIRTY-THREE

Miracle

Milo became directly involved in the activities of pre-fatherhood. Every month he accompanied Isabél to her visits with Dr. Cimarosa. Chiara, because of the ploy, was excluded. It didn't seem to bother her. She began spending time with Isabél in other ways. They would walk in the park and have lunches together. On weekends she and Milo would either cook dinner at their piso, or join Isabél, Vicenza and Felipe. Vicenza took an active roll to insure that Isabél had a nutritious diet. Isabél assisted in the chores. They developed a relationship similar to that of a mother and daughter. In many ways, the five of them grew into a family, and since Milo and Chiara were far from their own, they warmly embraced it.

All of them were excited about the arrival of the new member except Isabél. As her time approached, she became morose and depressed. Milo and Chiara worried she would change her mind. Milo suggested that they discuss it with Isabél. Chiara opposed it in that they might spook Isabél into backing out if she had doubts. Milo argued if she were going to back out, he didn't want it after the child was born. He put forward a plan. Felipe's brother would draw up a legal document, which would give custody of the child to Milo. The attorney pointed out that if she later changed her mind, they would have a legal basis to stand on, and the question of paternity would be his word against hers. At that time, there was no way to prove otherwise. The document would also be useful should the immigration authorities question Milo's status. Although Milo had some misgivings about expanding a deception, he saw no other way to give them some protection.

They used the U.S. immigration authorities as a reason for needing the document and approached Isabél. To their relief, she agreed. Though it gave them some security, they fretted over Isabél's state of mind. Milo decided to speak with Dr. Cimarosa about it on their next visit. "Dr. Cimarosa, I'm worried about Isabél. She has been depressed."

"It is not unusual, even in quite normal situations. In this case, she has also made a decision to give up her child. She has requested she be sedated before she has a chance to see it. Her wishes will be honored."

"Thank you, Doctor."

He smiled and spoke in a fatherly fashion. "*Calma*. Be calm and all will be well. By the way, my examination has shown that we will be seeing each other very soon. Please call my office when you are on your way."

Sure enough, Milo had left Isabél with Vicenza and returned home. There was a note on the door that there was a message at the front desk of the Príncipe Pio, Don Federico's hotel. They had no phone and he had arranged for them to have their messages taken there. Milo rushed up, and called Vicenza. It was time. He asked her to notify

Dr. Cimarosa, then hailed a cab.

At 2:00 in the afternoon, siesta traffic clogged the streets. The nerve-wracking trip to the hospital seemed to take forever. By the time they arrived, Milo feared she would deliver in the cab.

Dr. Cimarosa was waiting. With a hint of a smile on his face, but in a serious voice he said, "You seem unprepared for fatherhood, young man."

It was true. Milo didn't know quite how to act. Five months ago he would not have believed he would feel elated at the prospect of fatherhood.

"I would like to be present in the delivery room."

Cimarosa looked at him dumbfounded." That is not possible, I'm afraid."

"Why not?"

Cimarosa lifted his brows in thought. "Well . . . I don't know." Then, he said, "Calma — if you promise to stay calm, it can be arranged, I suppose."

Taken to a prep area, he dressed in the surgical garb given him and scrubbed according to instructions. The nurses, though skeptical at the unusual breach of procedure, were delighted and helpful. He looked about in curiosity when brought into the delivery room. Dr. Cimarosa merely pointed to a spot to his right and Milo stood there in awe of what he would soon witness.

Isabél looked up in surprise, smiled at Milo and took his hand. Within a short time, Milo could see the hairy top of the newborn's head begin to appear. With each contraction, the birth proceeded until a tiny, purple, and blood-streaked body emerged. Dr. Cimarosa clamped and cut the umbilical cord. A nurse suctioned the baby's air passages. Sedated, Isabél did not see her child. Offered the wailing infant, now a clean and healthy pink, he took the boy in his hands and marveled at its tiny fingers and toes.

A beaming Cimarosa said through his mask, "Congratulations, Papa."

In a daze, he quietly responded, "Thank you, Dr. Cimarosa."

As if in a dream, he walked to the maternity ward. He and the child were its only occupants. A short time later, they received their first visitors, Chiara and two trusted friends in on the secret. Lisandra, one of his English students, and Juan Miguel were to be godparents. Milo would never forget the look on Chiara's face when she saw and held her son for the first time. She beamed at Milo.

"It's a miracle! Thank you. I thought I'd never see this day, or even want to."

"Me either, but I'm glad we did."

They laughed, cried and talked about a suitable name and decided to call him Américo, meaning valiant prince. The charge nurse arrived, and in a motherly manner, shooed the guests out. She shook her head, laughed, and waved towards Milo, speaking in Spanish.

"The new mother and the baby must rest now."

After everyone had left, Américo needed to be changed. She instructed Milo on cleaning and diapering, and provided a bottle of formula. "This is to feed your son."

"When do I do it?"

"Give him the bottle when he's hungry."

"How will I know?"

She smiled. "You will know."

She picked up the child and held it to her chest, one hand holding its head. With the other, she patted it, Milo thought rather forcefully, on the back.

"This is to make him burp. You do this several times after he has taken some milk for a while. I will check on you later." She handed him the infant and left.

He sat on the bed cradling his son. He put the bottle in its mouth and Américo began to suck voraciously on the nipple. As he struggled to fit the diaper, he spoke with the son he hadn't wanted.

"There's no turning back now. We're stuck with each other for life." Américo yawned and pursed his lips. "I suppose you're going to keep me up all night. Fine, I'm not tired anyway. In a few weeks, you're going to be baptized. Don't take it too seriously. When you're older, I'll explain."

The next morning, Milo had just fed and changed Américo when Dr. Cimarosa sauntered through the door.

"Well, Papa, or should I say Mama," he chuckled, "let me see your son for a moment, please." He took the infant delicately. After examining the child, he said, "So, are you ready to take your son home?"

"I thought we had to be here for three days or something."

"That is only for the mother. Since you haven't done

him any damage over the night, he is fine and you may leave. Bring him to my office in two weeks. Okay?"

"Okay. How is Isabél?"

"She is fine. She will be staying another day or two."

A few days later, he met with Isabél. During her months of pregnancy, they'd established a bond as a result of their secret, and visits to Dr. Cimarosa. She'd rebelled against her faith, but hadn't abandoned it. One day Américo would know the truth about his birth mother and her fight to find him good parents. She looked pale and sad. He gave her a hug. He handed her an envelope containing her fare to Galicia and living expenses for six months.

"Are you sure you don't want to see the child? We named him Américo."

"It's a fine name. No, I think it's best if I do not."

"Thank you. Américo will someday know everything. Have a safe trip."

"I thank God for sending you and Chiara to me. I will never forget."

She asked nothing about her child. He did not see her again, but would remember her courage and determination. Her sacrifice and faith in him and Chiara would inspire them as parents. Milo wondered whether she selected them because they were special, or had she made them special by selecting them. Did it matter? He guessed not.

Fearful the authorities would somehow find them out, Milo decided that he must get a passport for Américo and leave Spain, a difficult decision because they'd been truly content. He loved the people, the culture, his English students, friends and neighbors. They'd become family. Most of all, a life steeped in music had brought him peace. The American Embassy informed him it would take ninety days or more to process the paperwork. It seemed more like ninety years. While they waited, he'd realized with a new family to support, flying, not music, would pay the bills.

After seeing an advertisement in the *International Tribune*, he wrote, asking for a position with Air General Helicopters, a company based near Boston. A shuttle service, it carried passengers from heliports on the "golden circle" to Logan airport. Many high-tech companies and major defense contractors, whose executives used the shuttle to avoid the horrific rush-hour traffic, were located near the highway encircling Boston.

He'd be flying turbine-powered Jet Rangers, replacing a drive of forty-five minutes with a flight of twelve. The chief pilot wrote back, telling Milo that Global Petrol Helicopters needed pilots. He suggested Milo apply for a job with them to increase his flight time, as Air General's insurance required all line pilots to have logged a minimum thousand hours of civilian flight operations. He wrote Global, and received an invitation to interview upon his return to the States.

In the meanwhile, the child's baptism was at hand. Don Federico dumbfounded them by graciously offering the use of the theater for the reception at his hotel, the Principe Pio and Milo's recital, which would follow.

Milo paid his mother's airfare first to Rome, then on to Spain, a way of keeping two promises. His mother arrived from a public audience with the Pope, a dream fulfilled. Now her baptized grandchild had his ticket to heaven, but Milo did not regret the concession. He'd never seen her more happy.

The baptism would be held at the local church, San Cristobal. Passing through the immense oak doors, Milo lifted his eyes to the massive dome, a canvas swathed in images of cherubs and angel faces glowing within auras of glory. The sheer purity of the art inspired by God could drive one to his knees in supplication. Cloaked in a veil of mysterious holiness, it brought shivers to those who yielded to its sacredness. Adornment and traces of wealth were everywhere. The ritual altar resembled a filigreed bank vault where the blood of Christ flowed in an endless procession of silver chalices offering salvation.

Chiara dutifully held the sacrificial child.

"*Benedictat vos omnipotens. Deus Pater, et Filius, et Spritu Sanctus. Amen.*

"*Dominus vobiscum.*"

"*Et cum spiritu tuo.*"

Out of the echoing silence, the words thumped against a pair of soundless drums. Milo swore his son would not honor an indenture he could not have understood, nor put pen to. The deed done, the fiesta would begin after the recital, as only Spaniards knew how.

Milo had never performed in public before. There would be hundreds in the audience: friends, students, neighbors and their families. Despite encouragement from Ortega and his friend, Juan Miguel, he felt inadequate. He'd never played in a dinner jacket. That alone meant trouble. Adding to the mix, Juan Miguel had composed a guitar suite for him at a level requiring more technique than he possessed. The final movement hadn't been finished until a month before the recital. At the expense of other pieces, Milo practiced hour after raw-fingered hour. It didn't matter. Disaster loomed with nothing to be done but suffer through it.

Milo took the stage to loud applause. With his mother and family in the front row, a sense of calm he hoped would materialize never happened. The trembling hand poised above the guitar obeyed a mind, but it wasn't his. He wondered how it would play the first note.

The first half proceeded shakily. At intermission, he spoke with Juan Miguel in the dressing room. "My brother, this is impossible. I can't play your suite. It will be a bust."

Juan laughed. "I have some inspiration for us." He held up a joint. Milo looked at him incredulously, "Are you loco? I can't play it straight! How will I play it stoned?"

"It will make you relaxed."

Juan Miguel lit up, took a hit, sucked it deep, held his breath and handed it off. He coughed, exhaled, and laughed. Milo thought, what the hell, how much worse can it get, and took a hit. Soon they were lost in a moment of hysteria. The warning bell chimed softly. Juan chuckled and winked a glazed eye. "Don't worry, my brother. It will be fine."

Milo walked onto the stage. A sympathetic audience politely applauded. He waited for silence. "My friends, thank you for such patience. You have suffered enough. I have a surprise. My dear friend, my brother, Juan Miguel, will perform his own composition!" Applause and whistles filled the hall.

From the first row, Juan looked at Milo, shaking his head, mouthing a word spoken the same in both languages — no. Milo smiled and beckoned, to another decibel of applause. Reluctant, Juan climbed three stairs to the stage. Back to the audience, he embraced Milo whispering through his laughter, "You fucked me good, my brother. I will remember."

"Have fun with your suite, since you're the only one who can play it."

The buzzed pair huddled on stage in hemp land. The oblivious audience erupted. Juan Miguel dazzled them with musical darts from his soul to their hearts.

True, the Spanish have their serious aspects; fiesta is not one of them. With the solemn and somber behind, the time for the wine, food, and love-fest began. In attendance at center stage, Américo settled for thumb and nap, oblivious to the pandemonium, a bittersweet celebration of friendship and farewell.

The new family departed Spain for a new life in America, symbolically Américo the only immigrant.

~ ~ ~

Flying put Milo in another place, but never as pilot-in-command. On the flight home, it wasn't a worry and thoughts flew through his mind like a 747 through clouds, sometimes dark, other times clear. Sebastian saw only light.

~ ~ ~

CHAPTER THIRTY-FOUR

Four Minor Children.
Hearse Gratis

Sebastian's failing eyesight grew dramatically worse in later years. It may have been due to a diabetic condition supported by the symptoms of eye pain, bad vision, and inflammation of the optic nerves. In April of 1749, it worsened to the point where city officials discussed options should he die, but Sebastian recovered, thanks to the services of an English oculist, Sir John Taylor, a specialist in cataract surgery.

The operation at first seemed successful, but ultimately failed. Sebastian opted for a second surgery, after which he deteriorated to a state of incessant illness. In July of 1750, now totally blind, Sebastian suffered a stroke. On July 28, racked with fever, his lucidity inexplicably returned when he opened his eyes and saw again his beloved Ana. The cool July evening was not inordinately so, but rare. The chill crept in despite fever. In a weakened voice he spoke, "Ana, my dear wife, perhaps a fire in the hearth will bring cheer and comfort to my bones."

She struck a fire, then tried to feed him soup. Sebastian refused. "Time hurries; I haven't much. I would dictate my last thoughts if you would accommodate your faithful husband by putting them to paper."

"Of course, my darling."

"I thank you for our years. You have been a loyal companion and mother. How could I have survived without you, since not a degree of help came forth from God?"

He laughed. She stopped writing as if to speak. With a weak forefinger to his lips, he bid she remain silent.

"Surely, you think I speak irreverently. Allow me to continue."

"But, you've just received communion; I don't understand."

"Only for the record, my dear, lest those council halfwits revoke my pension and leave you penniless. I've come to a different vision of God, not because I've suffered, though it did transform my thinking. The jealous, vengeful, punishing God in whose service I've been bound since birth shows human frailties. He reigns through fear and guilt. My God is not an image of me, but rather inseparable from me. In death I will not join God in an illusion of paradise. I'm already with him. Sorrows, joy and happiness are inseparable from life. Pain is not punishment for evil. I'm responsible for my spirituality, not for fear of retribution, but rather because God is the energy of pure love residing within. I cannot separate self from soul. Music is inspired by God within, not the three-part invention of man."

Thirstily, he asked for liquid and rested. Ana wrote for some time more. Eyes closed, he rested peacefully, hands folded over his heart. She thought he slept. He spoke.

"Have you noted my words?"

"Yes, Sebastian, I have."

"Good. Hand me the parchment, and draw the candle closer please."

For the first time in months he saw, carefully reading Ana's notes. He smiled and rolled them into a ball.

"My dearest Ana, perfection as usual. Burn it in the embers. The name Bach shall not be laden by what under-sized minds shall consider blasphemous."

Ana cast the crumpled parchment. It sprang to flame, briefly lighting the room, then turned to ash. Sebastian took a breath and slipped away. Faithfully, with honor, he'd dispatched his duties for more than twenty-five years. Yet after his death, the Leipzig town council voted to reduce Ana's pension. She died a pauper. Although he'd composed voluminous works, only a cantata was published in his lifetime. The original manuscripts were divided among his family, sold or lost. Not until long after his death did acclaim of his genius resonate. German composer, Richard Wagner, said of Bach, "the most stupendous miracle in all of music."

In the German language, Bach means little stream or brook. Ludwig van Beethoven said of Sebastian, "His name should not be Brook; it should be ocean."

An excerpt from the Leipzig burial register read: "1750, Thursday, July 30. A man, 67 years, Mr. Johann Sebastian Bach, Kapellmeister and Cantor of the St. Thomas School died Tuesday. Four minor children. Hearse gratis."

~ ~ ~

In an oddity of circumstance, all Milo had been taught by Sebastian would be needed for the next stage of his life.

~ ~ ~

CHAPTER THIRTY-FIVE

The Mission Continued

War and violence made little sense to Milo. His military service had served a single purpose, a flying career. Without regret, he would inter his memories of war without a funeral or any sense of loss. He looked forward to flying with Global. The company provided support service to the drilling and exploration industry worldwide.

Though Global hadn't been Milo's first choice, the work proved challenging and diversified. On a given shift he could be transporting passengers or equipment to rigs located a hundred miles or more offshore, along the Gulf from New Orleans to Galveston. On another, he might be flying external loads, laying pipe, or setting power line poles.

Milo logged enough hours with Global to qualify, and hired on with Air General, beginning in two weeks. A short-timer marking time, he wanted nothing more than to be home. Tonight would be his last with Global.

As the duty pilot at Morgan City, Louisiana, Milo would be on call from 9:00 PM to 6:00 the next morning. He and co-pilot, Sandy Peterson were on call for emergencies on rigs within two hundred miles. "Cocky" described Sandy, but Milo didn't mind, one of few pilots who didn't.

That they'd meet again had seemed unlikely. However, an explosion of oil exploration activities in the Gulf of Mexico and on the North Slope of Alaska fueled the company's rapid growth. The military, especially the Army, turned out to be its main source of pilots. Because of its willingness to accept higher insurance premiums, Global had become a transition point for military pilots seeking civilian flight time.

Sandy had hired on months before Milo returned from Spain, and decided to make a career with the company. He'd been flying a geological survey in South America. Assigned to Morgan City on his return, tonight would be the first time they'd seen each other since flight school.

On Milo's first work shift, Sandy hadn't yet arrived. Luckily they'd have minimal opportunity for more than superficial jabber. Milo's priorities didn't include social-izing, especially with ex-military types. He'd beg off to bed and avoid prolonged conversation. The restive state in which he now found himself demanded introspection — digging deep, picking scabs, probing wounds — or else continue in limbo between acceptance and change. Since there'd be no flying, Milo decided it a better use of time, preferable to an exchange of trivial pleasantries with a long-forgotten acquaintance.

Located below the control tower, the pilots' lounge sat high above the beach. It normally provided a spectacular view of the ocean. Not now in the fog and blowing scud. He looked out the window and saw nothing but his own reflection. The sound of rain grew louder, reminiscent of a platoon marching double-time, out of cadence. Rivulets of water on the pane seemed symbolic of all the tears he'd silently shed for the living, the dead, and himself.

Offshore flight operations in the Gulf were a challenge and at times dangerous. Waterspouts spawned from towering clouds could ruin a day. Frontal weather systems produced violent storms and furious seas. They didn't stop drilling, but did halt flight operations except for emergencies. Tonight's storm meant no flying, and Milo was glad. Besides being home and earning more, his new employment meant an end to offshore assignments. With things going his way, instead of elation, he felt depressed.

Milo poured a cup of coffee and opened the telegram that Chiara had forwarded to the Morgan City base. Postmarked from Germany, it was from Turan's sister. He hadn't seen or spoken to her since a visit to Berlin several years earlier. Oddly, Turan seemed to have dropped out of site again. As he tore open the message, he hoped it contained a way to contact her brother. Milo stared at the message as if the words would change. Turan had passed away a week earlier.

Shock pushed his body into the cushions of the chair, with all of its weight pressing out feelings of affection, sadness and regret. A fateful meeting with Turan had changed his life forever.

Turan had loved music, but ultimately abandoned the guitar in bitterness after spending almost a lifetime mastering it. Milo would never forget Turan's anger at the realization he'd lived not his own, but a father's passionate dream, and then missed an opportunity to reconcile it before his father died. Milo spoke to his inner voice.

"Turan is still helping me."

"Oh? How so?"

"I've just realized a couple of things."

"Shoot. I'm listening."

"For one, I'm fortunate to have resolved the issue of my dad's leaving before he died."

"What else?"

"I've never had to live someone else's idea of what my life should be."

"Right on."

"I now realize why I suddenly have regrets and deep sadness about Turan. If it hadn't been for him, I'd have never gone to Spain. Would never have met Antonio, or Juan Miguel. The list is endless."

"How about your great students? Wonderful food and wine is right up there."

"Most important of all, I wouldn't have met Isabél. Life is unimaginable without Américo. I never thanked him, or told him what a difference his friendship meant to me."

"There's an important lesson here — your first memory, Bach's *Chaconne*. Try to get above your life and observe it. From your first memory, a sequence of events transpired, and now, here you are. You will be able to see the uncontrollable events. More importantly, you will see the decisions and choices that were totally within your control. Certain things will become clear. You have total control of your thoughts, actions, and words, enough to create a masterpiece of your life."

"I'll work on it, but not now."

Milo tore up the telegram. The bad news and nasty night put a droop in his shoulders. A sure antidote would be the music of Bach's *Chaconne*. Written for violin, thanks to Turan, he now played it on the guitar. Intricate, majestic, a baroque dance.

He'd once read that an examination of the patterns in Bach's compositions and their careful placement suggested they were part of his prayer and meditation. Playing was the closest he'd come to prayer since abandoning any notion of God. Knowing Sebastian was deeply religious, he wondered what Bach knew, to flourish with his faith intact. Surely, he thought, the tragic events in Sebastian's life caused him to question the existence of God. Wouldn't they? Perhaps believing his music to be inspired by God, he feared the loss of inspiration. Milo smiled at the thought.

As he played it now, he thought how Sebastian's music had influenced him ever since he could remember — that and having lost his father. Gaining perspective or under-standing of his life seemed to him like trying to scrub a grease smudge with cold water. The emptiness wouldn't wash away.

On Sandy's arrival, Milo reluctantly put his guitar away. They sipped steaming coffee, noting the worsening weather. A cold frontal system, combined with the warm sea, produced heavy rain and violent thunderstorms.

Forty- to sixty-knot winds piled twelve- to fifteen-foot seas. Although fully instrumented, the Bell 204 would not make it any less dangerous a night to fly. All helicopter operations had been canceled. Emergency flights were at the discretion of the duty pilot.

"Well, Milo, great to see you again. It's been a while. See you made it back from Nam with all your parts."

"Got lucky, I guess. Good to see you, too."

"I hear this is your last night. What are your plans?"

"I took a job in Boston. I'll be flying out of Hanscomb Field, fifteen minutes from home. It'll be great to be with family. Besides, these fourteen days on and seven off are getting old."

Sandy chuckled, "The shifts don't bother me, but I wouldn't mind being closer to home. I lose two days out of my off time getting to Mississippi. I've decided to stay on. The benefits are great, and I may get a shot at managing a base on the North Slope."

"Why in hell do you want to go there? Winter is hell, and in summer, the mosquitoes are big enough to take you off for dinner."

"It's the money, man. They're paying big bonuses. After a couple of tours, you can come home with a good chunk of dough, enough to put a down on a house, or a small ranch."

"I suppose. How was your tour in Nam?"

"A joke. I got lucky."

He offered no further comment. Milo didn't pursue it and Sandy changed the subject.

"What a fucking lousy night, man. Hope it's quiet."

"Yeah! I don't want to be out in that shit, especially on my last shift."

"Hey, no problem, dude. It's your call. Nobody's going to get on your ass for not flying."

"True. Well, I'm going to turn in. I'm leaving for Boston tomorrow afternoon. Need some sack time. Later."

Tired but restless, he flopped on his bunk. He disliked bad weather. The stormy Gulf brought a memory of his rookie days, perhaps as a way to avoid the serious thoughts he'd promised himself to consider. It worked. Milo thought instead about "fat man."

Civilian flight operations had a totally different flavor about them — more than just not being shot at. Military helicopter pilots were prone to efficiency and expedience, not smoothness and finesse. Customers were not grunts outranked by pilots, and thanks for the ride, sir. Mostly high-ranking executives, engineers and technicians, they didn't appreciate a second helping of their last meal after rapidly falling like an elevator loose of its cables. A few such complaints and your job could be history.

Milo took pride in his skills. Even in emergency situations, his control movements were silken. Prudence is a large part of piloting. He would have been fired for the lack of it, but for intervention by a passenger, a friend of Global's president.

The mission seemed routine: transporting executives in Lafayette and New Orleans to Galveston. On arrival in New Orleans, he topped off his fuel tank. A large black man plodded towards the helicopter, a bag of tools in one hand and a newspaper to keep the weather off in the other.

At least three hundred pounds, he appeared wider than tall. A sleeveless shirt revealed Popeye arms. Milo knew trouble when he saw it. Already approaching gross allowable take-off weight with the passengers aboard, they'd be over max for certain. Flying out of a confined area, he would have bumped the man, but from an airport, the turf paralleling the runway could be used for a running take-off. He'd routinely flown over gross in Vietnam using that technique, and decided to bend the rules.

"New Orleans tower, this is Global Four-Six Golf requesting a running take-off parallel the active, en route VFR Galveston. Over."

"Roger Four-Six Golf. Winds northwest at fifteen knots, ceiling twelve hundred feet, visibility three miles in scud, altimeter 2992. Climb to and maintain nine hundred, immediate left turn heading 240 degrees to clear the pattern. Cleared for take-off. Over."

"Roger. Climb and maintain nine hundred, immediate left turn 240 degrees to clear. Global Four-Six Golf lifting off. Over."

"Roger, Global Four-Six Golf. Radar is showing what looks to be a squall line building about forty miles to the west. Might want to keep an eye on it. Over."

"Roger. Thanks. Four-Six Golf out."

The flight went as planned until weather had its way. Pea-sized hailstones peppered the fuselage. Visibility dropped to less than a quarter mile. Spotting a sandy beach along a lake rimmed with high trees, Milo circled and landed. A drum-roll of hail pelted the windscreen. When it abated, Milo tried tact. With a head thrust towards the green barrier, he singled out the fat man. "Sir, I'm sorry. I can't make it over those trees. We're carrying too much fuel."

"What? You got us in here, damn it." He pointed towards the rear. There's no tree over there."

"The winds are twenty-five knots and gusting. I can't take off downwind. You're going to have to wait here till we get another bird out."

"I gotta be in Galveston. If I don't get there, your ass is gonna be fired. Why doesn't one of the other guys stay?"

"Sir, both of them don't make one of you and your tools. Please help me out. Someone will be here as soon as possible."

"Fuck it, man. You can kiss your job goodbye."

Screw this fat fuck, he thought, but knew he shouldn't have taken him in the first place. There'd be no getting around that.

After clearing the trees, he circled for a last look. The hail had stopped, but the rain hadn't. Fat man sat on his toolbox, partly sheltered by pines, newspaper over his head. Serves the prick right for not carrying an umbrella, he thought, chuckling. He spoke to the passenger in the right seat.

"The guy can cost me my job. I took off from New Orleans over gross."

"Yes, but I did pressure you into it a bit, didn't I?"

Milo shot him a confused glance. The man winked. "Never mind. Just get me to Galveston."

Fat man reported and claimed Milo called him a nigger, and singled him out because of his color. The man who had cast the wink refuted the assertions.

Milo wondered about how easily he'd let his mind wander from serious contemplation. A chuckle could be better than a good cry. He'd had his fill of those; better than picking scabs too. He tucked the blanket under his chin and tried to sleep.

Sandy sat alone in the dome of the dimly lit control tower, sipping coffee. He ran his tongue along his military-trim moustache, cut flush with the top of his lip, a habit used to remove remnants of that which he'd imbibed. The lip bristle had been cultivated since his early teens, a symbol of manhood. Straggly ends drooped almost to his chin, serving to lengthen an already long face. With a sparse beard, useless to hide scars of acne, it took extra care to avoid a cut while shaving. Spotted dabs of toilet tissue dotted his cheeks like scarlet punctuation marks of futility. Scrawny, hopeless in sports and inept with females, if it weren't for success as a pilot, he'd likely have been a total failure. This sole triumph led to a smugness comrades found insufferable.

He had few interests outside flying, except a passion for comics. Daffy Duck and Superman were favorites, the latter perhaps because he was a pilot of sorts, and Clark may have possessed other qualities of envy. The night shift worked fine for him because flight operations ended at dusk, leaving him free of responsibility, other than emergencies. He stayed alert reading funnies.

A loud clap of thunder startled Sandy and made him uneasy. Bolts of fire pierced the darkness, a defiant counterpoint to the downpour and wind. Forgotten thoughts returned. A bullet had been his ticket out of Vietnam, but not from enemy fire or an accident. Anything could be bought there for a few cases of Salem menthols and your integrity.

He propped his feet on the desk and hunkered down with Daffy. The radio barked with urgency. Annoyed, he closed the comic.

"Morgan City, this is Fisher Two. Come in. Over." It was Jim Hartley, crew chief on Fisher Two, a drill rig.

"This is Morgan City. What's up?"

"We got a coon ass out here. Think his back is broke. He's in bad pain."

"Stand by. I'll let you speak to the duty pilot."

"Roger. Standing by."

Sandy buzzed Milo out of bed. Disheveled and fuzzy minded, he plodded to the radio room suppressing a yawn.

"Fischer, this is Milo. What's happening, Jim?"

"Guy out here. Think his back's broke. He's in a load of pain."

Sandy handed Milo the weather report. "Shit. Fisher Two, how about you put the guy on a crew boat?"

"Seas are high, rougher'n hell. Don't want to chance damagin' his spinal cord."

Milo took a deep breath. Flying conditions could not have been worse. He wanted to tell Jim no way. He spoke to his inner voice.

"Okay, what's going on?"

"You tell me."

"Why am I hesitant?"

"You tell me."

"Maybe it's because it's my last night?"

"Right, so why take unnecessary risks?"

"I can't be responsible for another death."

"Oh? Have you been responsible for others?"

"Knock it off. You know I have."

"I don't think so."

"What about the little girl who drowned?"

"What about her? If you'd gone in after her, you both could have drowned."

"Right, that's what I'm saying. I didn't try to save her, because I thought I might die."

"That's not about responsibility. You're talking fear and guilt."

"That's double-talk. I was afraid to die, so I couldn't save her."

"That's arrogance. What makes you think you could have saved her, even if you hadn't been afraid?"

"At least I'd have tried."

"That's another issue, courage."

"What about Erin?"

"Why are you punishing yourself? It was an accident."

"I was driving the car; she died. I was responsible."

"Was it because you were negligent?"

"No."

"It's pretty arrogant to think yourself responsible for unavoidable accidents. The way I see it, there's a lot of confusion here about fear, responsibility, guilt, and courage."

"Is that all?"

"Nope, there's anger."

Scenes came unbidden to his mind. A spring day turned dreadful and ugly. Guilt and pain still gnawed. So did anger. Would they never go away? Fuck! Not this time. I've got to get this guy. "Roger, Fisher, we're on the way."

"Sandy, let's boogie."

"Come on, buddy. Are you a nut cake? The weather stinks. You saw the reports, for Christ's sake."

"Cut the 'buddy' bullshit. We've got to get him in."

"You know the guidelines as well as I do. We don't have to do squat. Nobody will question it."

"That's beside the point. We've got to bring him in, so move it."

"Why, for God's sake?"

Leaning forward with challenge written in his eyes, Milo growled, "Are you flying or not?"

Sandy blinked, shaking his head. "Yeah, but it's nuts."

They gathered their gear and lit out for the hanger. Normally, the pre-flight inspection was done outdoors under floodlight, while topping the fuel. They'd do it under cover tonight. Hammering rain on the tin-sheathed roof meant shouting rather than talking normally. It suited a mood as foul as the weather. Adrenalin coursed through Milo's system with its typical response: elevated heart rate, sharpened focus, and a knotted gut.

Fear, which had always been a part of his life, came with a determination to overcome it. If not primary, it had proven a factor in choosing a flying career. It became an ally, an impetus for awareness, preparation, and technique. He'd need his hidden partner tonight.

Sandy did the preflight. Milo puzzled over stored bits of information in his brain. They wouldn't assemble or assimilate, not enough to give clarity to the niggling doubt about Sandy and the mission. It had been years since flight school. He had no knowledge of Sandy's competence during Vietnam except to what all pilots were subjected. Sandy had been tested, but evaded an attempt to flush out details. Many veterans were disinclined to discuss it.

Milo shrugged it off. Sandy's reluctance to fly in light of the dreadful weather conditions could not be construed as unreasonable. He'd ranked top dog in flight school, including instrument training, and survived Vietnam. You could screw up a simulation and get away with it, not the real thing, he thought. He exhaled a large lung-full of air. Sandy's credentials were impeccable.

The affirmation coursed through his body like a shot of morphine. On a personal basis, he thought, of all people to have as a co-pilot tonight, he wouldn't have chosen Sandy. Not a person he'd want to share a foxhole with either.

Sandy yelled, "She's fit to fly, but the log notes show a

bunch of radio problems."

The last pilot hadn't logged faulty electronics entries, but Milo didn't like the risk. He shouted to the mechanic, "Hey, Johnnie, got a spare radio lying around?"

The mechanic nodded.

"Okay, change it out."

Johnnie hustled a radio and towed the chopper to the helipad, pilots aboard. He topped off the fuel and connected an APU (auxiliary power unit) to conserve onboard battery power. Circling a forefinger, he signaled clearance to turn the turbines. Milo shouted "Clear," held the ignition switch in, and rolled on throttle, cranking in just enough fuel to avoid a hot start. It lit off with a muffled pop and the turbines whooshed to life. The rotor blades turned, flapping, as if trying to shed water, then became invisible. In the strobe effect, they re-appeared as a motionless solitary blade. Cockpit lights blinked in the blackness like cat's eyes watching. An instrument scan showed temperature and pressure gauges in the green. Sandy switched on the radios and keyed the intercom.

"How do you hear me?"

"Loud and clear. How me?"

"Loud and clear."

Sandy read off the cockpit checklist. Milo confirmed. They buckled in and adjusted their helmets, taking a few moments to gain night vision.

"What's our flight time out?"

Sandy did some calculations and gave an ETA.

"Morgan City base, this is Five-Four Tango. Over."

"Five-Four Tango, this is Morgan City."

"Roger, Johnnie. We're ready for lift-off. What are the winds?"

"Stand by. Winds are variable south to southwest at thirty, gusting to forty knots. Ceiling three hundred, visibility a quarter mile in rain and scud."

"Thanks, Johnnie. Estimate to the Fisher is one hour, three two minutes."

"Roger, Milo. I'll let them know you're on the way. Morgan City out."

He brought the helicopter to a hover, turned into the wind, and pushed forward on the cyclic. The chopper ascended into the dark and turbulent clouds. Nothing to be seen or said, they flew without conversation. Whining turbines and thumping blades underscored their silence and tension. In and out of visibility, they flew on instruments. Milo desperately hoped for a visual approach when they arrived.

The intercom came to life. Sandy groused, "What was that stupid fucker doing out there in this storm anyway? They should've shut down operations."

"They never shut down. Maybe it costs too much. It doesn't much matter."

"There are a thousand things I'd rather be doing right now."

"Forget it and focus on what you're supposed to do."

"My, aren't we testy."

With his shortened fuse, he wasn't of a mind to humor Sandy. Before he could respond, the radio squealed again.

"Five-Four Tango, this is Morgan City. Over."

"Roger, Johnnie. This is Five-Four Tango."

"Yeah, Milo, I just got an alert. The weather is deteriorating. Conditions are ripe for spouts along the front."

Shit, just what we need right now, he muttered. "Roger, Johnnie. Don't know how in hell we'd see them in this crap, but thanks. Five-Four Tango, out."

"That's roger. Morgan City out."

A few minutes from Fisher, Milo checked in. The radio crackled. He adjusted the squelch.

"Fisher Two, this is Five-Four Tango. Over."

"Five-Four Tango, this is Fisher Two."

"Roger, Fisher. We're about twelve miles north at three thousand on a long final. Fire flares. Over."

"Roger. On the way."

They broke out of the soup at about five hundred feet. The wipers couldn't keep up with the rain, and fierce winds slammed the chopper around the sky like a tennis ball. Milo had all he could handle to keep it airborne, straight, and level.

A glow illuminated the blackened clouds. Refracted by the raindrops, it shot thousands of laser-like beams in all directions, an unforgotten scene from hell, reminiscent of Vietnam. A thunderstorm rapidly closed on the rig. There'd be no getting around it, but it might be avoided if they moved fast. "Fisher, this is Five-Four Tango. Let's get it done before that monster hits."

"Roger that, Milo. We're ready."

Milo barely got the helicopter to the rain-slickened

helipad. Impatient, as two roughnecks and a paramedic placed the stretcher aboard, he scanned his instruments and prepared to lift off. The paramedic's voice came over the intercom.

"It's all clear back here."

Pre-flight done, Milo powered the turbines.

"Get on the gauges. I'll stay visual, and try to outrun that storm cell."

"Roger. I don't know, Milo. It's getting hairy. Are you sure we ought to do this?"

"I'm sure as hell not going to sit on this rig for two days. The food stinks, and the crew chief likes young pilots, buddy!"

The helicopter jumped off the pad into the gusts and Milo maneuvered into a climbing left turn, leveling off at four hundred feet in thick patches of fog. He decided to let Sandy go IFR (instrument flight rules).

"Okay, Sandy, we're on the gauges. Take her on up to three thousand. You've got it."

Sandy took the controls as if he'd be electrocuted by their touch. Like a python throttling its prey, fear slithered around him.

"Roger. I've got it."

Releasing the controls, Milo sucked in a deep breath. He watched the altimeter winding through the numbers, as Sandy climbed through twelve hundred feet. Slowly exhaling, his nerves settled. No matter his foreboding, Sandy's skills were above reproach. Whatever bugged him, Sandy was competent or he wouldn't be here. Am I competent, Milo wondered. Thoughts pinged in his head like radar, seeking to register a motive for the madness that exposed them. What am I trying to prove?

Milo settled in his seat and tried to relax by dialing in some soothing music. It was soothing, but not the music of his earliest memory. How did he get from then to now, he thought?

A loud explosion broke the spell. The helicopter lurched and the gauges went haywire. Milo shouted into the mike, "What the hell's going on?"

Sandy didn't respond. He sat like a stricken statue, head down. Milo grabbed the controls. "I've got it!"

Without a copilot, dependent solely on the magnetic compass, he flew by instinct. He bottomed the collective, sharply changing the pitch of the rotor blades, plunging them seaward. At two hundred feet, in a steep left turn, the visibility improved slightly. In the illumination of lightning bolts blasting aside, the dark, white caps appeared through the fog. Milo brought the helicopter straight and level a moment before disaster. In the middle of a vast ocean, they were trapped in a cocoon of raging elements. Silent flashing light gave Milo a glimpse of a horizon between water and hovering clouds, as he leveled off at fifty feet. A sudden down draft could plunk them in the sea at any time.

With limited visibility, he took an approximate heading towards Morgan City. After fifteen minutes, the situation worsened. Patches of fog swirled about like ghosts on a hunt, a dangerous mess at low altitude.

Without instruments, they hadn't a prayer. There were tall rigs all over the Gulf adding to his worries.

"It doesn't look great. This shit is getting thicker by the minute. Check with the medic and see if everything is okay back there."

Sandy didn't respond. Milo thought their chances of climbing up through the storm were next to nothing, especially without Sandy's help. Milo now had serious doubts about the rescue. Chances were now greater they'd end up as fish food. Shit! Get your head back into the cockpit, he thought.

"Sandy! Damn it! Check the fucking passengers. Then take a look at the map and find a rig. For Christ's sake, move it."

"Roger. Sorry, Milo."

"Forget it, man. Just find us a place to put this thing down."

Their only chance was to locate a platform while they still had visual reference. Then if they went blind, he could pop the pontoons. In these seas, chances they'd remain upright weren't great, but might get off an S.O.S and survive. Sandy's cockiness and self-assurance were gone but he'd deal with it later. His voice sounded hopeful.

"There's a rig about twelve miles northeast of Fisher. I figure we must be within a couple of miles. We could fly a map a segment search to locate it."

Well-mapped for navigation, the Gulf had been divided into numbered block segments to locate fixed rigs, but they were moved frequently. Thankfully, Sandy fastidiously kept his map current. "Sounds like a plan. Plot it and give me a read-out."

"Roger. Will do."

In this soup, the best chance would take luck — lots of it. Sandy calculated the coordinates and gave them to Milo. The fog thickened. In a matter of minutes they'd have to ditch. Without radio, the battery-powered beacon would output a distress signal. Sandy shouted, "I think I see lights. Turn right Zero-Five-Five degrees."

"Roger. Turning right, heading Zero-Five-Fiver degrees."

As it came into view, Milo's heart took an express elevator to the pit of his gut. "It's not a rig. It's a service vessel, with no fucking helipad. Might set down on a cleared deck with no guy wires though. Maybe the captain's savvy. If not, I'll ditch it here and they can pick us up. I'll circle."

He flew a tight pattern around the boat. Besides the deck being clear of obstacles, the vessel had to be into the wind. With a gust spread of thirty knots or more, and nine- to twelve-foot seas, it would take nerve, skill, and luck to get down on what looked to be a giant water coaster. The flurry of activity below appeared to be worker ants taking care of business. The captain knew his stuff, but could he get it done in time?

Fifteen minutes later, the vessel nosed into the wind. The ship heaved like a whale in heat. With poor visibility, spotlights on deck made matters worse. Milo started a practice approach to time the swells. If he miscalculated there'd be a meeting, but not the board of director's. The touchdown had to coincide with the downward motion of the vessel, and only one shot at it. Fog turned the rehearsal to show time instead, and Milo banked a hard turn to a short final approach.

The rolling deck seemed a target in a shooting gallery as Milo brought the helicopter to a hover over the stern. When it began to drop, he inched down and forward as the deck floated upward. He rolled off the throttle, hoping not to be heaved into the sea. Not finesse at its best, the helicopter slammed to the deck intact. Milo applied the rotor brake, and worried the blades wouldn't chop the tail boom. The crew lashed the chopper to the slick, rolling deck.

Milo relieved a chest-full of air, but an adrenaline-flooded heart took more time to normalize. Every nerve end yet quivered danger. Sandy patted Milo's arm. "Hairy, man. Great job, dude. Can't figure what the hell got into me. I just ate it."

"Yeah, lucky you found this tub. Thank Christ the skipper had it together. I want to kiss that man's ass without barfing on the poor bastard. I think I'm sick."

"Use the bag. Puke makes me vomit. I'll check on the medic and see if things are cool back there."

"Roger that."

They rode out the storm, sipping coffee on the bridge, watching stars peek through the fast-moving cloud breaks. The captain, nonchalantly deifying the rolling deck, waddled over with a printout. "Radar indicates weather improvement within the hour, but several large cells are still boiling along the front between here and the beach."

Milo didn't want conversation. Near disaster had left his tank empty, but he wondered at the euphoria of walking a wire between life and death. Fear and death, the boogie man twins. I'm still standing. That's the power of it, he thought.

"Thanks for the hospitality, skipper. We'd better crank her up, and move out."

"Yer' darned lucky, son, I'm glad to be in the right spot at the right time."

The captain maneuvered into the wind. Milo cranked up the turbine. "Sandy, give us a walk around. Make sure all tie downs are off. Ask the captain to radio Morgan City with our position, time of departure, and ETA."

Milo lifted off and climbed to six hundred feet. Still marginal, the weather markedly improved. They set course for Morgan City. The euphoric glow felt like a Tylenol with codeine. Sandy had come to grips with a hidden goblin and Milo understood. Without acting like a shrink, he made a gesture to get him over the hump.

"We ain't home free yet. Radar is showing a lot of weather between here and the beach and we've got nothing but a mag compass. My butt is whipped. I feel like cow shit in the middle of a stampede. I need a break. I'll bring her in when we hit the flats. You've got it."

Sandy's rump would have rocked and rolled to wag it off, if he'd had a tail, but his eyes were locked on the gauges.

"I've got it."

Milo let loose of the stick, leaned back and propped his feet on the outcrop below the windscreen. "What a helluva way to end my last shift. I've had my fill of this shit. I don't know how those guys do it out here for weeks on end. I ain't gonna miss it, guaranteed."

"Yeah, at least we get to the beach every day. Some of those poor bastards are out twenty-one days at a clip. Three weeks without pussy."

"Right, like the coon ass in the cabin. He won't be doing anything but his pillow for a long time."

"Been there, done that. Not the broken back, the pillow."

"What happened?"

"Clap, dude. Clap happened, but the sloe-eyed lady was worth it."

"Never had it, don't want it. Yup, ain't' nothing like pus drool to make you think with your higher brain."

"Listen, dude, not to change a juicy subject. I don't know what made me bail like that. I'm sorry."

"It could just as well have been the other way around. Probably something you ate, like a bad piece of snatch maybe?"

"Anyhow, I'm sure glad you were in the left seat."

"Well, I screwed up too, man. I should have topped this off on the boat; they run on diesel. We used our reserve hunting for anything but water to land on."

"Yeah, but we should make the beach with no sweat."

After they had flown for about forty minutes, Sandy shouted, "Well, I'll be dipped in shit! There's the light, I think."

"Yeah, I see it."

It was the pulsing beacon of Morgan City Hospital faintly blinking through the fog.

A weird vision of two bloody fingers dancing on a chopping block popped into Milo's head. "Morgan City, Ralph Bishop's home digs. Good old Ralph. If it hadn't been for him, I wouldn't be here at all." He wondered why it hadn't occurred to him before.

"Who's that?"

"Just an old ghost-friend from the past."

Milo adjusted his seat and scanned the gauges. Abruptly, the fuel warning light flashed and the audio blared in a frenetic duet. He switched off the acoustic and lightly took the stick.

"Right on. I've got it."

Sandy let loose the controls. "You've got it."

Visibility in the driven rain was next to nil. Milo banked tight right for a final approach. The moment he felt assured of survival, the turbine went silent. The blade thump stopped, his chest pump galloped. He bottomed the collective and put boot sole to the left pedal. It counteracted the torque and stopped the chopper from imitating an eggbeater.

It fell like a brick with blades. When the helipad just about slid from view through the windscreen, he pulled back on the stick to decelerate, pulled up on collective to increase blade pitch, which cushioned the landing. The helicopter lit dead center of the helipad.

Attendants rushed from the emergency room with a

gurney, but a sudden movement to Milo's right caught his attention — a man with a neck brace running, the man they had just rescued. Milo watched, astounded, as the man tore the brace off, and just kept trucking. It was almost comical. Bewildered, the attendants stood rooted as he disappeared into the pouring night. The man had been faking! He had apparently just wanted off the rig.

Angry and drained, Milo pulled off his helmet and slumped back in his seat. He covered his eyes and thought about having risked his life and that of others for a malingerer's selfish whim.

"What the hell, Sandy. Ain't that the cat's ass? Is this some kind of cosmic joke?"

"Naw, the dude probably just needed to get laid."

Milo laughed.

Several weeks after the Mission, Milo's physical exhaustion couldn't undermine the clarity of purpose, and sense of well-being he was feeling. The seeming aimlessness of his life path hadn't been so at all. While going in circles, he'd been in charge of both compass, and helm. Suddenly obvious, were the choices he made versus the ones he'd abdicated to the wind and tide. He realized it now, even with the events over which he had no control there was choice of response. He could react, or act, and reaction was nothing more than action, without thought. He spoke to his inner voice:

"What a trip. One mission completely changed my life. I've commuted a sentence of life self-imprisonment. I'm free. It feels so good!"

"Yes, you literally freed yourself from self-imposed condemnation and victimization. And this freedom was not bestowed or defined by God or man. You are your own redeemer."

"Holy shit, what a life!"

~ ~ ~

CHAPTER THIRTY-SIX

Coda

Many years later, Milo could not resist the exotic lure of Iberia and returned to retire in Spain. Today, on his ninety-fourth birthday, the descending Spanish sun silhouetted the willows in the glen, surrounding his villa in San Lorenzo de El Escorial. His son, Américo, and good friend Juan Miguel, had partnered in the country house in El Escorial, where he now lived.

Milo took a large breath of the 'aire del cielo.' The sweet fresh mountain air filled his lungs; flooded body and spirit with inner peace, harmonious with the tranquil scene around him. The immense palatial monastery, built by King Philip II in 1563, cast a mystic shadow of sapphire irony over the twilight landscape; a monument to a faith Milo had long ago discarded. In the soft autumn wind, willows in the surrounding glen seemed to wave farewell. He understood.

The falling dusk found busy barn swallows darting to and fro, on last-minute bedtime chores. In Spanish lore, a person who dared kill one forfeited eternal happiness and would be struck blind to the free blue sky. Eternal happiness, what is everlasting happiness, he mused.

Just then, Américo crept up behind his father and kissed him gently on the cheek. Milo touched his son's hand and pointed to the palace. "Look at those massive balustrades, Américo. They remind me of a poem. "In fear we seek to hide. Brick by brick the prison ramparts rise. Slowly blocking out the light until in dark and cold only breath, parts life from death.'"

Milo smiled and let the moment pass. He spoke with delight in his voice. "Your godfather is coming soon. We will dine together, only the three of us. Juan Miguel will prepare one of his feasts and treat us to some wonderful inspiration from Morocco!"

Américo's eyebrows skipped upward a notch. He grinned and said, "We will be very much inspired. He should cook enough for six!"

"Yes, and we will eat all of it. How is your mother?"

"Not well. She doesn't recognize me when I visit. You know, I always wished you'd still be together."

"Me too, I didn't know how to keep her."

Juan Miguel arrived carrying three glasses and a bottle of wine. "Américo, it's so good to see you."

"Tito, you look fantastic."

They embraced. "Thank you, Américo. I remember the first time you called me Tito. You were only four years old. It seems like two days ago."

Smiling, Juan Miguel turned to Milo and hugged him. "My brother, you look so happy."

But for the white hair, Milo thought his good friend looked almost as he had a half-century earlier. "How could I not be? Did you bring your baby?"

"No, not mine. Later I will play *your* guitar."

"You have my special cocktail, yes?"

Juan Miguel took Milo's hand and locked eyes. "As agreed, my brother."

The three sat in lively conversation sipping wine until the sun vanished below the horizon in a pretentious exodus. Américo spoke. "I'm starving. I'm going to be your chef's helper tonight, Tito."

"Yes, but first let us smoke some inspiration."

Juan Miguel lit and handed to Milo what appeared to be a cigarette, filter and all. Milo took a deep drag, and passed it to Américo, who took a puff and choked. When he had himself in control he said, "Are you trying to kill me, Tito?"

"No I'm not, but anyway, what a way to go!"

Milo looked on amused, as Juan Miguel and Américo appeared to have every possible kitchen utensil in use. Wine and weed entered their mouths as elixir and out flowed jovial banter.

Américo threw a couple of logs onto the hearth and within moments, flickering shadows capered about the den in a lively ballet. The three began to feast on a myriad of fare scattered about the table, which included many of Milo's favorites. As always, he reached first for the bread. Juan Miguel tossed him a knowing grin and said, "The crust is so perfect." Américo interjected. "Dip it into the chicken sauce, it's delicious."

Juan Miguel, mischief in his eyes, spoke over a mouthful of food, "It isn't chicken, it is *huevos de los toros*, you know? Bulls' balls."

Américo swallowed hard and took a gulp of wine. "What!" he coughed."

"Don't worry, they make you strong. You know? Like spinach does for Popeye."

Milo chimed in. "Try the cabezza de cordero. It's goat's brain. Prevents Alzheimer's."

"No thanks," said Américo. "I don't think I want to remember. Besides, Pop, it hasn't helped you any."

"It's because I keep forgetting to eat them."

For two hours they ate, drank, and enjoyed the Moroccan. Milo leaned back in his chair and rubbed his stomach. "It was exquisite, my brother."

"I couldn't eat another ball!" said Américo.

Juan Miguel guffawed. He rose, bowed with a sweeping gesture aimed towards Américo. "It was prepared with pleasure and love by me and my disabled collaborator."

A bottle of Lustau Solera Reserva suddenly appeared from behind his back. "This is the very best Spanish Brandy, so let's enjoy with a toast. *Hasta la vida infinita.*"

"Until infinite life," they chorused, and then Milo and Américo got into a conversation while Juan Miguel tidied up.

Milo lit a cigarette, took a puff, and blew out a swirl. He watched it rise to the rafters, and then smiled. "You've been a wonderful son. No father could ask or expect more."

"Thanks, Pop. You haven't been so bad yourself. You should really try to give those things up."

"Why? I enjoy it. Should I give up my scotch, and wine too? I'm ninety-two years old. It's not going to kill me. I guarantee it. If it bothers you, Tito and I can smoke outside."

"No, enjoy. It isn't any worse than downtown Madrid." He paused reflectively, and then continued. I'm thankful of how fate conspired to bring us together."

"Fate? We have the power to create it."

"That's what tonight is about isn't it?"

"Exactly."

"To prove it?"

"No, I have nothing to prove. My life is proof enough."

"Pop, you're not dying of a disease, are you?"

Milo chuckled. "As a matter of fact, I do have a terminal illness. It's called life."

Américo looked, straight-faced, into Milo's eyes. "Everything I've learned about truth shines in your eyes right now. Tell me straight on. What's happening here?"

"It is very interesting. Each day, I am less sentient, sometimes totally unaware of the corporal world. During those cataleptic episodes, my mind somehow still reasons."

"Wait, do you mean, you're not asleep, but sort of daydreaming? Is that what you're talking about?"

"Call it what you will, but while there, I can think, imagine, and see everything in my mind's eye."

"That's interesting. What's the problem, do you think you're delusional?"

"There is no problem. During those times I, for all purposes, no longer exist in the physical world. I'm totally alone."

"So, you're lonely."

"Not at all, but I'm spending more time out of touch, actually enjoying it.

Américo went solemn. He brought a chair around to face his father. He saw swaying willows and the stalwart stone citadel of El Escorial, reflected in Milo's eyes.

"Pop, all of my life, you've had this fascination with Bach's *Chaconne*. What is that all about?"

Milo took a momentary reflective look at a non-existent point off in the distance, and then his eyes re-focused on Américo. "The first time I heard my father play the *Chaconne*, I was three years old, I heard truth in it, and that led me on an astounding journey."

"Truth? How could you know what it meant when you were three years old?"

"When metaphorically spoken of as the ring of truth, it is an inner bell one hears. Once, when you were only weeks old, I asked Tito to try something. He played his guitar for you. You smiled when he played happy music, and cried when he played a sad piece. How did you know the music was happy or sad? The most important thing is to trust the pure knowledge you were born with. It is not filtered or tainted by ancestral influence, be it your mother's or mine, or that of educators, state, and most importantly, religious dogma."

A grin rippled across Milo's face like a banner of white.

Américo nodded knowingly. Milo sprawled stiffly back onto the divan, hands behind his head. He turned to Juan Miguel. "My brother, will you play for us?"

"Of course I will. Give me a moment."

He returned and handed Milo a dark goblet. Milo emptied it and embraced his friend and said, "Thank you for your friendship and acceptance of me, just as I am. I love you."

"*Gracias por todo que compartimos, a mi hermano. Te quiero mucho.*"

Juan Miguel took Milo's guitar, dark with age, out of its case, and tuned the sixth string to D. His right hand appeared to be motionless and the other ambled gracefully among the strings like a blindfolded high wire artist; the powerful first chord of Bach's *Chaconne* pervaded the room.

The euphony of Bach's musical prose settled around Milo like a down comforter. With a glow of warmth, it percolated deeply, seeming to reach to the very marrow of his bones.

In that epiphanic instant, Milo perceived a microcosm of the human condition and dualities; loss and triumph, fear and courage, pain and bliss, sorrow and joy, denial and acceptance, anger and everlasting love, all embodied in Bach's glorious dance of life, death, and continuum. He smiled.

Américo embraced and kissed his father, and whispered. "You're right. It is beautiful, pop."

"Yes, everything you need to know about life is

expressed in it. I love you too, Américo. Having you in my life has brought me more joy than I deserve. Forgive me, but I'm sleepy now."

Milo lay back closed his eyes, enjoying the music he so dearly loved. Américo stroked his father's brow. "I love you, Dad."

As always, Milo spoke to his inner voice.

"Life gave me more than my money's worth."

"But for everywhere you have gone there are more places to go. For everything you have touched there is more to touch. For all you have seen there is more to see. For all you have heard, there is more to hear. For all you have smelled, there is more to smell. For all you have tasted, there is more to taste. For all you have carried in your heart, there is more to carry. For all that you have conceived in your mind, there is more to conceive."

"I know the poem. It goes on — "My spirit is connected to all that is. It has no beginning and no end. It is a good day to die."

"Yes, it sure is."

"Hey, I'm not alone. I've still got you. It's just you and me now!"

"That's very funny."

"Thank you, Sebastian!"

Juan Miguel finished playing. In the last note rang Bach's acceptance of his beloved wife's death. Juan Miguel gently placed the guitar back in the velvet-lined case and closed the lid.

~ ~ ~